WATCH OUT FOR
THE KILLING FROSTS ...

"The Garden of Smoke" by G. K. Chesterton
When a young woman accepts employment as a companion to a woman artist, she finds herself in a household where evil seems to flourish, a neighbor carries a dagger, and something deadly is waiting in the garden.

"A Curtain of Green" by Eudora Welty
A descent into madness and a killing rage are pulling the widowed Mrs. Larkin toward a horrifying deed in her beloved garden ... in a small Southern town where malevolence seems to seep into the earth with the summer rain.

"Rappaccini's Daughter" by Nathaniel Hawthorne
This classic tale, filled with brooding symbolism and twisted love, tells of a beauty that may be a lure for destruction ... and a poison that can seep into the very soul of a prideful man.

"The Azalea War" by Wyc Toole
When two retirees become neighbors, and instant enemies, they fight over a dog bite, a boundary line, and an azalea bush until an explosive climax seems inevitable. But the final twist in this story makes it an earth-shaking surprise.

*And many more superb stories
of murder in the garden*

MYSTERY ANTHOLOGIES

☐ **MURDER ON TRIAL** *13 Courtroom Mysteries By the Masters of Detection.* Attorney and clients, judges and prosecutors, witnesses and victims all meet in this perfect locale for outstanding mystery fiction. Now, subpoenaed from the pages of *Alfred Hitchcock's Mystery Magazine* and *Ellery Queen Mystery Magazine*—with the sole motive of entertaining you—are tales brimming with courtroom drama.
(177215—$4.99)

☐ **ROYAL CRIMES, New Tales of Blue-Bloody Murder, by Robert Barnard, Sharyn McCrumb, H. R. F. Keating, Peter Lovesey, Edward Hoch and 10 others. Edited by Maxim Jakubowski and Martin H. Greenberg.** From necromancy in the reign of Richard II to amorous pussyfooting by recent prime ministers, heavy indeed is the head that wears the crown, especially when trying to figure out whodunit . . . in fifteen brand new stories of murder most royal.
(181115—$4.99)

☐ **MURDER FOR MOTHER by Ruth Rendell, Barbara Collins, Billie Sue Mosiman, Bill Crider, J. Madison Davis, Wendy Hornsby, and twelve more.** These eighteen works of short fiction celebrate Mother's Day with a gift of great entertainment . . . a story collection that every mystery-loving mama won't want to miss.
(180364—$4.99)

☐ **MURDER FOR FATHER** 20 Mystery Stories by Ruth Rendell, Ed Gorman, Barbara Collins, and 7 More Contemporary Writers of Detective Fiction. Here are proud papas committing crimes, solving cases, or being role models for dark deeds of retribution, revenge, and of course, murder.
(180682—$4.99)

*Prices slightly higher in Canada

GARDEN OF DEADLY DELIGHTS

Stories from
Ellery Queen's Mystery Magazine
and
Alfred Hitchcock Mystery Magazine

Edited by Cynthia Manson

A SIGNET BOOK

SIGNET
Published by the Penguin Group
Penguin Books USA Inc., 375 Hudson Street,
New York, New York 10014, U.S.A.
Penguin Books Ltd, 27 Wrights Lane,
London W8 5TZ, England
Penguin Books Australia Ltd, Ringwood,
Victoria, Australia
Penguin Books Canada Ltd, 10 Alcorn Avenue,
Toronto, Ontario, Canada M4V 3B2
Penguin Books (N.Z.) Ltd, 182–190 Wairau Road,
Auckland 10, New Zealand

Penguin Books Ltd, Registered Offices:
Harmondsworth, Middlesex, England

First published by Signet, an imprint of Dutton Signet,
a division of Penguin Books USA Inc.

First Printing, April, 1996
10 9 8 7 6 5 4 3 2 1

Grateful acknowledgment is made to the following for permission to reprint their copyrighted material:

"The Price of Tomatoes" by William Bunce, copyright © 1987 by Davis Publications, Inc., reprinted by permission of the author; "One Last Picture" by Sherita Saffer Campbell, copyright © 1987 by Davis Publications, Inc., reprinted by permission of the author; "The Ghost in the Garden" by Dan Crawford, copyright © 1990 by Davis Publications, Inc., reprinted by permission of the author; "The Azalea War" by W. D. Toole, Jr., copyright © 1986 by Davis Publications, Inc., reprinted by permission of the author; "The Ronnie" by K. D. Wentworth, copyright © 1991 by Davis Publications, Inc., reprinted by permission of the author; all stories previously appeared in *Alfred Hitchcock Mystery Magazine,* published by Dell Magazines, Inc.

"Garden of Evil" by Carol Cail, copyright © 1974 by Davis Publications, reprinted by permission of the author; "The Garden of Smoke" by G. K. Chesterton, copyright © 1946 by G. K. Chesterton, reprinted by permission of A. P. Watt, Ltd. on behalf of the Royal Literary Fund; "How Does Your Garden Grow?" by Agatha Christie, copyright © 1935 by The Curtis Publishing Company © renewed 1962 by Agatha Christie Mallowan, reprinted by permission of Harold Ober Associates, Inc; "Parrots in My Garden" by Dorothy B. Davis, copyright © 1993 by Dorothy B. Davis, reprinted by permission of the author,

(The following page constitutes an extension of this copyright page.)

Contents

Garden of Deadly Delights presents a mixed bouquet of mystery stories from *Ellery Queen's Mystery Magazine* and *Alfred Hitchcock Mystery Magazine*. Mystery fans will be treated to perennial favorites, such as Agatha Christie, G. K. Chesterton, Ruth Rendell, Eudora Welty, and Nathaniel Hawthorne, as well as newly discovered practitioners of the art.

Gardens, for all their serene beauty, can be tempting environments to murderers, concealing lethal poisons in the guise of delicate blooms. Insecticides designed to protect plants can prove all too fatal to an unsuspecting victim. Another word of caution: Beware the owner of a prizewinning garden, the fertilizer could be a very special mixture. Gardens may be depicted as places of total enchantment and fantasy, as in Dan Crawford's "The Ghost in the Garden," and K. D. Wentworth's "The Ronnie," or they may be places of terror, as illustrated in Carol Cail's "Garden of Evil" and Lord Dunsany's "Three Men in a Garden."

The masterful authors whose work appears in this collection cultivate a variety of lovely but deadly crops. Enjoy the fruits of their labor as they plant doubts in your mind and seed their plots with clues, all in the best tradition of classical detection.

—Cynthia Manson

How Does Your Garden Grow?
by *Agatha Christie*

Hercule Poirot arranged his letters in a neat pile in front of him. He picked up the topmost letter, studied the address for a moment, then neatly slit the back of the envelope with a little paper knife that he kept on the breakfast table for that express purpose and extracted the contents. Inside was yet another envelope, carefully sealed with purple wax and marked *Private and Confidential*.

Hercule Poirot's eyebrows rose a little on his egg-shaped head. He murmured, "Patience! *Nous allons arriver!*" and once more brought the little paper knife into play. This time the envelope yielded a letter, written in a rather shaky and spiky handwriting. A few words were underlined.

Hercule Poirot unfolded it and read. The letter was headed once again *Private and Confidential*. On the right-hand side was the address—Rosebank, Charman's Green, Bucks—and the date, March twenty-first.

Dear M. Poirot: I have been recommended to you by an old and valued friend of mine who knows the *worry* and *distress* I have been in lately. Not that this friend knows the actual *circumstances*—those I have kept *entirely* to myself—the matter being strictly private. My friend assures me that you are *discretion* itself—and that there will be no fear of my being involved in a *police* matter which, if my suspicions should prove correct, I should *very much* dislike. But it is of course possible that I am *entirely* mistaken. I do not feel myself clearheaded enough nowadays—suffering as I do from insomnia and the result of a severe illness last winter—to investigate things for myself. I have neither the *means* nor the *ability*. On the other hand, I must reiterate that this is a very delicate family matter and that for many reasons I may want the *whole thing hushed up*. If I am once assured of the *facts,* I can deal with the matter myself and should prefer to do so. I hope that I have made myself clear on this point. If you will undertake this investigation, perhaps you will let me know?

> Yours very truly,
> AMELIA BARROWBY.

Poirot read the letter through twice. Again his eyebrows rose slightly. Then he placed it on one side and proceeded to the next envelope in the pile.

At 10 o'clock precisely he entered the room where Miss Lemon, his confidential secretary, sat awaiting her instructions for the day. Miss Lemon was 48 and of unprepossessing appearance. Her general effect was that of a lot of bones flung together at random. She had a passion for order almost equaling that of Poirot himself; and though capable of thinking, she never thought unless told to do so.

Poirot handed her the morning correspondence. "Have the goodness, mademoiselle, to write refusals couched in correct terms to all of these."

Miss Lemon ran an eye over the various letters, scribbling a hieroglyphic on each of them. These marks were legible to her alone and were in a code of her own: "Soft soap"; "slap in the face"; "purr purr"; "curt"—and so on. Having done this, she nodded and looked up for further instructions.

Poirot handed her Amelia Barrowby's letter. She extracted it from its double envelope, read it through and looked up inquiringly.

"Yes, M. Poirot?" Her pencil hovered—ready—over her shorthand pad.

"What is your opinion of that letter, Miss Lemon?"

With a slight frown Miss Lemon put down the pencil and read through the letter again.

The contents of a letter meant nothing to Miss Lemon except from the point of view of composing an adequate reply. Very occasionally her employer appealed to her human, as opposed to her official, capacities. It slightly annoyed Miss Lemon when he did so—she was very nearly the perfect machine, completely and gloriously uninterested in all human affairs. Her real passion in life was the perfection of a filing system beside which all other filing systems should sink into oblivion. She dreamed of such a system at night. Nevertheless, Miss Lemon was perfectly capable of intelligence on purely human matters, as Hercule Poirot well knew.

"Well?" he demanded.

"Old lady," said Miss Lemon. "Got the wind up pretty badly."

"Ah! The wind rises in her, you think?"

Miss Lemon, who considered that Poirot had been long enough in Great Britain to understand its slang terms, did not reply. She took a brief look at the double envelope.

"Very hush-hush," she said. "And tells you nothing at all."

"Yes," said Hercule Poirot. "I observed that."

Miss Lemon's hand hung once more hopefully over the shorthand pad. This time Hercule Poirot responded.

"Tell her I will do myself the honor to call upon her at any time she suggests, unless she prefers to consult me here. Do not type the letter—write it by hand."

"Yes, M. Poirot."

Poirot produced more correspondence. "These are bills."

Miss Lemon's efficient hands sorted them quickly. "I'll pay all but these two."

"Why those two? There is no error in them."

"They are firms you've only just begun to deal with. It looks bad to pay too promptly when you've just opened an account—looks as though you were working up to get some credit later on."

"Ah!" murmured Poirot. "I bow to your superior knowledge of the British tradesmen."

"There's nothing much I don't know about them," said Miss Lemon grimly.

The letter to Miss Amelia Barrowby was duly written and sent, but no reply was forthcoming. Perhaps, thought Hercule Poirot, the old lady had unraveled the mystery herself. Yet he felt a shade of surprise that in that case she should not have written a courteous word to say that his services were no longer required.

It was five days later when Miss Lemon, after receiving her morning's instructions, said, "That Miss Barrowby we wrote to—no wonder there's been no answer. She's dead."

Hercule Poirot said very softly, "Ah—dead." It sounded not so much like a question as an answer.

Opening her handbag, Miss Lemon produced a newspaper clipping. "I saw it in the tube and tore it out."

Just registering in his mind approval of the fact that, though Miss Lemon used the word "tore," she had neatly cut the entry out with scissors, Poirot read the announcement taken from the Births, Deaths, and Marriages in the *Morning Post:* "On March 26th—suddenly—at Rosebank, Charman's Green, Amelia Jane Barrowby, in her seventy-third year. No flowers, by request."

Poirot read it over. He murmured under his breath, "Suddenly." Then he said briskly, "If you will be so obliging as to take a letter?"

The pencil hovered. Miss Lemon, her mind dwelling on the intricacies of the filing system, took down in rapid and correct shorthand:

Dear Miss Barrowby: I have received no reply from you, but as I shall be in the neighborhood of Charman's Green on Friday, I will call upon you on that day and discuss more fully the matter you mentioned to me in your letter.

                                Yours, etc.

"Type this letter, please; and if it is posted at once, it should get to Charman's Green tonight."

On the following morning a letter in a black-edged envelope arrived by the second post:

Dear Sir: In reply to your letter my aunt, Miss Barrowby, passed away on the twenty-sixth, so the matter you speak of is no longer of importance.

                            Yours truly,
                            MARY DELAFONTAINE.

Poirot smiled to himself. "No longer of importance . . . Ah—that is what we shall see. *En avant*—to Charman's Green."

Rosebank was a house that seemed likely to live up to its name, which is more than can be said for most English houses of its class and character.

Hercule Poirot paused as he walked up the path to the front door and looked approvingly at the neatly planned beds on either side of him. Rose bushes that promised a good harvest later in the year, and at present daffodils, early tulips, blue hyacinths. The last bed was partly edged with oyster shells.

Poirot murmured to himself, "How does it go, the English rhyme the children sing?

> *Mistress Mary, quite contrary,*
> *How does your garden grow?*
> *With cockle-shells, and silver bells,*
> *And pretty maids all in a row.*

"Not a row, perhaps," he considered, "but here is at least one pretty maid to make the little rhyme come right."

The front door had opened and a neat little maid in cap and apron was looking somewhat dubiously at the spectacle of a heavily mustached foreign gentleman talking aloud to himself in the front garden. She was, as Poirot had noted, a very pretty little maid, with round blue eyes and rosy cheeks.

Poirot raised his hat with courtesy and addressed her: "Pardon, but does a Miss Amelia Barrowby live here?"

The little maid gasped and her eyes grew rounder. "Oh, sir, didn't you know? She's dead. Ever so sudden it was. Tuesday night."

She hesitated, divided between two strong instincts: the first, distrust of a foreigner; the second, the pleasurable enjoyment of her class in dwelling on the subject of illness and death.

"You amaze me," said Hercule Poirot, not very truthfully. "I had an appointment with the lady for today. However, I can perhaps see the other lady who lives here."

The little maid seemed slightly doubtful. "The mistress? Well, you could see her, perhaps, but I don't know whether she'll be seeing anyone or not."

"She will see me," said Poirot, and handed her a card.

The authority of his tone had its effect. The rosy-cheeked maid fell back and ushered Poirot into a sitting room on the right of the hall. Then, card in hand, she departed to summon her mistress.

Hercule Poirot looked round him. The room was a perfectly conventional drawing room—oatmeal-colored paper with a frieze round the top, rose-colored cushions and curtains, a good many china knickknacks and ornaments. There was nothing in the room that stood out, that announced a definite personality.

Suddenly Poirot, who was very sensitive, felt eyes

watching him. He wheeled round. A girl was standing in the entrance of the French window—a small, sallow girl, with very black hair and suspicious eyes.

She came in, and as Poirot made a little bow she burst out abruptly, "Why have you come?"

Poirot did not reply. He merely raised his eyebrows.

"You are not a lawyer—no?" Her English was good, but not for a minute would anyone have taken her to be English.

"Why should I be a lawyer, mademoiselle?"

The girl stared at him sullenly. "I thought you might be. I thought you had come perhaps to say that she did not know what she was doing. I have heard of such things—the not due influence; that is what they call it, no? But that is not right. She wanted me to have the money, and I shall have it. If it is needful I shall have a lawyer of my own. The money is mine. She wrote it down so, and so it shall be." She looked ugly, her chin thrust out, her eyes gleaming.

The door opened and a tall woman entered and said, "Katrina."

The girl shrank, flushed, muttered something, and went out through the French window.

Poirot turned to face the newcomer who had so effectually dealt with the situation by uttering a single word. There had been authority in her voice, and contempt and a shade of well-bred irony. He realized at once that this was the owner of the house, Mary Delafontaine.

"M. Poirot? I wrote to you. You cannot have received my letter."

"Alas, I have been away from London."

"Oh, I see; that explains it. I must introduce myself. My name is Delafontaine. This is my husband. Miss Barrowby was my aunt."

Mr. Delafontaine had entered so quietly that his arrival had passed unnoticed. He was a tall man with grizzled hair and an indeterminate manner. He had a nervous way of fingering his chin. He looked often toward his wife, and it was plain that he expected her to take the lead in any conversation.

"I much regret that I intrude in the midst of your bereavement," said Hercule Poirot.

"I realize that it is not your fault," said Mrs. Delafontaine. "My aunt died on Tuesday evening. It was quite unexpected."

"Most unexpected," said Mr. Delafontaine. "Great blow." His eyes watched the window where the foreign girl had disappeared.

"I apologize," said Hercule Poirot. "And I withdraw." He moved a step toward the door.

"Half a sec," said Mr. Delafontaine. "You—er—had an appointment with Aunt Amelia, you say?"

"Parfaitement."

"Perhaps you will tell us about it," said his wife. "If there is anything we can do—"

"It was of a private nature," said Poirot. "I am a detective," he added.

Mr. Delafontaine knocked over a little china figure he was handling. His wife looked puzzled.

"A detective? And you had an appointment with auntie? But how extraordinary!" She stared at him. "Can't you tell us a little more, M. Poirot? It—it seems quite fantastic."

Poirot was silent for a moment. He chose his words with care.

"It is difficult for me, madame, to know what to do."

"Look here," said Mr. Delafontaine. "She didn't mention Russians, did she?"

"Russians?"

"Yes, you know—Reds, all that sort of thing."

"Don't be absurd, Henry," said his wife.

Mr. Delafontaine collapsed. "Sorry—sorry—I just wondered."

Mary Delafontaine looked frankly at Poirot. Her eyes

were very blue, the color of forget-me-nots. "If you can tell us anything, M. Poirot, I should be glad if you would do so. I can assure you that I have a—a reason for asking."

Mr. Delafontaine looked alarmed. "Be careful, old girl—you know there may be nothing in it."

Again his wife quelled him with a glance. "Well, M. Poirot?"

Slowly, gravely, Hercule Poirot shook his head. He shook it with visible regret, but he shook it. "At present madame," he said, "I fear I must say nothing."

He bowed, picked up his hat, and moved to the door. Mary Delafontaine came with him into the hall. On the doorstep he paused and looked at her.

"You are fond of your garden, I think, madame?"

"I? Yes, I spend a lot of time gardening."

"Je vous fait mes compliments."

He bowed once more and strode down to the gate. As he passed through it and turned to the right, he glanced back and registered two impressions—a sallow face watching him from a first-floor window, and a man of erect and soldierly carriage pacing up and down on the opposite side of the street.

Hercule Poirot nodded to himself. *"Definitivement,"* he said. "There is a mouse in this hole! What move must the cat make now?"

His decision took him to the nearest post office. Here he put through a couple of telephone calls. The result seemed to be satisfactory. He bent his steps to Charman's Green police station, where he inquired for Inspector Sims.

Inspector Sims was a big, burly man with a hearty manner. "M. Poirot?" he inquired. "I thought so. I've just this minute had a telephone call through from the chief constable about you. He said you'd be dropping in. Come into my office."

The door shut, the Inspector waved Poirot to one chair, and settled himself in another.

"You're very quick onto the mark, M. Poirot. Come to see us about this Rosebank case almost before we know it is a case. What put you onto it?"

Poirot drew out the letter he had received and handed it to the Inspector. The latter read it with some interest.

"Interesting," he said. "The trouble is, it might mean so many things. Pity she couldn't have been a little more explicit. It would have helped us now."

"Or there might have been no need for help."

"You mean?"

"She might have been alive."

"You go as far as that, do you? H'm—I'm not sure you're wrong."

"I pray of you, Inspector, recount to me the facts. I know nothing at all."

"That's easily done. Old lady was taken bad after dinner on Tuesday night. Very alarming. Convulsions—spasms—whatnot. They sent for the doctor. By the time he arrived she was dead. Idea was she'd died of a fit. Well, he didn't much like the look of things. He hemmed and hawed, but he made it clear that he couldn't give a death certificate. And as far as the family go, that's where the matter stands. They're awaiting the result of the postmortem. We've got a bit farther. The doctor gave us the tip right away—he and the police surgeon did the autopsy together—and the result is in no doubt whatever. The old lady died of a large dose of strychnine."

"Aha!"

"That's right. Very nasty bit of work. Point is, who gave it to her? It must have been administered very shortly before death. First idea was it was given to her in her food at dinner—but, frankly, that seems to be a washout. They had artichoke soup, served from a tureen, fish pie, and apple tart."

" 'They' being?"

"Miss Barrowby, Mr. Delafontaine and Mrs. Delafontaine. Miss Barrowby had a kind of nurse-attendant—a half-Russian girl—but she didn't eat with the family. She had the remains as they came out from the dining room. There's a maid, but it was her night out. She left the soup on the stove and the fish pie in the oven, and the apple tart was cold. All three of them ate the same thing—and, apart from that, I don't think you could get strychnine down anyone's throat that way. Stuff's as bitter as gall. The doctor told me you could taste it in a solution of one in a thousand, or something like that."

"Coffee?"

"Coffee's more like it, but the old lady never took coffee."

"I see your point. Yes, it seems an insuperable difficulty. What did she drink at the meal?"

"Water."

"Worse and worse."

"Bit of a teaser, isn't it?"

"She had money, the old lady?"

"Very well to do, I imagine. Of course, we haven't got exact details yet. The Delafontaines are pretty badly off, from what I can make out. The old lady helped with the upkeep of the house."

Poirot smiled a little. He said, "So you suspect the Delafontaines. Which of them?"

"I don't exactly say I suspect either of them in particular. But there it is; they're her only near relations, and her death brings them a tidy sum of money, I've no doubt. We all know what human nature is!"

"Sometimes inhuman—yes, that is very true. And there was nothing else the old lady ate or drank?"

"Well, as a matter of fact—"

"Ah, *voilà!* I felt that you had something, as you say, up your sleeve—the soup, the fish pie, the apple tart—a *bêtise!* Now we come to the hub of the affair."

"I don't know about that. But as a matter of fact, the

old girl took a cachet before meals. You know, not a pill or a tablet; one of those rice-paper things with a powder inside. Some perfectly harmless thing for the digestion."

"Admirable. Nothing is easier than to fill a cachet with strychnine and substitute it for one of the others. It slips down the throat with a drink of water and is not tasted."

"That's all right. The trouble is, the girl gave it to her."

"The Russian girl?"

"Yes. Katrina Rieger. She was a kind of lady-help, nurse-companion to Miss Barrowby. Fairly ordered about by her, too, I gather. Fetch this, fetch that, fetch the other, rub my back, pour out my medicine, run round to the chemist—all that sort of business. You know how it is with these old women—they mean to be kind, but what they need is a sort of slave!"

Poirot smiled.

"And there you are, you see," continued Inspector Sims. "It doesn't fit in what you might call nicely. Why should the girl poison her? Miss Barrowby dies and now the girl will be out of a job, and jobs aren't so easy to find—she's not trained or anything."

"Still," suggested Poirot, "if the box of cachets was left about, anyone in the house might have the opportunity."

"Naturally we're onto that, M. Poirot. I don't mind telling you we're making our inquiries—quiet like, if you understand me. When the prescription was last made up, where it was usually kept; patience and a lot of spade work—that's what will do the trick in the end. And then there's Miss Barrowby's solicitor. I'm having an interview with him tomorrow. And the bank manager. There's a lot to be done still."

Poirot rose. "A little favor, Inspector Sims. You will send me a little word how the affair marches? I would esteem it a great favor. Here is my telephone number."

"Why, certainly, M. Poirot. Two heads are better than one; and, besides, you ought to be in on this, having had that letter and all."

"You are too amiable, Inspector." Politely, Poirot shook hands and took his leave.

He was called to the telephone on the following afternoon. "Is that M. Poirot? Inspector Sims here. Things are beginning to sit up and look pretty in that little matter you and I know of."

"In verity? Tell me, I pray of you."

"Well, here's item No. 1—and a pretty big item. Miss B. left a small legacy to her niece and everything else to K. In consideration of her great kindness and attention—that's the way it was put. That alters the complexion of things."

A picture rose swiftly in Poirot's mind. A sullen face and a passionate voice saying, "The money is mine. She wrote it down so, and so it shall be." The legacy would not come as a surprise to Katrina—she knew about it beforehand.

"Item No. 2," continued the voice of Inspector Sims. "Nobody but K. handled that cachet."

"You can be sure of that?"

"The girl herself doesn't deny it. What do you think of that?"

"Extremely interesting."

"We only want one thing more—evidence of how the strychnine came into her possession. That oughtn't to be difficult."

"But so far you haven't been successful?"

"I've barely started. The inquest was only this morning."

"What happened at it?"

"Adjourned for a week."

"And the young lady—K.?"

"I'm detaining her on suspicion. Don't want to run any risks. She might have some friends in the country who'd try to get her out of it."

"No," said Poirot. "I do not think she has any friends."

"Really? What makes you say that, M. Poirot?"

"It is just an idea of mine. There were no other 'items,' as you call them?"

"Nothing that's strictly relevant. Miss B. seems to have been monkeying about a bit with her shares lately—must have dropped quite a tidy sum. It's rather a funny business, one way and another, but I don't see how it affects the main issue—not at present, that is."

"No, perhaps you are right. Well, my best thanks to you. It was most amiable of you to ring me up."

"Not at all. I'm a man of my word. I could see you were interested. Who knows, you may be able to give me a helping hand before the end."

"That would give me a great pleasure. It might help you, for instance, if I could lay my hand on a friend of the girl Katrina."

"I thought you said she hadn't got any friends?" said Inspector Sims, surprised.

"I was wrong," said Hercule Poirot. "She has one."

Before the Inspector could ask a further question, Poirot had rung off.

With a serious face he wandered into the room where Miss Lemon sat at her typewriter. She raised her hands from the keys at her employer's approach and looked at him inquiringly.

"I want you," said Poirot, "to figure to yourself a little history."

Miss Lemon dropped her hands into her lap in a resigned manner. She enjoyed typing, paying bills, filing papers, and recording appointments. To be asked to imagine herself in hypothetical situations bored her very much, but she accepted it as a disagreeable part of a duty.

"You are a Russian girl," began Poirot.

"Yes," said Miss Lemon, looking intensely British.

"You are alone and friendless in this country. You have reasons for not wishing to return to Russia. You are employed as a kind of drudge, nurse-attendant and companion to an old lady. You are meek and uncomplaining."

"Yes," said Miss Lemon obediently, but entirely failing to see herself being meek to any old lady under the sun.

"The old lady takes a fancy to you. She decides to leave her money to you. She tells you so." Poirot paused.

Miss Lemon said "Yes" again.

"And then the old lady finds out something; perhaps it is a matter of money—she may find that you have not been honest with her. Or it might be more grave still—a medicine that tasted different, some food that disagreed. Anyway, she begins to suspect you of something and she writes to a very famous detective—*enfin*, to the most famous detective—me! I am to call upon her shortly. And then, as you say, the dripping will be in the fire. The great thing is to act quickly. And so—before the great detective arrives—the old lady is dead. And the money comes to you . . . Tell me, does that seem to you reasonable?"

"Quite reasonable," said Miss Lemon. "Quite reasonable for a Russian, that is. Personally, I should never take a post as a companion. I like my duties clearly defined. And of course I should not dream of murdering anyone."

Poirot sighed. "How I miss my friend Hastings. He had such an imagination. Such a romantic mind! It is true that he always imagined wrong—but that in itself was a guide."

Miss Lemon was silent. She had heard about Captain Hastings before, and was not interested. She looked longingly at the typewritten sheet in front of her.

"So it seems to you reasonable," mused Poirot.

"Doesn't it to you?"

"I am almost afraid it does," sighed Poirot.

The telephone rang and Miss Lemon went out of the room to answer it. She came back to say, "It's Inspector Sims again."

Poirot hurried to the instrument. " 'Allo, 'allo. What is that you say?"

Sims repeated his statement. "We've found a packet of strychnine in the girl's bedroom—tucked underneath the mattress. The sergeant's just come in with the news. That about clinches it, I think."

"Yes," said Poirot. "I think that clinches it." His voice had changed. It rang with sudden confidence.

When he had rung off, he sat down at his writing table and arranged the objects on it in a mechanical manner. He murmured to himself, "There was something wrong. I felt it—no, not felt. It must have been something I saw. *En avant,* the little gray cells. Ponder—reflect. Was everything logical and in order? The girl—her anxiety about the money; Mme. Delafontaine; her husband—his suggestion of Russians—imbecile, but he is an imbecile; the room; the garden—ah! Yes, *the garden.*"

He sat up very stiff. The green light shone in his eyes. He sprang up and went into the adjoining room.

"Miss Lemon, will you have the kindness to leave what you are doing and make an investigation for me?"

"An investigation, M. Poirot? I'm afraid I'm not very good—"

Poirot interrupted her. "You said one day that you knew all about tradesmen."

"Certainly I do," said Miss Lemon with confidence.

"Then the matter is simple. You are to go to Charman's Green and you are to discover a fishmonger."

"A fishmonger?" asked Miss Lemon, surprised.

"Precisely. The fishmonger who supplied Rosebank with fish. When you have found him you will ask him a certain question."

He handed her a slip of paper. Miss Lemon took it, noted its contents without interest, then nodded and slipped the cover on her typewriter.

"We will go to Charman's Green together," said Poirot. "You to the fishmonger and I to the police station. It will take us but half an hour from Baker Street."

On arrival at his destination, he was greeted by the surprised Inspector Sims. "Well, this is quick work, M. Poirot. I was talking to you on the phone only an hour ago."

"I have a request to make to you—that you allow me to see this girl Katrina."

"Well, I don't suppose there's any objection to that."

The girl Katrina looked even more sallow and sullen than ever.

Poirot spoke to her very gently. "Mademoiselle, I want you to believe that I am not your enemy. I want you to tell me the truth."

Her eyes snapped defiantly. "I have told the truth. To everyone I have told the truth! If the old lady was poisoned, it was not I who poisoned her. It is all a mistake. You wish to prevent me having the money." Her voice was rasping. She looked, he thought, like a little cornered rat.

"Tell me about this cachet, mademoiselle," M. Poirot went on. "Did no one handle it but you?"

"I have said so, have I not? They were made up at the chemist's that afternoon. I brought them back with me in my bag—that was just before supper. I opened the box and gave Miss Barrowby one with a glass of water."

"No one touched them but you?"

"No." A cornered rat—with courage!

"And Miss Barrowby had for supper only what we have been told. The soup, the fish pie, the tart?"

"Yes." A hopeless "yes"—dark, smoldering eyes that saw no light anywhere.

Poirot patted her shoulder. "Be of good courage, mademoiselle. There may yet be freedom—yes, and money—a life of ease."

She looked at him suspiciously.

As he went out Sims said to him, "I didn't quite get what you said through the telephone—something about the girl having a friend."

"She has one, Me!" said Hercule Poirot, and had left the police station before the Inspector could pull his wits together.

At the Green Cat tearooms, Miss Lemon did not keep her employer waiting. She went straight to the point.

"The man's name is Rudge, in the High Street, and you were quite right. A dozen and a half exactly. I've made a note of what he said." She handed it to him.

"Arrr." It was a deep, rich sound like the purr of a cat.

Hercule Poirot betook himself to Rosebank. As he stood in the front garden, the sun setting behind him. Mary Delafontaine came out to him.

"M. Poirot?" Her voice sounded surprised. "You have come back?"

"Yes, I have come back." He paused and then said, "When I first came here, madame, the children's nursery rhyme came into my head when I saw your garden:

> *Mistress Mary, quite contrary,*
> *How does your garden grow?*
> *With cockle-shells and silver bells,*
> *And pretty maids all in a row.*

Only they are not *cockle* shells, are they, madame? They are *oyster* shells." His hand pointed.

He heard her catch her breath and then stay very still. Her eyes asked a question.

He nodded. "*Mais, oui,* I know! The maid left the dinner ready—she will swear and Katrina will swear that that is all you had. Only you and your husband know that you brought back a dozen and a half oysters—a little treat *pour la bonne tante.* So easy to put the strychnine in an oyster. It is swallowed—*comme ça!* But there remain the shells. They must not go in the bucket—the maid would see them. And so you thought of making an edging of them to a flower bed. But there were not enough—the edging is not complete. The effect is bad—it spoils the symmetry of the otherwise charming garden. Those few oyster shells struck an alien note—they displeased my eye on my first visit."

Mary Delafontaine said, "I suppose you guessed from the letter. I knew she had written—but I didn't know how much she'd said."

Poirot answered evasively, "I knew at least that it was a family matter. If it had been a question of Katrina there would have been no point in hushing things up. I understand that you or your husband handled Miss Barrowby's securities to your own profit, and that she found out—"

Mary Delafontaine nodded. "We've done it for years—a little here and there. I never realized she was sharp enough to find out. And then I learned she had sent for a detective; and I found out, too, that she was leaving her money to Katrina—that miserable little creature!"

"And so the strychnine was put in Katrina's bedroom? I comprehend. You save yourself and your husband from what I may discover, and you saddle an innocent child with murder. Had you no pity, madame?"

Mary Delafontaine shrugged her shoulders—her blue forget-me-not eyes looked into Poirot's. He remembered the perfection of her acting the first day he had come and the bungling attempts of her husband. A woman above the average—but inhuman.

She said, "Pity? For that intriguing little rat?" Her contempt rang out.

Hercule Poirot said slowly, "I think, madame, that you have cared in your life for two things only. One is your husband."

He saw her lips tremble.

"And the other—is your garden."

He looked round him. His glance seemed to apologize to the flowers for that which he had done and was about to do.

The Cop Who Loved Flowers
by Henry Slesar

Spring comes resolutely, even to police stations, and once
again Captain Don Flammer felt the familiar, pleasant
twitching of his senses. Flammer loved the springtime—
the green yielding of the earth, the flourishing trees, and
most of all, the flowers. He liked being a country cop,
and the petunia border around the Haleyville Police
Headquarters was his own idea and special project.

But by the time June arrived, it was plain that there was
something different about Captain Flammer this spring.
Flammer wasn't himself. He frowned too much; he neglected the garden; he spent too much time indoors. His
friends on the force were concerned, but not mystified.
They knew Flammer's trouble: he was still thinking about
Mrs. McVey.

It was love of flowers that had introduced them. Mrs.
McVey and her husband had moved into the small two-
story house on Arden Road, and the woman had waved a
magic green wand over the scraggly garden she had inherited. Roses began to climb in wild profusion; massive
pink hydrangea bloomed beside the porch; giant pansies,
mums, peonies showed their faces; violets and bluebells
crept among the rocks; and petunias, more velvety than
the Captain's, invaded the terrace.

One day the Captain had stopped his car and walked
red-faced to the fence where Mrs. McVey was training
ivy. Flammer was a bachelor, in his forties, and not at
ease with women. Mrs. McVey was a few years younger,

a bit to thin for prettiness, but with a smile as warming as the sunshine.

"I just wanted to say," he told her heavily, "that you have the nicest garden in Haleyville." Then he frowned as if he had just arrested her, and stomped back to his car.

It wasn't the most auspicious beginning for a friendship, but it was a beginning. Flammer stopped his car in the McVey driveway at least one afternoon a week, and Mrs. McVey made it clear, with smiles, hot tea, and homemade cookies, that she welcomed his visits.

The first time he met Mr. McVey, he didn't like him. McVey was a sharp-featured man with a mouth that looked as if it were perpetually sucking a lemon. When Flammer spoke to him of flowers, the sour mouth twisted in contempt.

"Joe doesn't care for the garden," Mrs. McVey said. "But he knows how much it means to me, especially because he travels so much."

It wasn't a romance, of course. Everybody knew that—even the town gossips. Flammer was a cop, and cops were notoriously stolid. And Mrs. McVey wasn't pretty enough to fit the role.

So nobody in Haleyville gossiped, or giggled behind their backs. Mrs. McVey and the Captain met, week after week, right out in the open where the whole town could see them. But he was in love with her before the autumn came, and she was in love with him; yet they never talked about it.

She did talk about her husband. Little by little, learning to trust Flammer, inspired by her feelings for him, she told him about Joe.

"I'm worried because I think he's sick," she said. "Sick in a way no ordinary doctor can tell. There's such bitterness in him. He grew up expecting so much from life and he got so little."

"Not so little," Flammer said bluntly.

"He hates coming home from his trips. He never says

that in so many words, but I know. He can't wait to be off again."

"Do you think he's—" Flammer blushed at the question forming in his own mind.

"I don't accuse him of anything," Mrs. McVey said. "I never ask him any questions, and he hates to be prodded. There are times when—well, I'm a little afraid of Joe."

Flammer looked from the porch at the pink hydrangea bush, still full-bloomed at summer's end, and thought about how much he would enjoy holding Mrs. McVey's earth-stained hand. Instead, he took a sip of her tea.

On September 19th Mrs. McVey was shot with a .32 revolver. The sound exploded in the night, and woke the neighbors on both sides of the McVey house.

It was some time before the neighbors heard the feeble cries for help that followed the report of the gun, and called the Haleyville police. Captain Flammer never quite forgave the officer on duty that night for not calling him at home when the shooting occurred. He had to wait until morning to learn that Mrs. McVey was dead.

No one on the scene saw anything more in Captain Flammer's face than the concern of a conscientious policeman. He went about his job with all the necessary detachment. He questioned Mr. McVey and made no comment on his story.

"It was about two in the morning," McVey said. "Grace woke up and said she thought she heard a noise downstairs. She was always hearing noises, so I told her to go back to sleep. Only she didn't; she put on a kimono and went down to look for herself. She was right for a change—it was a burglar—and he must have got scared and shot her the minute he saw her ... I came out when I heard the noise, and I saw him running away.

"What did he look like?"

"Like two feet running," Joe McVey said. "That was all I saw of him. But you can see what he was doing here."

Flammer looked around—at the living room debris, the opened drawers, the scattered contents, the flagrant evidence of burglary, so easy to create, or fabricate.

The physical investigation went forward promptly. House and grounds were searched, without result—no meaningful fingerprints or footprints were found, no weapon turned up—indeed, they found no clue of any kind to the murderous burglar of Arden Road. Then they searched for answers to other questions: Was there really a burglar at all? Or had Joe McVey killed his wife?

Captain Flammer conducted his calm inquiry into the case, and nobody knew of his tightened throat, of the painful constriction in his heart, of the hot moisture that burned behind his eyes.

But when he was through, he had discovered nothing to change the verdict at the coroner's inquest: Death at the hands of person or persons unknown. He didn't agree with that verdict, but he lacked an iota of proof to change it. He knew who the Unknown Person was; he saw his hateful, sour-mouthed face in his dreams.

Joe McVey disposed of the two-story house less than a month after his wife's death—sold it at a bargain price to a couple with a grown daughter. Joe McVey then left Haleyville—went to Chicago, some said—and Captain Flammer no longer looked forward to spring, and the coming of the flowers, with joyful expectation.

But spring came again, resolutely as always, and despite the Captain's mood of sorrow and resentment at his own inadequacy, his senses began to twitch. He began driving out into the countryside. And one day he stopped his car in front of the former McVey house.

The woman who stood on the porch, framed by clumps of blue hydrangea, lifted her arm and waved. If a heart can somersault, Flammer's did. He almost said Grace's name aloud, even after he realized that the woman was only a girl, plumpish, not yet twenty.

"Hello," she said, looking at the police car in the driveway. "Beautiful day, isn't it?"

"Yes," Flammer said dully. "Are the Mitchells at home?"

"No, they're out. I'm their daughter Angela." She smiled uncertainly. "You're not here on anything official, I hope?"

"No," Flammer said.

"Of course, I know all about this house, about what happened here last year—the murder and everything." She lowered her voice. "You never caught that burglar, did you?"

"No, we never did."

"She must have been a very nice woman—Mrs. McVey, I mean. She certainly loved flowers, didn't she? I don't think I ever saw a garden as beautiful as this one."

"Yes," Captain Flammer said. "She loved flowers very much."

Sadly, he touched a blue blossom on the hydrangea bush, and started back toward his car. He found that his eyes were filling up, and yet they had seen things clearly.

For suddenly he stopped and said, "Blue?"

The young woman watched him quizzically.

"Blue," he said again, returning and staring at the flowering hydrangea bush. "It was pink last year—I know it was. And now it's blue."

"What are you talking about?"

"Hydrangea," Flammer said. "Do you know about hydrangea?"

"I don't know a thing about flowers. As long as they're pretty—"

"They're pretty when they're pink," Flammer said. "But when there's alum in the soil—or iron—they come up blue. Blue like this."

"But what's the difference?" the girl said. "Pink or blue, what difference? So there's iron in the soil—"

"Yes," Captain Flammer said. "There must be iron in

the soil. And now, Miss Mitchell, I'll ask you to please fetch me a shovel."

She looked bewildered, but then she got him the shovel. There was no triumph on Flammer's face when he dug up the revolver at the base of the hydrangea bush, its barrel rusted, its trigger stiff.

He didn't rejoice even when the gun had been identified, as both the weapon that had killed Grace McVey and as the property of Joe McVey. He didn't rejoice when the killer had been brought back to face justice. But while he felt no sense of victory, Captain Flammer admitted one thing: there was a great deal of satisfaction to be derived from the love of flowers.

Garden of Evil
by Carol Cail

Leaning on the kitchen table, washing yesterday's dishes, she could see the garden waiting for her. The August sun bouncing off the parched Kentucky clay made the landscape quiver and weave. All that motion and not a breath of wind. All that warm dishwater and still her fingers would scarcely bend.

Why am I so scared of that garden, she kept wondering. Me, 82 years a country girl and wife. This garden is the same as the others year after year. First you stir up the sleeping dirt, then you mix seeds in it, then you guard it against weeds and rabbits, and, when the time comes, you take what's due you. What did I plant different this spring out there with all the usual peas and beans?

She knew she'd be gnawing hungry in a couple hours, and she'd have to brave the garden. She had stayed in the house three days straight living off the pantry, and now it was depleted except for a bag of sugar and one of flour. Breakfast this morning had been a slice of dry toast and two cups of tea.

The first time she'd sensed the evil in the garden had been one steamy July evening as she waded among the scrambled tomato vines looking for some supper. She had been lazy early in the season, not putting up the poles or tying the plants. Now she was paying for it, thinking about snakes and finding spiders, rot, and rabbit leavings.

The apparently perfect red fruit she wrapped her fingers around had a slimy underside; her hand came up dripping sour-smelling tomato entrails that she hastily wiped on the nearest plantain. An outraged grasshopper sprang at her, and her step backward crushed a cluster of green tomatoes, the seeds squirting and clinging to her legs.

She had fled to a bare space, one of the rows she'd had the energy to weed, and stood there breathing hard, taking stock.

This familiar patch of truck garden where she had spent hours of her life buzzed and hissed and rustled. She saw the ground teeming with bees and beetles and ants and worms. She felt the fire of mosquitoes and oats bugs and flies devouring her. Perspiration trickled down her spine, and she twitched around to see what had touched her. A spire of Johnson grass tapped the back of her knee, and again she jumped.

She could summon up neither humor nor reason. So she had retreated, abandoning the half-filled basket, to the sanctuary of the kitchen, where she immediately felt foolish.

That was the first time the garden had menaced her. She couldn't count how often it had happened since.

At two o'clock she sat on the front porch swing, pretending she couldn't hear the growling in her stomach. The sun would slither behind the mountain in another hour or so, and the garden would be cooler, she'd rationalized.

From the porch she could see far, or could when she was younger. The view was up, not down. She lived in a cup of land surrounded by wooded cliffs. She counted distance by the ridges, one hill to her nearest neighbor, three hills to the nearest crossroads, and so on. The closest store, where she traded her social security for what she couldn't grow, was five hills away.

She'd never been lonely. Not even when Calvin passed away a year ago. It had been something of a relief to have the place to herself after all those years of doing for him.

Now she could sleep late if she wanted, let the housework slide. Let the woods grow.

"Hey!"

She shaded her eyes and peered into the little wild yard. Long red hair swinging was what she picked out first.

"Hey, Granny! What you doing?" the girl yelled, climbing onto the porch.

"Donna, I swan," she welcomed, her voice coming out wobbly and hoarse from disuse. "My only kin in the whole world and ain't you the stranger!"

"Now don't go expecting me to stay or anything. I'm just passing by on my way from California to New York. I couldn't find a job I liked out west, so now I'm going to try the east."

"What kind of work you looking for?" she asked, remembering how to sound interested. She hadn't seen Donna since Calvin's funeral, and not often before that. The child was obviously a hippie. All that hair, and, from the way she jiggled, no underwear.

"Oh, something glamorous. I studied acting at the university. Maybe you'll read about me on Broadway."

"How'd you get here?"

"A friend of mine." She paused and simpered to make clear the friend was male. "Lent me his car. It's up on the road. So I can't stay. Not long enough to let the local yokels strip it down."

The old woman plotted. "My neighbors usually fetch me in supplies every week, but this time I'm short. You go get me a few things at the store, and we'll have us a nice supper and talk."

"No, I don't think so. I really need to be getting on."

"Just a bite to eat. I won't keep you overnight. It would do me good to hear what you been doing and all," she lied.

"Well—" and the right mixture of guilt and vanity made her say yes.

While Donna was gone, the old woman set the table. She knew she ought to at least sweep the floor, but she knew, too, that Donna didn't care about the place being rundown. When she inherited it, she would sell it for whatever she could get and as fast as she could get it. A clean floor wouldn't bring up the price any. Come to that, Donna didn't look too clean herself.

So she sat at the table gazing out toward the garden, thinking how she'd tell Donna to pick extra vegetables to insure having leftovers. "They're just as good warmed over, and it'll save me a heap of work," she'd say. Then she'd watch out the window to see if the garden did anything to Donna.

Not that it had ever really done anything to *her*. But there had been the rabbit.

That was the last time she'd worked up the spunk to go out there. It was three days ago, in early August. The beans and corn needed canning, but she didn't want the job. She'd told herself, Why bother? You probably won't live out the winter anyway.

So this was to be her usual hurried trip into the now weed-infested garden to harvest a meal's worth. She had started for the carrot row, holding the spade in front of her chest like a cross warding off dark powers. The sides of her eyes saw little movements, but if she looked directly at the spot, nothing stirred. She'd learned it was no good to sneak into the garden, so she plunged headlong.

She overshot the carrots, had to retrace her steps to find them underneath a swarm of morning-glory vines. She put the spade into a likely space and raised one foot to shove it home. That's when she saw the rabbit.

He was in among the vines, and she knew he was dead, but never in all her years had she seen an animal look like this in death. He wasn't lying sideways and limp. He lay on his back, spreadeagled, each foot entangled in morning-glory tendrils, and a bindweed wrapped around his neck.

The spade was still out there. Probably covered by vines now, too. She'd thought about that rabbit a lot, but she couldn't shake off the impression of the garden watching her and swaying around her and whispering that it had killed him.

Of course, she knew the garden couldn't have killed the rabbit. Though come to think, it had killed Calvin, in a way.

He'd been out there hoeing and pruning and thinning all day in the hot sun, just like always, early spring to late fall, taming the wilderness and bending it to his will. When he came in for supper, he was all trembly limbed and dizzy, too weak to eat a mouthful. Just climbing the stairs to bed was the last straw.

She'd heard him from the kitchen. There was a scrabbling on the stairwell wall and then a soft thud thud thud as he hit the three steps down from the first landing.

She didn't try to fetch anyone. She knew it was too late. She did get him to the sofa, and that's where he died sometime during the night, still wearing his garden shoes, the soles caked with dried mud.

Ashes to ashes, dust to dust . . .

The house shuddered as feet hit the front porch. Donna staggered through the door, a grocery bag in each arm. The table squeaked when she set them down.

"Here you are. Don't let me forget to give you your change."

The old woman reached into one bag and yanked back her hand as if it had been slapped.

"You, girl. What did you buy bacon for? You know I got no use for meat."

"Oh, Granny, I'm sorry. I just picked it up out of habit. You're still a vegetarian, huh?"

"A dollar and eighty-nine cents for something I'll just chuck out," she grieved.

"Well, I'll eat some. Where's your skillet?"

"No. I'll cook. You got to get some vegetables."

She gave the girl the basket and the instructions about quantity, then watched out the window as Donna sashayed into the garden, squatted down in the string-bean row, and commenced to work.

Minutes ticked by. Donna moved on to the sweet corn. After she'd wrested a dozen ears from their stalks, she stood and shucked them all. Next she started on the tomatoes. Her industry was a pleasant surprise.

The old woman walked out to the edge of the garden. Donna glanced up. "No need to help—I'm through."

"Let's just check if any melons has come ready," she said and boldly entered.

She pretended to be inspecting muskmelons. The garden surrounded them in perfect tranquility. Tan earth smelling dusty sweet. Humming insect songs. Bone-warming sun. Viceroy butterflies dancing.

Donna had found the perennial bed, and she was breaking stems—gloriosa daisies, chrysanthemums, asters, scabiosa, statice. "What's the use of having posies out here where you can't enjoy them?"

Some of the fibrous stems she had to twist back and forth as if she were snapping wires, leaving the stumps bruised and shredded. A tough old aster uprooted in Donna's grip. The garden bided.

The old woman had to say it. "Sometimes—something—out here makes me afraid."

Donna went on plundering the flowers, her face peering over an armload of color. "Well, of course you must be. Alone all the time. You ought to have a dog."

"Paaah. No dog. And no cat neither. I'd be more scared of them than of being alone."

"You used to have a dog," Donna said unkindly.

She didn't answer, remembering the dog. Charlie. A 'coon hound they'd raised from a pup. A vision of Donna as a toddler, teasing Charlie till he cried. Donna's mother, looking white and sickly even then, twisting a switch off the willow tree and stinging the chubby legs. And then, years later, the foaming muzzle sinking poisoned teeth into Donna's pappy's, her son's, hand. She'd mourned them both, dog and man. She could never have another son, and she wouldn't have another dog.

Donna said, "Let's get on into the house. I got to leave before it's too dark to find the way up the road."

They made the meal together. Donna was a fast, steady worker, maybe because she was in a hurry to eat and leave; she ate fast and steady, too. The old woman ate carefully, thankful that her fast had had a fortuitous ending. With each mouthful her opinion of her granddaughter improved. She had not let Donna fry the bacon, but now she said the girl must take the package with her as "a present."

"Oh, Granny, in this heat?" she laughed. "It would just spoil and smell up the car before I'm anywhere to use it." She had a carrot stick that she waved around between bites, and, while she chewed and swallowed, she talked. "You really ought to try the bacon yourself. It's delicious. Honest. You don't know what you're missing, not eating meat."

"I'd gag. Thinking of the poor innocent animal. I haven't eaten flesh for prit' near seventy years, and I'm proud and thankful for it."

"Well, now, Granny, if you're feeling righteous about it," Donna teased, "maybe you'd feel even prouder and thankfuler if you didn't eat vegetables either. One time in psychology class the professor was telling us about how plants feel pain same as humans."

When the falling sensation passed, she said, "What do you mean? How does he know?"

"He mentioned it, is all. I guess the class had discussed it another day when I wasn't there."

Her fingers wouldn't support the fork any longer. She asked, amazed, "Didn't you wonder about it? Didn't it worry you?"

"Well, of course," Donna bristled. "But the kids said he wasn't going to test us on it, so it was okay."

The bouquet Donna had crowded into one Mason jar smelled like a funeral.

"Listen, Granny, I hate to eat and run, but I just must be scooting along. Thanks for supper. I'll do all the dishes next time," she promised, laughing and winking. She didn't try to bestow a goodbye kiss, only waved and ran out.

The old woman sat staring at the dishes of leftovers. She wondered if the pain stopped once the ear of corn left the stalk, or did it go on as the husk was ripped away. Was it there while the knife severed kernels from cob, and was it there for the scalding water flood? She saw herself forking and chewing and swallowing. At last she rose and scraped out every dish into the slop bucket.

She left the kitchen as it was, hoisting herself upstairs. The first landing had always groaned. This time it froze her in her tracks.

If it is true, she thought, then life is impossible. The house a tomb, made of tree bones. The bedstead, an oak slaughtered by her own father, holding her every night like an open coffin. Books, rugs, pictures, all, all maimed, skinned, murdered. Not just here. Everywhere.

She ground her knuckles into her eyes and moaned, "The tree was crucified first."

She went downstairs slowly, full of dread. She found a shovel in the tool shed, dug a hole by the front porch, and committed to it Mason jar and all. When she'd tamped the dirt and put away the shovel, she walked to the brink of the garden.

Light was fading fast. Crickets had begun gnashing their legs. She sensed the grass blades straining beneath her shoes. The garden crouched before her.

She was trembling so hard she ached. Her voice shook loose and said, "Listen." She hugged herself to keep from flying apart. "If you can understand English," she added hesitantly.

There was no answer.

"I didn't know. I didn't! But now I do, so I won't be bothering you again. Never."

She backed away and turned and made for the house. The skin of her skull pricked with expectation.

Nothing happened.

She went inside and straight upstairs. She fell onto the bed and lay rigid, watching the ceiling disappear. Later she slept, but she didn't rest.

The old woman died the first week of September. She didn't know it because she was in bed asleep. The coroner said it was from natural causes—old age and malnutrition.

Another friend let Donna borrow his black car. When the funeral ended, Donna drove to her inheritance to meet the county's leading realtor.

The two of them strolled around the rocky, weedy yard discussing possibilities. Mr. Howard was reluctant to quote any figure till he'd felt out some potential buyers. Donna wondered if an auction wouldn't be the quickest easiest way. They stopped at the verge of the garden.

"This place looks a lot worse than it is," Donna prompted. "Why, I was in this garden just about a month ago, and what a world of difference. Not a weed in sight. Now look at it. A jungle. Of course, if I'd realized how sick Granny was I'd have stayed right here. But she never let on she wasn't the same as always."

Donna broke a tall blade of grass to chew. She said, "Well, she *was* talking kind of funny part of the time. I guess I should have guessed from that. Do you know they say she didn't eat or drink a single thing but milk for three weeks? Milk is supposed to be the perfect food, I know, but, like the Bible says, Man can't live by milk alone."

Mr. Howard opened his mouth, saw she was serious, and snapped it shut again.

"Anyway, like I was saying, the place needs cleaning up is all. Why, Mr. Howard, just clearing out this mess of overgrown truck patch would do wonders. Maybe I could borrow a riding mower before you bring anybody out to look at the property. Or better yet, I could just set fire to it. Pour kerosene on and throw in a match. Maybe I should do that to the house, too." And she laughed, so Mr. Howard laughed.

"Well, first I got to get the antiques out," she went on. "There's a man coming from Corbin this afternoon to see what's valuable and what's just old."

Mr. Howard said he must go, that he'd check around and give her a ring. He left her beside the garden.

Donna watched him pick his way past the house and out of sight up the hill. She sighed, frowned at her watch, and scuffed a sandy anthill shut with the toe of her shoe. She gazed across the tangled garden, thinking about New York. Her eyes fixed on a blur of color; they focused.

She didn't know her flowers, but this one looked like some kind of rose. Dark red and waxy petaled, it seemed to lean toward her, begging to be picked. She measured the distance with her eyes. Two giant steps in and out— that was all it would take. She chose her foothold carefully, a grassy patch that stuck up above the weedy sea.

As she took the leaping step, some taller plants brushed against her inner thighs. She teetered, steadied, reached to break the stem. The flower swayed aside, and she pinched vacant air, startled to have felt no breeze. That same split second something coiled around her left leg. Snake! her mind squealed before she looked. Her pupils contracted in horror. Her throat scraped with one scream as she fell.

The antiques dealer found her.

Since she wasn't at the house, but her car was still parked on the road, he made a search. He said he was drawn to the garden by the smell, but that was hardly possible, as she had been dead only a few hours.

There were many theories offered by the many people who discussed the event. The most widely accepted, because it seemed the most reasonable, was that the girl had been in the garden when an epileptic fit had seized her. She'd fallen down and rolled around till she was hopelessly tangled in the plants.

The coroner studied on it half a day; then he typed "accidental strangulation" on his report and went outside to groom his privet hedge.

Clubbed to Death
by Donald Olson

When Royden Smith retired after forty years with the Gresham Board of Public Utilities, his sole ambition was to buy a modest camper-trailer and do a bit of traveling, see something of the country before he and his wife May were too old to stir from home. It was a very pleasant home in that section of town known as the Glade, not so pretentious as Pleasantview Heights, but with its own unique woodsy charm.

As May had always shared Royden's dream of traveling, or certainly had given him the impression of doing so, he was unprepared for the damper she cast on the camper idea, even more vigorous a damper than she'd cast on his early retirement with its consequent reduction in pension benefits.

"Time enough for all that gallivanting," May declared, assuming her most imperious expression. "We must tighten our belts, not expand our horizons." Liking the sound of this, she smiled like a politician expecting applause.

Royden didn't applaud, neither did he argue, having learned long ago that arguing with May was a pointless exercise in frustration. Instead he proposed a compromise: they could take a bus tour to Williamsburg, the first of many national historic sites he'd looked forward to visiting.

"Forget that," said May. "I'm entertaining the Garden and Tree ladies on the second. We'll be making final plans for the house and garden tour. Which reminds me, I want you to get started on my English garden before it's too late."

"I don't know the first thing about English gardens," Royden protested. He enjoyed puttering around outside, but planning an English garden lay well beyond his scope.

"You can learn, can't you? That's what libraries are for."

The Garden and Tree Club was only one of May's enthusiasms, but until he retired Royden had had only a vague awareness of just how active a clubwoman May had become.

"Now you must make yourself scarce this afternoon," May informed him. "I'm having the Mozart Club for lunch and study. Poor Betty. You should have seen her face when I was elected president. She'd set her heart on it."

"What am I supposed to do?" Royden quibbled.

"Be *resourceful,* dear. You're retired, remember? You can do whatever you want. Go to the library and read up on English gardens. There's nothing more annoying than having husbands popping in and out when a meeting's in progress."

Royden soon discovered the extent of his wife's club activities, which clearly she had no intention of curtailing to satisfy his whims. Every day she seemed to be off to one or another meeting. There was the Quilters, the Newcomers Club, the Fortnightly, the Garden and Tree, the Mozart Club, the Doreas Circle, the Browning Society, to name but a few. That May had kept herself busy during his working years had pleased Royden, but he'd assumed that once he'd retired she would be devoting her time to sharing his pleasures and pursuits. Such was plainly not to be the case.

What astonished him was the amount of political infighting in these organizations, the subtle conspiracies, the constant jockeying for position. To see her name in the Club Activities column of the *Register* seemed to bring May inordinate satisfaction, and until now Royden had been unaware of the intense rivalry between May and her neighbor Betty Fairbaugh; each aspired to be the Guiding Force in their various clubs.

"Can you imagine?" May exploded one afternoon when she arrived home from a meeting of the Browning Society. "We all know how pushy Betty is, but we had an *agreement*, for heaven's sake. And she betrayed me. I'd promised to back her for president of the Fortnightly if she did the same for me at the Browning. The woman's totally devoid of scruples."

"You could resign," Royden meekly suggested.

"Re*sign?* Are you mad? I should give her the satisfaction?"

"But what about Williamsburg?"

May stared at him as if he'd uttered the most unfathomable of non sequiturs. "Williamsburg?"

"We have to book for the tour before the seats are all taken."

"Royden, weren't you *listening?* How can I go traipsing off to Williamsburg when I've got my plate full with all this planning for the house and garden tour? Be reasonable."

"I'm trying, dear, but every time I suggest we do something together there's always one of these infernal club meetings to interfere."

"You should have thought of that before you took early retirement. You must find things to occupy your time. You know Henry Fairbaugh offered to sponsor you for the Rod and Gun."

"I'm not the least bit interested in rods or guns."

"Silly, it's a *social* club, you don't have to shoot or fish."

"I'm not a joiner. I've never been, you know that."

"Well, you can't simply vegetate. I won't let you."

Royden could imagine nothing more fruitful to the spirit than vegetating in peace, unless it might be traveling about the country visiting historic sites, neither of which pleasures was evidently to be allowed. Early retirement was fast losing its appeal.

Thursday-night bridge with the Fairbaughs had been a ritual for years; Royden found it a relaxing diversion, he and Henry being companionable if not intimate friends. Until now he'd remained oblivious of the immoderate bickering over club matters that May and Betty engaged in over the bridge table.

"Did you know," said Betty, pondering her cards, "that Mrs. Lionel Asperson has agreed to open Bellwood for the first time to the house and garden tour?"

Mrs. Lionel Asperson was the town's richest woman, widow of a department store magnate; May wondered aloud how she had come to make so magnanimous a gesture.

"Little me talked her into it," said Betty with the merest trace of a simper. "What's more, she's all but agreed to join the Garden and Tree."

May lifted her great prow of a nose. "How on earth did you manage that?"

"Well, never mind how I found out, but it seems her gardener's run off with the maid. I suggested she might wish to employ the services of our Pedro. She jumped at the chance."

May winced at the "our Pedro." Pedro Martinez worked part time for a number of Gresham families, not exclusively and not very frequently for the Fairbaughs.

"I dare say," boasted Betty, "that when the club girls learn how I pulled off that little coup there'll be no contest when it comes to choosing our next president."

May simmered beneath her most august smile, decided it best to change the subject. "Did I tell you that Royden is putting in an English garden?"

"How quaint," Betty murmured. "So lucky your having Royden at your beck and call now he's retired. Without Pedro our garden would be a shambles."

Henry winked at Royden. "See why I'm not eager to retire?"

Royden looked glum. "I thought *we* were going to travel when I quit work."

May laughed. "All he does is sputter about seeing the country. Join the Rotary Club, I tell him. They put on some very interesting travelogues."

"Travelogues are not at all the same thing," said Royden crossly. "We can save them for our old age."

"Mrs. Lionel Asperson just returned from a trip to Egypt," said Betty.

"Rich widows like her can afford to travel," Henry replied.

"Which reminds me," said Betty in a confidential tone, "Mrs. Asperson told me she's been asked to form a local chapter of the W.C.A."

"What's that?" asked Royden. "Anything like the S.P.C.A.?"

"Hardly," May replied. "It's a club. Very exclusive. I'm afraid neither Betty nor I are eligible," she added with a sigh.

"Not yet, anyway," said Betty with a coy glance at May. "Unless we were to *pull a few strings,* if you know what I mean." Titter, titter.

May looked blank for a moment, then giggled. "You're very naughty, shame on you."

At the end of the evening, May had to admit that Betty had scored a few points. "I tell you, Royden, that woman won't rest until she's president of every club in town. And talk about coups. Wait till she learns I've roped in one of the country's foremost poets to read for us at the G.L.S. in August."

The Greshan Literary Society was one of May's partic-

ular favorites; she was a charter member and its acknowledged Guiding Force.

Royden scowled. "You know very well we talked about
Mount Rushmore in August."

"*You* talked about Mount Rushmore. And Williamsburg, and Gettysburg, and Stone Mountain, and the Great
Smokies. Have I missed anything? Gracious me, you'd
have us turning into gypsies in our golden years."

"But hang it all, May, why else do you think I took an
early retirement? To travel was our dream."

May regarded him with a smile of patient fortitude.
"Your dream, dear. Of course I had to humor your whims.
That's what wives are for."

Like a child betrayed out of a trip to the circus, Royden
looked around as if for a favorite toy to smash, but he
was too accustomed to containing his anger to do more
than mutter his displeasure.

The following day Royden took himself off to the public library, solved with a little help the mysteries of the
Dewey decimal system, and climbed to the upper tier,
where he found to his dismay shelf upon shelf of books
on gardens and gardening, flowers and plants. So many!
How was he to find one that would tell him what he had
to know about planting an English garden? Browsing the
shelves he did find British books by a Beverley Nichols
and a V. Sackville-West about English gardens, but they
were less than instructive.

He was about to give up—let May plant her own English garden if she was so hot on the idea—when his
weary eyes fell upon a fat little tome with the intriguing
title, *Poisonous Plants*. Wanting something to wile away
an hour or so, Royden carried the book to a small desk in
an alcove and sat down to read.

He'd had no idea there was such a variety of poisonous
plants, and how deceptively pretty they looked in the col-

ored plates: nux vomica, water hemlock, black night-shade, monkshood, henbane, death camass, belladonna, foxglove. So exotic-sounding, yet many of them apparently could be found growing among the commoner wildflowers in rural areas.

"That's no way to research a subject," complained May when Royden reported his failure to acquire any useful information on English gardens. "You don't just paw blindly through the shelves. What do you think reference librarians are there for? Time is wasting, you can't muddle about. You must go back tomorrow and ask for assistance."

"I'll do that," he said musingly, with a secret smile. "I'll go back tomorrow."

"And goodness knows you'll find all manner of books on travel. No need to go careering around in a camper. Let your mind do the traveling. Use your imagination."

Which was precisely what Royden had begun to do.

The following day, a day Royden had spent not only in the library but in rambling about the woods and fields around Gresham, May arrived home from the Garden and Tree in a mood of extreme irritation.

"Can you believe it? Betty Fairbaugh actually *promised* that Mrs. Lionel Asperson would open her home to the house and garden tour if the club would agree to make Betty chairperson of the event. And they *did*."

"So what's wrong with that?" Royden asked.

"My dear man, Betty Fairbaugh has no more organization talent than a snail. This is *the* event of the summer. Oh, I tell you if I could think of a way to put that woman's nose out of joint, I'd do it. I'm in a very bad mood, so don't you dare tell me you wasted another day at the library without learning anything about English gardens."

"No, dear, I didn't waste my time at all."

"And?"

"The librarians were very helpful."

"Well that's more like it. My English garden *must* be planted in time for the house and garden tour."

With the help of Pedro, a fair amount of progress was made on the project, although Royden felt sure the garden's resemblance to an *English* garden would be purely literary, not that May was likely to know the difference.

"Well, I've kept my end of the bargain," said Royden once the plantings had been finished. "I expect you to keep yours, May."

"Bargain? What bargain?"

"As soon as this famous house and garden tour is history, you and I are going to buy that camper and head for the Great Smokies. After Williamsburg."

May snorted, most unbecomingly. "What absolute nonsense. Bargain, indeed. You must be dreaming. I shall be far too busy this fall to do any traveling."

Royden drew himself up. "Would you rather I went by myself?"

"Are you out of your mind? I never heard of anything so preposterous. What would people say?"

Royden smiled broadly. "I've retired from caring what people say."

"You're just trying to get my goat."

"I'm trying to get your attention. Something I haven't been able to do since the day I retired."

"You're being impossible," she snapped.

"No, dear, I'm being serious."

"I don't like being threatened, Royden. I don't like it one little bit."

Royden turned his back and headed for the kitchen. The library, he'd told May, had inspired him with an interest in the culinary arts as a hobby. Not the sort of hobby May would have chosen for him, although she had to admit the omelets Royden had cooked for them in the past few days hadn't been all that bad.

* * *

The accident happened a couple of nights later. Royden was in the living room reading the newspaper when suddenly the lights went out.

May came scurrying out of the kitchen. "I've done it again, dear. I know you told me I shouldn't plug the mixer into that bad outlet but I forgot. A fuse has blown. You'll have to go down cellar and replace it."

Royden muttered under his breath as he fumbled in a kitchen drawer for the flashlight. It wasn't there. May claimed not to have seen it. "You can find your way to the fusebox without a flashlight," she told him.

Royden crossed the dark room to the cellar door. The stairs were treacherously steep and he felt for the handrail screwed into the wall. Two things happened at once. His foot seemed to catch on something and the rail came loose in his hand. Losing his balance, he plunged down into the darkness.

"You were lucky, old boy," said Henry Fairbaugh when it was discovered Royden had suffered no more than a cracked rib. "The way May was carrying on when she came screaming to the door, I thought I'd find you dead on the cellar floor. Bit careless, weren't you?"

"I tripped over something. It caught on my instep. I felt it just before I fell."

Henry shook his head. "I didn't see anything. Maybe it was your shoelace. You know what they say about most accidents happening in the home."

To anyone who didn't know May well, her reaction to the accident might have seemed to be somewhat perfunctory. Royden expected no more. In fact, he was sure Henry's remark about May rushing to his door screaming for help must have been exaggerated; he couldn't imagine anything causing May to lose control of her emotions.

"I'm afraid you'll have to forget about your plans, imaginary or otherwise," she said, "to travel off into the sunset of the Smokies."

"I only cracked a rib, not a hip."

"If you must have a hobby you'd better stick to cooking, it's much less expensive."

Royden, assembling the ingredients for a green salad, nodded agreement. "You're right as always, my dear. Besides, every man should know how to cook in case the day comes when he has to look after himself."

Like many casual observations, it was only in retrospect that Royden's remark acquired a portentous significance. Preparing for bed a few nights later, May, who had been complaining of a nagging abdominal disorder, became deathly ill. Royden summoned dear old Dr. Chumley, who was all but in his dotage, yet still practicing. Regrettably, nothing could be done. May passed away shortly after midnight.

Acute gastritis was noted as the cause of death when Dr. Chumley signed the certificate.

As he paid farewell visits to all their friends, Royden felt for the first time in his memory that sense of unfettered freedom that follows the perilous escape from a confinement seemingly doomed to last forever. In Henry Fairbaugh's eyes he detected a wistful envy as he described the camper he was picking up in the morning before taking off for Williamsburg and points south.

Betty Fairbaugh squeezed out a mournful tear. "How us girls will miss May's forceful presence. There wasn't a club in town she didn't belong to, except of course the W.C.A."

"I remember you mentioned that one," said Royden. "You said May wasn't eligible?"

"Nor ever will be, poor dear. W.C.A. stands for the Widows Clubs of America. Mrs. Lionel Asperson has just formed the local chapter."

Royden drove away in a reflective mood, nagged by certain thoughts about May that left him vaguely ashamed. Her club memberships meant the world to May, and she did say she'd do anything to put Betty Fairbaugh's nose out of joint, but even she wouldn't go that far to make herself eligible for a club Betty couldn't join. What was that quip Betty had made when the W.C.A. was first mentioned at the bridge table, about her and Betty being excluded? *Unless we were to pull a few strings?*

Like maybe stretching a length of twine across a cellar step?

Oh, wicked, wicked thought; but it was funny what crazy ideas could pop into a man's head.

Royden decided to stop at the library and read more about Williamsburg. How true it was, a person could glean much useful information about so many subjects at the library. About gardening, for instance, and cooking, and of course botany.

The Garden of Smoke
by *Gilbert K. Chesterton*

The end of London looked very like the end of the world:
and the last lamppost of the suburbs like a lonely star in
space. It also resembled the end of the world in another
respect: that it was a long time coming.

The girl, Catharine Crawford, was a good walker; she
had the fine figure of the mountaineer; there almost went
with her a wind from the hills through all the gray labyrinth of London. For she came from the high villages of
Westmoreland, and seemed to carry the quiet colors of
them in her light-brown hair, her open features, irregular
yet the reverse of plain, the framework of two grave and
very beautiful gray eyes. But the mountaineer began to
feel the labyrinth of London suburbs interminable and in-
tolerable, swiftly as she walked. She knew little of the details of her destination, save the address of the house, and
the fact that she was going there as a companion to a Mrs.
Mowbray, or rather to *the* Mrs. Mowbray; a famous lady
novelist and fashionable poet, married, it was said, to
some matter-of-fact medical man reduced to the permanent status of Mrs. Mowbray's husband. And when she
found the house eventually, it was at the end of the very
last line of houses, where the suburban gardens faded into
the open fields.

The whole heavens were full of the hues of evening,
though still as luminous as noon, as if in a land of endless
sunset. It settled down in a shower of gold amid the twin-
kling leaves of the thin trees of the gardens, most of

which had low fences and hedges, and lay almost as open to the yellow sky as the fields beyond. The air was so still that occasional voices, talking or laughing on distant lawns, could be heard like clear bells. One voice, more recurrent than the rest, seemed to be whistling and singing the old sailors' song of "Spanish Ladies"; it drew nearer and nearer, and when she turned into the last garden gate at the corner the singer was the first figure she encountered. He stood in a garden red with very gorgeous ranks of standard roses, and against a background of the golden sky and a white cottage, with touches of rather fanciful color; the sort of cottage that is not built for cottagers.

He was a lean, not ungraceful man in gray, with a limp straw hat pulled forward above his dark face and black beard, out of which projected an almost blacker cigar; which he removed when he saw the lady.

"Good evening," he said politely, "I think you must be Miss Crawford. Mrs. Mowbray asked me to tell you that she would be out here in a minute or two, if you cared to look around the garden first. I hope you don't mind my smoking. I do it to kill the insects, you know, on the roses. Need I say that this is the one and only origin of all smoking? Too little credit, perhaps, is given to the self-sacrifice of my sex, from the club-men in smoking-rooms to the navvies on scaffoldings, all steadily and firmly smoking, on the mere chance that a rose may be growing somewhere in the neighborhood. Handicapped, like most of my comrades, with a strong natural dislike of tobacco, I yet contrive to conquer it and—"

He broke off, because the gray eyes regarding him were a little blank and even bleak. He spoke with gravity and even gloom; and she was conscious of humor, but was not sure that it was good humor. Indeed she felt, at first sight, something faintly sinister about him; his face was aquiline and his figure feline, almost as in the fabulous griffin; a creature molded of the eagle and the lion, or perhaps the leopard. She was not sure that she approved of fabulous animals.

"Are you Dr. Mowbray?" she asked, rather stiffly.

"No such luck," he replied, "I haven't got such beautiful roses, or such a beautiful—household, shall we say. But Mowbray is about the garden somewhere, spraying the roses with some low scientific instrument called a syringe. He's a great gardener; but you won't find him spraying with the same perpetual, uncomplaining patience as you'll find me smoking."

With these words he turned on his heel and hallooed his friend's name across the garden in a style which, along with the echo of his song, somehow suggested a ship's captain; which was indeed his trade. A stooping figure disengaged itself from a distant rosebush and came forward apologetically.

Dr. Mowbray also had a loose straw hat and a beard, but there the resemblance ended; his beard was fair and he was burly and big of shoulder; his face was good-humored and would have been good-looking, but that his blue and smiling eyes were a little wide apart; which rather increased the pleasant candor of his expression. By comparison the more deep-sunken eyes on either side of the dark captain's beak seemed to be too close together.

"I was explaining to Miss Crawford," said the latter gentleman, "the superiority of my way of curing your roses—of any of their little maladies. In scientific circles the cigar has wholly superseded the syringe."

"Your cigars look as if they'd kill the roses," replied the doctor. "Why are you always smoking your very strongest cigars here?"

"On the contrary, I am smoking my mildest," answered the captain, grimly. "I've got another sort here, if anybody wants them."

He turned back the lapel of his square jacket, and showed some dangerous-looking sticks of twisted leaf in his upper waistcoat pocket. As he did so they noticed also that he had a broad leather belt round his waist, to which was buckled a big crooked knife in a leather sheath.

As he spoke the French windows of the house opened abruptly, and a man in black came out and passed them, going out at the garden gate. He was walking rapidly, as if irritably, and putting on his hat and gloves as he went. Before he put on his hat he showed a head half bald and bumpy, with a semicircle of red hair; and before he put on his gloves he tore a small piece of paper into yet smaller pieces, and tossed it away among the roses by the road.

"Oh, one of Marion's friends from the Theosophical or Ethical Society, I think," said the doctor. "His name's Miall, a tradesman in the town, a chemist or something."

"He doesn't seem in the best or most ethical of tempers," observed the captain. "I thought you nature-worshippers were always serene. Well, he's released our hostess at any rate; and here she comes."

Marion Mowbray really looked like an artist, which an artist is not supposed to do. This did not come from her clinging green draperies and halo of Pre-Raphaelite brown hair, which need only have made her look like an esthete. But in her face there was a true intensity; her keen eyes were full of distances, that is of desires, but of desires too large to be sensuous. If such a soul was wasted by a flame, it seemed one of purely spiritual ambition. A moment after she had given her hand to the guest, with very graceful apologies, she stretched it out toward the flowers with a gesture that was quite natural, yet so decisive as to be almost dramatic.

"I simply must have some more of those roses in the house," she said, "and I've lost my scissors. I know it sounds silly, but when the fit comes over me I feel I must tear them off with my hands. Don't you love roses, Miss Crawford? I simply can't do without them sometimes."

The captain's hand had gone to his hip, and the queer crooked knife was naked in the sun; a shining but ugly shape. In a few flashes he had hacked and lopped away a long spray or two of blossom, and handed them to her with a bow, like a bouquet on the stage.

"Oh, thank you," she said, rather faintly; and one could fancy, somehow, a tragic irony behind the masquerade. The next moment she recovered herself, and laughed a little. "It's absurd I know; but I do so hate ugly things, and living in the London suburbs, though only on the edge of them. Do you know, Miss Crawford, the next-door neighbor walks about his garden in a top hat. Positively in a top hat! I see it passing just above that laurel hedge about sunset; when he's come back from the city, I suppose. Think of the laurel, that we poor poets are supposed to worship," and she laughed more naturally, "and then think of my feelings, looking up and seeing it wreathed round a top hat."

And, indeed, before the party entered the house to prepare for the evening meal, Catharine had actually seen the offending headdress appear above the hedge, a shadow of respectability in the sunshine of that romantic plot of roses.

At dinner they were served by a man in black like a butler, and Catharine felt an unmeaning embarrassment in the mere fact. A man-servant seemed out of place in that artistic toy cottage, and there was nothing notable about the man addressed as Parker except that he seemed especially so—a tall man with a wooden face and dark flat hair like a Dutch doll's. He would have been proper enough if the doctor had lived in Harley Street, but he was too big for the suburbs.

Nor was he the only incongruous element, nor the principal one. The captain, whose name seemed to be Fonblanque, still puzzled her and did not altogether please her. Her northern Puritanism found something obscurely rowdy about his attitude. It would be hardly adequate to say he acted as if he were at home; it would be truer to say he acted as if he were abroad in a *café* or tavern in some foreign port. Mrs. Mowbray was a vegetarian; and though her husband lived the simple life in a rather simpler fashion, he was sufficiently sophisticated to drink water. But Captain Fonblanque had a great flagon of rum all to himself, and did not disguise his relish; and the meal ended in smoke of the most rich and reeking description. And throughout the captain continued to fence with his hostess and with the stranger, with the same flippancies that had fallen from him in the garden.

"It's my childlike innocence that makes me drink and smoke," he explained. "I can enjoy a cigar as I could a sugarstick; but you jaded dissipated vegetarians look down on such sugarsticks." His irony was partly provocative, whether of her hosts or herself; and Catharine was conscious of something slightly Mephistophelean about his blue-black beard and ivory-yellow face amid the fumes that hung round his head.

In passing out, the ladies paused accidentally at the open French windows, and Catharine looked out upon the darkening lawn. She was surprised to see that clouds had already come up out of the colored west, and the twilight was troubled with rain. There was a silence and then Catharine said, rather suddenly:

"That neighbor of yours must be very fond of his garden. Almost as fond of the roses as you are, Mrs. Mowbray."

"Why, what do you mean?" asked that lady, turning back.

"He's still standing among his flowers in the pouring rain," said Catharine, staring, "and will soon be standing in the pitch dark too. I can still see his black hat in the dusk."

"Who knows," said the lady poet, softly, "perhaps a sense of beauty has really stirred in him in a strange, sudden way. If seeds under black earth can grow into those glorious roses, what will souls even under black hats grow into at last? Don't you like the smell of the damp earth, and that deep noise of all the roses drinking?"

"All the roses are teetotalers, anyhow," remarked Catharine, smiling.

Her hostess smiled also. "I'm afraid Captain Fonblanque shocked you a little; he's rather eccentric, wearing that crooked Eastern dagger just because he's traveled in the East, and drinking rum of all ridiculous things, just to show he's a sailor. But he's an old friend, you know."

"Yes, he reminds me of a pirate in a play," said Catharine, laughing. "He might be stalking round this house looking for hidden treasure of gold and silver."

Mrs. Mowbray seemed to start a little, and then stared out into the dark in silence. At last she said, in a changed voice:

"It is strange that you should say that."

"And why," inquired her companion in some wonder.

"Because there is a hidden treasure in this house," said Mrs. Mowbray, "and such a thief might well steal it. It's not exactly gold or silver, but it's almost as valuable, I believe, even in money. I don't know why I tell you this; but at least you can see I don't distrust you. Let's go into the other room." And she rather abruptly led the way in that direction.

Catharine Crawford was a woman whose conscious mind was full of practicality; but her unconscious mind had its own poetry; which was all on the note of purity. She loved white light and clear waters, boulders washed smooth in rivers, and the sweeping curves of wind. It was perhaps the poetry that Wordsworth, at his finest, found in the lakes of her own land, and in principle it could repose in the artistic austerity of Marion Mowbray's home. But whether the stage was filled too much by the almost fantastic figure of the piratical Fonblanque, or whether the summer heat, with its hint of storm, obscured such clarity, she felt an oppression. Even the rose garden seemed more like a chamber curtained with red and green than an open place. Her own chamber was curtained in sufficiently cool and soothing colors, yet she fell asleep later than usual, and then heavily.

She woke with a start from some tangled dream of which she recalled no trace. With senses sharpened by darkness, she was vividly conscious of a strange smell. It was vaporous and heavy, not unpleasant to the nostrils, yet somehow all the more unpleasant to the nerves. It was not the smell of any tobacco she knew; and yet she connected it with those sinister black cigars to which the captain's brown finger had pointed. She thought half-consciously that he might be still smoking in the garden; and that those dark and dreadful weeds might well be smoked in the dark. But it was only half-consciously that she thought or moved at all; she remembered half rising from her bed; and then remembered nothing but more dreams, which left a little more recollection in their track. They were but a medley of the smoking and the strange smell and the scents of the rose garden; but they seemed to make up a mystery as well as a medley. Sometimes the roses were themselves a sort of purple smoke. Sometimes they glowed from purple to fiery crimson, like the butts of a giant's cigars. And that garden of smoke was haunted by the pale yellow face and blue-black beard, and she awoke with the word "Bluebeard" on her mind and almost on her mouth.

Morning was so much of a relief as to be almost a surprise; the rooms were full of the white light that she loved, and which might well be the light of a primeval wonder. As she passed the half-open door of the doctor's scientific study or consulting room, she paused by a window, and saw the silver daybreak brightening over the garden. She was idly counting the birds that began to dart by the house; and as she counted the fourth she heard the shock of a falling chair, followed by a voice crying out and cursing again and again. The voice was strained and unnatural; but after the first few syllables she recognized it as that of the doctor. "It's gone!" he was saying, "The stuff's gone, I tell you!"

The reply was inaudible; but she already suspected that it came from the servant Parker, whose voice was as baffling as his face. The doctor answered again in unabated agitation:

"The drug, you devil or dunce or whatever you are! The drug I told you to keep an eye on!"

This time she heard the dull tones of the other who seemed to be saying, "There's very little of it gone, sir."

"Why has any of it gone?" cried Doctor Mowbray. "Where's my wife?"

Probably hearing the rustle of a skirt outside, he flung the door open and came face to face with Catharine, falling back before her in consternation. The room into which she now looked in bewilderment was neat and even severe; except for the fallen chair still lying on its back on the carpet. It was fitted with bookcases, and contained a rack of bottles and phials, like those in a chemist's shop, the colors of which looked like jewels in the brilliant early daylight. One glittering green bottle bore a large label of "Poison," but the present problem seemed to revolve round a glass vessel, rather like a decanter, which stood on the table, more than half full of a dust or powder of a rich reddish brown.

Against this strict scientific background the tall servant looked more important and appropriate; in fact she was soon conscious that he was something more intimate than a servant who waited at table. He had at least the air of a doctor's assistant; and indeed, in comparison with his distracted employer, might also at that moment have been the attendant in a private asylum.

"It's the cursed plague breaking out again," said the doctor hastily. "Go and see if my wife is in the dining room."

He pulled himself together as Parker left the room, and

picked up the chair that had fallen on the carpet, offering it to the girl with a gesture.

"Well, I suppose you ought to have been told. Anyhow you'll have to be told now."

There was another silence, and then he said: "My wife is a poet, you know; a creative artist and all that. And all enlightened people know that a genius can't be judged quite by common rules of conduct. A genius lives by a recurrent need for a sort of inspiration."

"What do you mean?" asked Catharine almost impatiently, for the preamble of excuses was a strain on her nerves.

"There's a kind of opium in that bottle," he said abruptly, "a very rare kind. She smokes it occasionally; that's all. I wish Parker would hurry up and find her."

"I can find her, I think," said Catharine, relieved by the chance of doing something; and not a little relieved, also, to get out of the scientific room. "I think I saw her going down the garden path."

When she went out into the rose garden it was full of the freshness of the sunrise; and all her smoke nightmares were rolled away from it. The roof of her green and crimson room seemed to have been lifted off like a lid. She went down many winding paths without seeing any living thing but the birds hopping here and there; then she came to the corner of one turning, and stood still.

In the middle of the sunny path, a few yards from one of the birds, lay something crumpled like a great green rag. But it was really the rich green dress of Marion Mowbray; and beyond it was her fallen face, colorless against its halo of hair, and one arm thrust out in a piteous stiffness toward the roses, as she had stretched it when Catharine saw her for the first time. Catharine gave a little cry, and the birds flashed away into a tree. Then she bent over the fallen figure; and knew, in a blast of all the trumpets of terror, why the face was colorless, and why the arm was stiff.

An hour afterward, still in that world of rigid unreality that remains long after a shock, she was but automatically, though efficiently, helping in the hundred minute and aching utilities of a house of mourning. How she had told them she hardly knew; but there was no need to tell much. Mowbray the doctor soon had bad news for Mowbray the husband, when he had been but a few moments silent and busy over the body of his wife. Then he turned away; and Catharine almost feared he would fall.

A problem confronted him still, however, even as a doctor, when he had so grimly solved his problem as a husband. His medical assistant, whom he had always had reason to trust, still emphatically asserted that the amount of the drug missing was insufficient to kill a kitten. He came down and stood with the little group on the lawn where the dead woman had been laid on a sofa, to be examined in the best light. He repeated his assertion in the face of the examination; and his wooden face was knotted with obstinacy.

"If he is right," said Captain Fonblanque, "she must have got it from somewhere else as well, that's all. Did any strange people come here lately?"

He had taken a turn or two of pacing up and down the lawn, when he stopped with an arrested gesture.

"Didn't you say that Theosophist was also a chemist?" he asked. "He may be as theosophical or ethical as he likes; but he didn't come here on a theosophical errand. No, by gad, nor an ethical one."

It was agreed that this question should be followed up first; Parker was despatched to the High Street of the neighboring suburb; and about half an hour afterward the black-clad figure of Mr. Miall came back into the garden, much less swiftly than he had gone out of it. He removed his hat out of respect for the presence of death; and his face under the ring of red hair was whiter than the dead.

But though pale, he also was firm; and that upon a point that brought the inquiry once more to a standstill.

He admitted that he had once supplied that peculiar brand of opium, and he did not attempt to dissipate the cloud of responsibility that rested on him so far. But he vehemently denied that he had supplied it yesterday, or even lately, or indeed for long past.

"She must have got some more somehow," cried the doctor, in dogmatic and even despotic tones, "and where could she have got it but from you?"

"And where could I have got it from anybody?" demanded the tradesman, equally hotly. "You seem to think it's sold like shag. I tell you there's no more of it in England—a chemist can't get it even for desperate cases. I gave her the last I had months ago, more shame to me; and when she wanted more yesterday, I told her I not only wouldn't but couldn't. There's the scraps of the note she sent me, still lying where I tore it up in a temper."

The doctor seemed to regard the hitch in the inquiry with a sort of harassed fury. He browbeat the pale chemist even more than he had browbeaten his servant about his first and smaller discovery. His desire at the moment, so concrete as to be comic in such a scene, seemed to be the desire to hang a chemist.

The figures in the little group on the lawn had fallen into such angry attitudes, that one could almost fancy they would strike each other even in the presence of the dead; when an interruption came, as soft as the note of the bird, but as unexpected as a thunderbolt. A voice from several yards away said mildly but more or less loudly:

"Permit me to offer my assistance."

They all looked around and saw the next-door neighbor's top hat, above a large, loose, heavy-lidded face, leaning over the low fringe of laurels.

"I'm sure I can be of some little help," he said. And the next moment he had calmly taken a high stride over the low hedge and was walking across the lawn toward them. He was a large, heavily walking man in a loose frock-coat; his clean-shaven face was at once heavy and cadaverous. He spoke in a soft and even sentimental tone, which contrasted with his impudence and, as it soon appeared, with his trade.

"What do you want here?" asked Dr. Mowbray sharply, when he had recovered from sheer astonishment.

"It is you who want something—sympathy," said the strange gentleman. "Sympathy and also light. I think I can offer both. Poor lady, I have watched her for many months."

"If you've been watching over the wall," said the Captain, frowning, "we should like to know why. There are suspicious facts here, and you seem to have behaved in a suspicious manner."

"Suspicion rather than sympathy," said the stranger, with a sigh, "is perhaps the defect in my duties. But my sorrow for this poor lady is perfectly sincere. Do you suspect me of being mixed up in her trouble?"

"Who are you?" asked the angry doctor.

"My name is Traill," said the man in the top hat. "I have some official title; but it was never used except at Scotland Yard. We needn't use it among neighbors."

"You are a detective, in fact?" observed the Captain. But he received no reply, for the new investigator was already examining the corpse, quite respectfully but with a professional absence of apology. After a few moments he rose again, and looked at them under the large drooping eyelids which were his most prominent features, and said simply:

"It is satisfactory to let people go, Dr. Mowbray; and your druggist and your assistant can certainly go. It was not the fault of either of them that the unhappy lady died."

"Do you mean it was a suicide?" asked the other.

"I mean it was a murder," said Mr. Traill. "But I have a very sufficient reason for saying she was not killed by the druggist."

"And why not?"

"Because she was not killed by the drug," said the man from next door.

"What?" exclaimed the Captain, with a slight start. "How else could she have been killed?"

"She was killed with a short and sharp instrument, the point of which was prepared in a particular manner for the purpose," said Traill in the level tones of a lecturer. "There was apparently a struggle but probably a short, or even a slight one. Poor lady, just look at this;" and he lifted one of the dead hands quite gently, and pointed to what appeared to be a prick or puncture on the wrist.

"A hypodermic needle, perhaps," said the Doctor in a low voice. "She generally took a drug by smoking it; but she might have used a hypodermic syringe and needle after all."

The detective shook his head, so that one could almost imagine his hanging eyelids flapping with the loose movement. "If she injected it herself," he said sadly, "she would make a clean perforation. This is more a scratch than a prick and you can see it has torn the lace on her sleeve a little."

"But how can it have killed her," Catharine was compelled to ask, "if it was only a scratching on the wrist?"

"Ah," said Mr. Traill; and then, after a short silence, "I think," he said, "that when we find the dagger, we shall find it a poisoned dagger. Is that plain enough, Captain Fonblanque?"

The next moment he seemed to droop again with his rather morbid and almost maudlin tone of compassion. "Poor lady," he repeated. "She was so fond of roses, wasn't she? Strew on her roses, roses, as the poet says. I really feel somehow that it might give a sort of rest to her, even now."

He looked around the garden with his heavy, half-closed eyes, and addressed Fonblanque more sympathetically. "It was on a happier occasion, Captain, that you last cut flowers for her; but I can't help wishing it could be done again now."

Half unconsciously, the Captain's hand went to where the hilt of his knife had hung, then his hand dropped, as if in abrupt recollection. But as the flap of his jacket shifted for an instant, they saw that the leather sheath was empty and the knife was gone.

"Such a very sad story, such a terrible story," murmured the man in the top hat distantly, as if he were talking of a novel. "Of course it is a silly fancy about the flowers. It is not such things as that that are our duties to the dead."

The others seemed still a little bewildered; but Catharine was looking at the Captain as if she had been turned to stone by a basilisk. Indeed that moment had been for her the beginning of a monstrous interregnum of imagination, which might well be said to be full of monsters. Something of such mythology had hung about the garden since her first fancy about a man like a griffin. It lasted for many days and nights, during which the detective seemed to hover over the house like a vampire; but the vampire was not the most awful of the monsters. She hardly defined to herself what she thought, or rather refused to think. But she was conscious of other unknown emotions coming to the surface and co-existing, somehow, with that sunken thought that was their contrary.

For some time past the first unfriendly feelings about the Captain had rather faded from her mind; even in that short space he had improved on acquaintance, and his sensible conduct in the crisis was a relief from the wild grief and anger of the husband, however natural these might be. Moreover the very explosion of the opium secret, in accounting for the cloud upon the house, had cleared away another suspicion she had half entertained about the wife and the piratical guest. This she was now disposed to dismiss, so far at least as he was concerned; and she had lately had an additional reason for doing so.

The eyes of Fonblanque had been following her about, in a manner in which so humorous and therefore modest a lady was not likely to be mistaken; and she was surprised to find in herself a corresponding recoil from the idea of this comedy of sentiment turning suddenly to a tragedy of suspicion.

For the next few nights she again slept uneasily; and, as is often the case with a crushed or suppressed thought, the doubt raged and ruled in her dreams. What might be called the Bluebeard *motif* ran through even wilder scenes of strange lands, full of fantastic cities and giant vegetation; through all of which passed a solitary figure with a blue beard and a red knife. It was as if this sailor not only had a wife, but a murdered wife, in every port. And there recurred again and again, like a distant but distinct voice speaking, the accents of the detective: "If only we could find the dagger, we should find it a poisoned dagger."

Yet nothing could have seemed more cool and casual than the moment, on the following morning, when she did find it. She had come down from the upper rooms and gone through the French windows into the garden once more; she was about to pass down the paths among the rose bushes, when she looked round and saw the Captain leaning on the garden gate. There was nothing unusual in his idle and somewhat languid attitude; but her eye was fixed, and as if it were frozen, on the one bright spot where the sun again shone and shifted on the crooked blade. He was somewhat sullenly hacking with it at the wooden fence; but stopped when their eyes met.

"So you've found it again?" was all that she could say.

"Yes, I've found it," he replied rather gloomily, and then after a pause; "I've also found several other things, including how I lost it."

"Do you mean," asked Catharine, unsteadily, "that you've found out about—about Mrs. Mowbray?"

"It wouldn't be correct to say I've found it out," he answered. "Our depressing neighbor with the top hat and the eyelids has found it out, and he's upstairs now, finding more of it out. But if you mean do I know how Marion was murdered, yes, I do; and I rather wish I didn't."

After a minute or two of objectless chipping on the fence, he stuck the point of his knife into the wood; and faced her abruptly.

"Look here," he said, "I should like to explain myself a little. When we first knew each other, I suppose I was very flippant. I admired your gravity and great goodness so much that I had to attack it; can you understand that? But I was not entirely flippant—no, nor entirely wrong. Think again of all the silly things that annoyed you, and of whether they have turned out so very silly? Are not rum and tobacco really more childlike and innocent than some things, my friend? Has any low sailors' tavern seen a worse tragedy than you have seen here? Mine are vulgar tastes, or if you like, vulgar vices. But there is one thing to be said for our appetites; that they are appetites. Pleasure may be only satisfaction; but it can be satisfied. We drink because we are thirsty; but not because we want to be thirsty. I tell you that these artists thirst for thirst. They want infinity, and they get it, poor souls. It may be bad to be drunk; but you can't be infinitely drunk; you fall down. A more horrible thing happens to them; they rise and rise, forever. Isn't it better to fall under the table and snore, than to rise through the seven heavens on the smoke of opium?"

She answered at last, with an appearance of thought and hesitation.

"There may be something in what you say; but it doesn't account for all the nonsensical things you said." She smiled a little and added, "You said you only smoked for the good of the roses, you know. You'll hardly pretend there was any solemn truth behind that."

He started, and then stepped forward leaving the knife standing and quivering in the fence.

"Yes, by Gad, there was!" he cried. "It may seem the

maddest thing of all, but it's true. Death and hell would not be in this house today, if they had only trusted my trick of smoking the roses."

Catharine continued to look at him wildly; but his own gaze did not falter or show a shade of doubt, and he went slowly back to the fence and plucked his knife out of it. There was a long silence in the garden before either of them spoke again.

"Do you think," he asked, in a low voice, "that Marion is really dead?"

"Dead!" repeated Catharine. "Of course she's dead."

He seemed to nod in brooding acquiescence staring at his knife; then he added: "Do you think her ghost walks?"

"What do you mean? Do you think so?" demanded his companion.

"No," he said, "but that drug of hers is still disappearing."

She could only repeat, with a pale face: "Still disappearing?"

"In fact, it's nearly disappeared," remarked the Captain. "You can come upstairs and see, if you like." He stopped and gazed at her a moment very seriously. "I know you are brave," he said. "Would you really like to see the end of this nightmare?"

"It would be a much worse nightmare if I didn't," she answered. The Captain, with a gesture at once negligent and resolved, tossed his knife among the rosebushes and turned toward the house.

She looked at him with a last flicker of suspicion. "Why are you leaving your dagger in the garden?" she asked abruptly.

"The garden is full of daggers," said the Captain as he went upstairs. Mounting the staircase with a catlike swiftness, he was some way ahead of the girl, in spite of her own mountaineering ease of movement. She had time to reflect that the grays and greens of the dados and decorative curtains had never seemed to her so dreary and even inhuman. And when she reached the landing and the door of the Doctor's study, she met the Captain again, face to face. For he stood now, with his face as pale as her own, and not any longer as leading her, but rather as barring her way.

"What is the matter?" she cried; and then, by a wild intuition, "Is somebody else dead?"

"Yes," replied Fonblanque, "somebody else is dead."

In the silence they heard within the heavy and yet soft movements of the strange investigator; Fonblanque spoke again with a new impulsiveness:

"Catharine, I think you know how I feel about you; but what I am trying to say now is not about myself. It may seem a queer thing for a man like me to say; but somehow I think you will understand. Before you go inside, remember the things outside. I don't mean my things, but yours. I mean the empty sky and all the good gray virtues and the things that are clean and strong like the wind. Believe me, they are real, after all; more real than the cloud on this accursed house."

"Yes, I think I understand you," she said. "And now let me pass." Apart from the detective's presence there were but two differences in the Doctor's study as compared with the time when she stood in it last; and though they bulked very unequally to the eye, they seemed almost equal in a deadly significance. On a sofa under the window, covered with a sheet, lay something that could only be a corpse; but the very bulk of it, and the way in which the folds of the sheet fell, showed her that it was not the corpse she had already seen. For herself she had hardly need to glance at it; she knew almost before she looked, that it was not the wife, but the husband. And on the table stood the glass vessel of the opium and the other green bottle labeled "Poison." But the opium vessel was quite empty.

The detective came forward with a mildness amounting to embarrassment.

"You are naturally prejudiced against me, my dear," he said. "You feel I am a morbid person; I think you sometimes feel I was probably a murderer. Well, I think you were right; not about the murder, but about the morbidity. I can't help being interested in tragedies that are my trade; and you're quite wrong if you think my sentiment's all hypocritical."

Catherine did not doubt his good nature. But the unanswered riddle still rode her imagination.

"But I thought you said," she protested, "that Mrs. Mowbray was not killed by the drug."

"She was not killed by the drug. She was killed *for* the drug. Did you notice anything odd about Dr. Mowbray, when you were last in his room?"

"He was naturally agitated," said the girl doubtfully.

"No, unnaturally agitated," replied Traill; "more agitated than a man so sturdy would have been even by the revelation of another's weakness. It was his own weakness that rattled him like a storm that morning. He was indeed angry that the drug was stolen by his wife; for the simple reason that he wanted all that was left for himself. I have rather an ear for distant conversation, Miss Crawford, and I once heard you talking at the window about a pirate and a treasure. Can't you picture two pirates stealing the same treasure bit by bit, till one of them killed the other in rage at seeing it vanish? That is what happened in this house; and perhaps we had better call it madness, and then pity it. The drug had become that unhappy man's life, and that a horribly happy life. He had long resolved that when he had really emptied this bottle," and Traill touched the receptacle of opium, "he would at once turn to this"—and he laid his lean hand on the green bottle of poison.

Catharine's face was still puzzled.

"You mean her husband killed her, and then killed himself?" she said, in her simple way. "But how did he kill her, if not with the drug? Indeed how did he kill her at all?"

"He stabbed her," replied Traill. "He stabbed her in a strange fashion, when she was far away at the other end of the garden."

"But he was not there!" cried Catharine. "He was up in this room."

"He was not there when he stabbed her," answered the detective.

"I told Miss Crawford," said the Captain, in a low voice, "that the garden was full of daggers."

"Yes, of green daggers that grow on trees," continued Traill. "You may say if you like that she was killed by a wild creature, tied to the earth but armed."

His morbid fancy in putting things moved in her again her vague feeling of a garden of green mythological monsters.

"He was committing the crime at the moment when you first came into that garden," said Traill. "The crime that he committed with his own hands. You stood in the sunshine and watched him commit it.

"I have told you the deed was done for the drug, but not by the drug. I tell you now it was done with a syringe, but not a hypodermic syringe. It was being done with that ordinary garden implement he was holding in his hand when you saw him first. But the stuff with which he drenched the green rose trees came out of this green bottle."

"He poisoned the roses?" asked Catharine, almost mechanically.

"Yes," said the Captain, "he poisoned the roses. And the thorns."

He had not spoken for some time; but the girl was gazing at him distractedly.

Then she said, "And the knife . . .?"

"That is soon said," answered Traill. "The presence of the knife had nothing to do with it. The absence of the knife had a great deal. The murderer stole it and hid it, partly perhaps with some idea that its loss would look black against the Captain, whom I did in fact suspect, as I think you did. But there was a much more practical reason; the same that had made him steal and hide his wife's scissors. You heard his wife say she always wanted to tear off the roses with her fingers. If there was no instrument to hand, he knew that one fine morning she would. And one fine morning she did."

Catharine left the room without looking again at what lay in the light of the window under the sheet. She had no desire but to leave the room, and leave the house, and above all leave the garden behind her. And when she went out into the road she automatically turned her back on the fringe of fanciful cottages, and set her face toward the open fields and the distant woods of England. And she was already snapping bracken and startling birds with her step before she became conscious of anything incongruous in the fact that Fonblanque was still strolling in her company.

And, as the tales go, it was like the end of the world in that it was the beginning of a better one.

The Price of Tomatoes
by William Bunce

"Hope springs eternal"—that's what Edie Sangroff said to herself when, from the kitchen window of her retirement home, she watched her husband Morton once more attack the stubborn clay of the back yard garden.

Outside, in the glassy afternoon sunshine, Morton jabbed the spade viciously at the ground. Perspiration trickled over his salt-and-pepper eyebrows and down his flushed cheeks. Every time he turned a clump of earth, his spine felt like a hot wire shooting sparks through his arms and legs.

Years ago Dr. Traub had suggested gardening as a way of reducing Morton's blood pressure. "Great recreation," he remembered the physician saying, "and you can beat the supermarket out of a few bucks, what with the price of fresh produce nowadays." Morton took his advice to heart. Now the good doctor was resting comfortably in the shade of a concrete archangel, while his ex-patient toiled like a Chinese coolie. Each year he drove himself to his gardening chores, but only recently had he begun to ask himself why.

He might just as well ask himself why he put his fist through two wall lockers after he captained the Crimson Cougars to their loss of the state championship in '38. Or why he left his squad behind to be one of the first infantrymen off Omaha Beach during D-Day. Morton was a sucker for competition. The plaque that rode his office desk for forty years was now over his front door. It read: When the going gets tough, the tough get going.

Of course, he had his detractors. Some even thought him a poor loser. These he dismissed as envious cretins. As evidence of his lack of sportsmanship, critics would refer to the celebrated "doubles incident," which continued to run the rounds of senior tennis buffs. Skip Solarski, a retired podiatrist from Brooklyn, still took medication as a result of that little blowup. After a brief executive session, the rules committee voted to banish Morton from the sports complex pending a written apology. This, needless to say, was not forthcoming.

That left tomatoes. Every summer, Harmony Village's weekly tabloid, the *Sunday Sentinel*, awarded a prize for the biggest tomato grown within the confines of the community. For three straight years he had carried away the trophy without much trouble. Then Archie Ledbetter moved in next door, and Morton became a has-been. Sure, his fruit continued to ripen on schedule, large-globed and sweet as heaven; but they were nothing compared to Ledbetter's. His were the size of small cantaloupes and the color of clotted blood.

In fact, the first time Archie took Grand Prize, Morton suspected chicanery. His neighbor had erected a six-foot cedar fence to shield his plot from prying eyes and, for insurance, posted an ill-humored Doberman pinscher near the gate. From his bedroom window, however, Morton had a bird's eye view of Ledbetter's secret nook. In the interests of fair play, he was determined to observe the development of his neighbor's garden and report any irregularity to the judges.

The first surprise: Ledbetter grew nothing but tomatoes. No peppers, squash, cucumbers—just a few stringy plants he picked up on sale at the local K-Mart.

The second surprise: Morton's neighbor took little or no interest in his crops after shoving them rudely into the ground. Not once did Morton see him breaking his back

weeding or squishing loathsome hornworms from the
fragile transplants—just as he did night after night while
the mosquitoes took their due.

After a week of such negligence, to Morton's amaze-
ment, Ledbetter's plants simply took off. The stalks grew
as thick as a man's arm, and the leaves turned as green as
a spring grasshopper. At contest time Ledbetter could
have randomly picked any of his tomatoes and walked
away with first prize.

Morton vowed this year would be different. He was no
more willing to let his rival push him out of the picture
than he was willing to let the Germans push him into the
sea that fateful day in 1944. It was just another kind of
war; and as he leaned on the shovel, exhausted after digging only one row, Morton decided the first step in any
campaign was to gather intelligence.

Accordingly, the next night he set out for Archie
Ledbetter's front door with a bottle of his best blackberry
wine. He leaned on the doorbell for five minutes before
deciding it was out of order. Typical. The man hadn't
fixed a thing since he moved in. The front gutter waved
ominously in the light breeze; the plastic-potted plants
dangling from the porch were shriveled skeletons; the little jockey lying on the front lawn had toppled with his
lamp in a rainstorm. All of which pointed to someone
who just didn't care, who thumbed his nose at his neighbors and let the world go to rack and ruin.

Morton transferred the wine bottle to his left hand and
banged on the door with his fist. Somewhere in the depths
of the house he heard what sounded like heavy furniture
being moved about, an anthropoid grunt, and finally footsteps shuffling towards the door. Morton smoothed down
the front of his sportshirt and looked as pleasant as possible. The door opened a chain's length and a watery blue
eye looked him up and down.

"Hi, neighbor," said Morton in a voice so loud it even
startled himself. "Just thought you'd appreciate a bottle

of my blackberry wine." He thrust the bottle at the crack in the doorway. "Make it myself with a press I have in the cellar."

The eye narrowed. "That you, Mort Sangroff?"

"The same."

"You look different in the dark—skinnier."

Morton was losing patience. After all, nobody chained their doors in Harmony Village; there hadn't been a single robbery in five years. Who was he afraid of, anyway? "Listen, do you want this or not?" Once more he held up the unlabeled bottle before the eye. This time the chain rattled a few times, and the door finally swung open.

Ledbetter was in his striped pajamas. Most of the buttons were missing from the jacket, and his huge, hairy belly sagged obscenely over the elastic. He looked as if he hadn't shaved in several days, and he smelled like a damp horse. "How strong is that stuff?" he said, extending one of his sausage fingers.

"Strong enough," muttered Morton, putting a foot inside the doorway. "Why don't you invite me in, and we'll find out?"

The neighbor rubbed his stubbled chin for a moment. "I *was* going to hit the liquor store," he said. "Gin ran out yesterday, but now you saved me the trouble." He made a mock cavalier gesture with one arm. "Come into my parlor, please."

He led Morton into the kitchen, then hunted in the cupboards for some glasses. He came up with two dusty jelly jars. "It's only homemade stuff," he cracked. "No need to get fancy."

Morton dispensed the wine, making sure that Ledbetter got twice as much. "I had a couple before I got here," he explained.

Ledbetter shrugged. "All the same to me, buddy-boy." Just as he put the glass to his lips, he hesitated. "Say, you wouldn't poison me, would you?"

"Why would I do that?"

The gurgling laugh started at the bottom of Ledbetter's belly and slowly rose to the top until his whole flabby body rippled with mirth. Finally he trained his gaze on Morton, deadly serious. " 'Cause I beat you out of that Grand Prize year after year." Another wave of laughter. "I don't care about the tomatoes. That pukey look you get when they hand me that award is reward enough."

Overcoming his urge to throttle the beast right then and there, Morton forced a smile. "So don't drink if you think I'd poison you."

For a minute there was silence between them. Ledbetter's lips twisted into an ugly leer, and he drained off the glass in one gulp. "Not bad," he said, using the back of his hand to erase the stain of the wine. "Let's belly up and have another go." He slammed the jar down on the table for seconds.

They drank into the night. When the first bottle ran out, Morton scurried back for another, then another, until he lost track of the trips he made back to the house. All he knew was that Ledbetter's kitchen kept shifting and distorting until he felt as if he were inside an abstract picture.

The conversation returned to tomatoes. "I've got to admit I can't grow them as good as you, Ledbetter. Nobody's seen specimens like yours—around here, anyway."

As far gone as he was, Ledbetter's radar picked up the insinuation at once. He pounded a hammy fist on the table. "Well, I grow 'em back of the house. I don't care what anybody thinks." He leaned forward secretively. "I bet you'd like to know how I do it, buddy-boy?"

Morton stifled his curiosity for the moment. "Everybody has their own recipe. Mrs. Gebhardt buries tea leaves, Gabe Hoffsteder spreads chicken manure. . . ."

"Boneheads," announced Ledbetter. He gripped Morton's arm, and his fingers reached all the way around the biceps. "If I show you how it's done, you promise to keep it to yourself?"

This was exactly what Morton had wanted. It was simply a matter of letting the liquor do its work. He would have enjoyed his victory more, though, if strange things weren't happening inside his stomach. "I promise," he said solemnly.

Ledbetter disappeared for a minute and returned with a New York newspaper. He threw it down in front of Morton. "What do you see on the front page?"

He really tried to focus, but it was difficult for Morton. All he could make out was a fuzzy young blonde. "It's a girl," he said.

"What does the caption read?"

The words stumbled off Morton's tongue: "PROSTITUTE FOUND SLASHED." He looked at Ledbetter blankly. "So what does that have to do with tomatoes?"

His neighbor looked at him slyly and emptied the dregs of the bottle into his jelly jar. "Just this: After I got out the navy, I worked my way around South America as a straw boss, building bridges, roads, and such. I was working in a little town in Peru called Ayaquipo—just a bunch of shacks on the side of a dead volcano. Anyway, I get in tight with the old priest. He tells me his people are the descendants of the ancient Incas, that they still honor the old gods. At the beginning of every growing season they sacrifice a young woman in supplication to these spirts; and in return, they nourish and protect the crops. At first I think the old man is just talking through his hat, but then he takes me along as a witness. The whole village trails up the side of this volcano with the girl and the priest in the lead. She kneels at a certain point and. . . ." Ledbetter sliced his hand across his throat. "Best corn I ever tasted."

When Morton shoved his chair back from the table, it made an unnerving screech against the linoleum. For a moment he had no idea what Ledbetter was driving at. Then it dawned on him. "You're saying— Let me get this straight. You're saying you kidnapped this girl from New

York and cut her throat in your back garden?" The whole
idea seemed like a joke, but his neighbor wasn't smiling.

"Kidnap?" he roared. "Those hookers swarm over the
city like maggots in a garbage can. I just give one a few
bucks temporarily and put her out of her misery."

"There's a big difference between Acapulco—or whatever you call it—and New Jersey," countered Morton.

Ledbetter seemed to enjoy his guest's discomfiture.
"I'll tell you what the old man told me: The gods are always around us, like the sun and the wind. All you have
to do is give 'em what they want."

"I don't believe a word of it."

"Fine." Ledbetter lurched to his feet. "Follow me."

The humid night air pressed around Morton like damp
cotton as he followed in the tracks of his partner. A dark
figure slid towards them. "Lie down, Satan," Ledbetter
ordered, and the figure retreated into the shadows. He
flung open the gate to the tomato garden, then pulled
Morton into the jungle of vines.

"Go ahead," he said. "Reach down and grab a handful
of dirt."

Morton did as he was told. It felt sticky. He lifted it to
his nose. He remembered the smell from the slaughter-
house in Omaha.

Back in the kitchen, both men collapsed into their
chairs. Morton happened to glance at the hand that had
held the soil. It was still a dark crimson. All at once his
stomach began to heave. Although the sink was only a
few feet away, he made it just in time. As spasms of nausea jolted through his body, he could hear the raucous
laughter behind him. "If you want anything bad enough,"
Ledbetter thundered, "you gotta pay the price!"

After that night, Morton began doing something he had
not done since his army days, before Edie was there to
smooth out the kinks in his life. He began to drink heavily. Only in the blurred world of intoxication could he forget Ledbetter's challenge. At bottom, Morton was a

sensitive man; and unable to cope with a perverse alliance of spirit and flesh, he felt robbed of his one last chance for recognition.

Like others who feel set upon by the world, he struck out at those closest to him. In the weeks that followed, Morton managed to alienate most of his friends. He quarreled over the smallest matters and frequently resorted to physical threats when his drunken pronouncements were not immediately accepted.

His wife was alarmed one night to find him attacking his glass trophy case with a hammer. "What are you doing?" she screamed. When Morton wheeled to face her, she thought she was looking at a stranger. His clothes and demeanor reminded Edie of the derelicts in the city who wiped your windshield for a quarter. He still had the hammer above his head when he approached her, and for the first time in her life she was terrified of her husband.

Suddenly he relaxed. Like a puppet whose strings are cut, he went limp, and the hammer slipped to the carpet. "Sorry," he mumbled. "This tomato thing is getting to me. I can't bear to think of that fat slob Ledbetter rubbing my face in the dirt again."

Edie wrapped her arms around her husband. "It's not important, dear." She looked down at the splinters of glass that lay before the trophy case. "Now let's clean up this mess before somebody gets cut."

"Let me show you something first." His voice was flat, toneless; but his eyes had the restless glitter of a man who hadn't slept in days. "Out in the garden. There's something you have to see."

"Of course, dear." Happy to see the revival of his old interests, Edie took his hand, and they walked out into the moonlight. "You know," she began as they strolled along the path, "years ago we used to take walks together like this all the time. When did we ever stop?"

But Morton didn't answer. Instead, he pointed to a spot close to the biggest tomato plant. "Down there," he said.

"Look real close and you can see it." Obediently, Edie kneeled and put her head close to the ground. She never saw the flash of the paring knife as it came across her throat, nor did she hear the howl of Satan, barely ten yards away, as he turned in his sleep.

All afternoon Archie Ledbetter lay in his rusting lawn chair watching the show. He went through two bags of Fritos chuckling at the boneheads gathering around the patrol cars in front of the Sangroff rancher.

A red pickup with MILLER'S GARDENING SUPPLIES stenciled on the front door pulled up across the street, and a boy carrying a gallon jug ran over to Ledbetter's front yard. Archie gave him a brief wave of recognition. Jimmy put the jug on the grass next to the recliner and pulled on his baseball cap.

"Who'd expect something like this—in Harmony Village?" he said, nodding toward the police cars.

"People are people," growled Ledbetter. He twisted off the cap to the jug and took a deep sniff. Satisfied with its contents, he placed it back on the grass.

"Where did you come up with the idea of rabbit blood, anyway?"

Ledbetter winked. "Little trick I picked up in Peru. Feeds the plants and keeps the critters away."

The boy's gaze returned to the crowd, now beginning to disperse for dinner. "Still beats me how a guy with everything he could want would up and kill a sweet old lady like Mrs. Sangroff."

Archie Ledbetter was already trundling towards his front door with the jug cradled in his arms. "I'll tell you one thing buddy-boy didn't have," he said, jerking a fat thumb over his shoulder. "He didn't have no sense of humor, that's for sure."

Early Retirement
by Frances Usher

It was in mid-July that Tony Minnifer loaded his books for the last time into the boot of his car and drove away from the comprehensive school from which he was taking early retirement. By early September he had decided to murder his sister.

It was a logical decision; Tony was a lifelong math teacher, after all. The package of early-retirement measures thrust upon him by his education authority, desperate for staff cutbacks, and by his new headmaster, who believed that anyone who remembered the twelve-sided threepenny bit must be kept away from the young, had not left Tony a wealthy man.

"Only a pittance really." He stared morosely out into the large neglected back garden.

"Never mind, dear." His wife Stella lifted her head from a leaflet she'd picked up in the library. It was called *Golden Age: Golden Stage*. Only a month before, she'd been made redundant from her own job with a building society. "It says here the retirement years can be the most fulfilling, satisfying, and fun-packed time of your life."

"*Can* be."

Beaming grey-haired couples were pictured all over the leaflet, sitting outside their immaculate country cottages, leaning on the rails of cruise liners, hugging their unnaturally friendly grandchildren on some distant airport tarmac.

"Never mind that lot," said Tony. "All I want is to get

this garden in decent shape now there's a bit of spare time. But I can't even afford to do that properly."

It was then that a picture of his only sister Marjorie came into his mind.

He blinked. Now, there *was* an idea. For the first time, early retirement began to hold out a possibility or two.

"We could always sell the car," Stella was saying. "See if we could get bus passes instead."

"No," said Tony. "I think I might be needing the car for a while."

Marjorie lived in Worthing. It was a dark, drizzling evening when Tony drew up outside her house.

"Well, Tony. Quite a surprise."

Marjorie led him into the warm sitting room. Clearly, her accountant husband had left her well provided for.

"You don't mind, do you?" She eased herself back into her armchair, her eyes fixed on the blue-bathed television screen. It was a Conservative Party political broadcast. "Only another moment or two."

"Of course," said Tony. He fingered the rolled-up tie in his pocket. He hadn't worn a tie since the day he'd left the school.

The Tories would be holding their annual conference in a week or two. Unless he took action now, Marjorie would be there in the conference hall as usual, gazing adoringly at the platform with the rest of her well-fed sisterhood. He'd glimpsed her once on a news bulletin, taking part in a fourteen-minute ovation. He'd felt sick.

"Only a moment or two," he said.

Perhaps she saw his reflection in the screen. Perhaps it was a sixth survival sense. She turned at the last second, saw him coming towards her with the tie stretched taut between his hands, screamed . . . and suddenly collapsed over the arm of her chair, her hands scrabbling at her blue twin set, her face purple with pain, terror, and plain simple astonishment.

Tony watched in awe as her chest ceased to heave. Then, slowly, he rolled up the tie again and put it back in his pocket.

"Damn," he said. Trust Marjorie.

He reached for the telephone and began to dial for an ambulance.

The legacy made quite a difference to the Minnifers' life. Once the Worthing house was sold Tony was able to buy all sorts of equipment and start laying out the garden in the way that recently he'd been dreaming of. He spent hours ploughing up the rough grass, moving earth, and scooping out trenches. On wet days, he drew plans on squared paper.

Stella, meanwhile, was extending her social life, attending coffee mornings and enrolling in afternoon art classes.

"Tony?" She stumbled towards him across the garden one November dusk. "Whatever are all those stones doing on the drive?"

Tony straightened up, wiping his glasses.

"I'm going to make a rockery," he said. "Over there in the corner. I'll see to it all tomorrow. I'm just off to the garden centre now. See if they've got any alpines I can buy. It won't take long."

The familiar door no longer said "Headmaster." It said "Director of Educational Policy (Studies)." Tony drew a deep breath. Along a distant corridor he could hear the hum of a floor polisher. He pushed open the door.

The headmaster looked up, startled.

"Tony?"

In the shaded lamplight Tony could read upside-down headings on the documents spread on the desk. "Rationalisation of School Dinner Services," he read, and "English in the Service of Industry."

"Was there something you wanted . . ." The headmaster smiled uncertainly. ". . . Tony?"

"Yes," he said, and moved round to the back of the desk. He braced himself against the notice board covered with flow charts and reached into his pocket.

"Oh yes," he said. "Indeed there was."

It was quite dark outside. He'd brought a large plastic compost sack with him and it wasn't too difficult to drag the body, decently wrapped and trussed, over the polished floor the short distance to the outside door. He'd already backed the car close up. Lifting the bundle high enough to topple into the car boot was harder, but he managed it safely and soon he was driving into his garage at home with a warm sense of satisfaction.

Pleasurable, he decided. That was the word. It had been perverse of Marjorie to have had that heart attack at the last moment. Saved trouble, of course. But the plan had been ready, and it had been disappointing not to carry it through.

Still, he'd done it this time. He'd made a start.

The rockery looked very nice in the corner of the garden.

"Sort of substantial," said Stella, viewing it from the kitchen window. "Gives the garden quite a focus."

"So will the pool," said Tony, drying a plate. "That's my next job. It's going to be—"

"Shush a minute." Stella turned up the radio. "Did you hear that? About those young criminals? Whatever are things coming to?"

"I know." Tony nodded his head. "Makes you think, doesn't it?"

The research had taken some time, but time was what he had plenty of. And he'd tracked him down now.

Wayne Wilkinson.

To Tony's relief, Stella hadn't argued when he'd told her he was going up to London for the weekend.

"Feel a bit—well—cooped up at home," he said. "After all the hurly-burly of school. Thought I'd look up old Alan again. Get him to take me round some of the sights for a day or two. If it's all right with you, dear."

"Of course." Stella smiled, shuddering faintly to herself. She remembered Tony's old friend Alan and how he'd behaved at their wedding. "You go and enjoy yourself, Tony. Do you good to get away from the garden."

He followed him all day Saturday, the pale pink scalp under the cropped hair unchanged since classroom days. He remembered how the boy used to sprawl back on his chair when reprimanded, digging the point of his pen deep into the back of his hand, and the light blue eyes that stared insolently into his own.

"So?" he'd say. "Gonna make me or somefing?"

Wayne Wilkinson.

There were tattoos now on the backs of his hands and a swastika glittered on his black T-shirt. Tony watched him from across the street, selling illiterate racist magazines. He observed him on the football terraces, jostling and spitting, screaming obscenities with his mates. He trailed him round the streets, saw him shoplifting. Finally he came to rest in the shadows outside a gay disco. Wayne and a group of others were operating a stakeout.

It was nearly three in the morning before the chance came. Wayne had set off alone behind a couple in blue denim, their heads bent, their hands linked.

The boy was so intent on keeping up with them that he knew nothing of Tony's presence at all, until he felt the whip of the tie around his throat.

"Coffee, dear?"

"Lovely."

Stella took the mug and sipped, lifting her face gratefully to the warm spring sunshine. A blackbird was singing in the apple tree.

"Oh, I do like sitting here," she said. "All that work you put into it, Tony."

Tony smiled. "Worth it, dear," he said. "Even digging that huge great hole half the night, putting in the plastic liner—all of it. All worth it."

His eyes followed the flashing Golden Orfes as they darted and turned in the clear, sparkling water. The purple irises were already tall and budding at the margins of the pool. Soon dragonflies would skim across the surface like threads of shot silk.

Clean, he thought. Clean and pure and washed. Couldn't wish for a better place myself when my time comes.

The main project in the garden after that was the herbaceous border.

"Plenty of mulch, Mr. Minnifer," advised the man at the garden centre. He'd become quite a friend of Tony's by now. "That's what herbaceous borders need. Lost of well-rotted manure, compost, anything like that. Anything you can get your hands on."

"Oh, right," said Tony.

He'd seen the woman on the lunchtime news. She was a member of a think tank on education. She was declaring there was no possible connection between the size of a school class and the quality of learning that took place.

"It just needs a bit of discipline by the teachers," she said. The interviewer's hair blew in the wind but her blond curls remained unmoved. "All it takes is competence." Her voice reminded Tony of a cut-glass vase his mother had once owned.

It was almost too easy. Her address was listed in an old *Who's Who* he picked up at a jumble sale.

He was waiting for her one warm evening as she drove towards the wrought-iron gates that led to her eighteenth-century manor house home. Seeing him step out of the bushes, she faltered and reached to wind up the window, but there was no time.

If there had been, she might have told him about her son, about how she'd just taken him to boarding school. But as the maximum number of pupils in a class at that school was twelve, this might not have helped her plight as far as Tony was concerned one little bit.

The lupins were splendid that year, and so were the delphiniums and peonies. When Stella brought her new friends Jane and Angus round one evening for a drink by the pool, Jane was full of envy.

"What I'd give for a husband like yours," she said to Stella. "Angus—" she gave a little laugh. "Not much use in the garden, I'm afraid."

Stella gazed at Angus thoughtfully. He was tall and fair, with warm, dark-brown eyes.

"Never mind," she said. "Gardens aren't everything in life, are they?"

It was perhaps soon after this that Tony Minnifer began to grow a little irritable. Somehow, even now, he still hadn't achieved the fulfilling, satisfying, fun-packed early retirement that *Golden Age: Golden Stage* had promised.

He'd tried to make the world a better place, a cleaner place. And yet . . .

It was Wimbledon Fortnight, perfect weather for once. This would be the first year he wasn't in the classroom, condemned to evening highlights while he still wearily marked exercise books.

He lay back on the sofa, trying to enjoy it. Surely he'd earned a rest.

"Not watching this, Stella?" he said. "Thought you liked tennis."

"It's my local history group," Stella said. "We're ex-

ploring the environment today. I might be a bit late." She
was gone.

Tony shrugged and turned back to the screen.

There was a new whiz kid this year, a teenage girl born
in Eastern Europe, trained in Florida, her hair in bunches
and a nasal twang of a voice that spat out insults through
a mouthful of teethbraces.

The media loved her. By the end of the first day she'd
collected a nickname and a clutch of fans who followed
her everywhere, hoping for worse excesses. The newspapers had begun begging for someone to "Crush this kid."

A challenge, Tony thought. Idly, he began working out
how it could be done. A quick trip to London, mingle
with the autograph hunters, then—

Better not. Kid like that would be surrounded by security. Shame, though.

The lawn would have been the place for her, smooth
and green and velvety as the Centre Court itself.

There was one more, in October. But it wasn't the
same. It was almost as if he were just keeping his hand in.

The man had had to go, of course; a local builder responsible for buying up a perfectly harmless copse, grub-
bing up all the trees, dotting around some "Luxury
Executive-Style Homes"—each completed by a triple garage and a stunted rhododendron bush—and christening
the whole revolting result Woodland Way.

"I'll woodland way him," Tony promised himself,
heaving the sack-covered heap out of the boot. The
builder had been a hefty man and Tony wasn't getting any
younger.

"Under the new patio for you, I think," he said to the
builder. "See how you like the feel of concrete running
over you."

He slaved to get the patio finished by the weekend.
Somehow the joy had gone out of it a bit; the purity. And

where was Stella? She never seemed to be around now when he needed a bit of praise.

On impulse, he rang Angus and Jane and invited them to a barbecue, beginning to savour the notion of roasting meat on the patio.

"Yes, lovely," said Jane, but her voice was listless. "Angus isn't actually here at the moment, but I'm sure he'll come along."

"Good," said Tony heartily. "Great."

But, by the day of the barbecue, everything had changed.

Angus didn't feel much like going, but he supposed one had to make an effort. He walked round to the Minnifers' road and in at their front gate.

He sniffed. There didn't seem to be any whiff of smoke from their back garden. Odd, that. Surely it was time to get the thing lit up.

"*Left* you?" said Stella.

Angus nodded. "Last Monday. Found a note on the table. Bit hackneyed, really. I hadn't realised. She knew all about it, you see."

"About—?"

"Us."

"Ah."

Stella fiddled with her bracelet, leaning back against the freezer. Outside the kitchen window, it was already dark.

After a minute, Angus said, "Stella?"

"Mmm?"

"Where's Tony?"

Stella smiled sadly.

"He's . . . gone, Angus. I don't think we'll be seeing him again."

"You mean—" Angus frowned. "He knew about us, so he buggered off like Jane?"

Stella shook her head. "I thought it was enough," she said. "More than enough, perhaps."

She stroked the lid of the freezer lovingly, and then straightened up and crossed to the window. They stood close together, arms round each other, looking out at the dark garden.

"Fulfilled," she said. "Satisfied. He was happy while it lasted. And, really, he'd got the garden into very good shape. Who was I to stop him? Early retirement isn't easy, you know, Angus."

"I suppose not." His eyes were puzzled, searching her face.

"It was time," she said. "It could have been cabinet ministers ... royals ... So much trouble there'd have been ..."

She summoned a smile.

"We mustn't get downhearted. There's a lot we can do, Angus, to cheer each other up."

He nodded, a little doubtful.

"Gardening, for instance," she said. "I'm thinking of going down to the garden centre tomorrow to buy a sundial. I thought it would look nice all laid out with fancy paving." She gestured into the darkness. "Out there, in the middle of the roses."

Her voice became pleading.

"A memorial sort of thing, to Tony. To mark the passing hours. You'd help me, Angus, wouldn't you? Wouldn't you, Angus?"

Venus's-Flytrap
by *Ruth Rendell*

As soon as Daphne had taken off her hat and put it on Merle's bed, Merle picked it up and rammed it on her own yellow curls. It was a red felt hat and by chance it matched Merle's red dress.

"It's a funny thing, dear," said Merle, looking at herself in the dressing-table mirror, "but anyone seeing us two— any outsider, I mean—would never think that I was the single one and you'd had all those husbands and children."

"I only had two husbands and three children," said Daphne.

"You know what I mean," said Merle, and Daphne, standing beside her friend, had to admit she did. Merle was so big, so pink and overflowing and female, while she—well, she had given up pretending she was anything but a little dried-up widow, 70 years old and looking every day of it.

Merle took off the hat and placed it beside the doll whose yellow satin skirts concealed Merle's nightgown and bag of hair rollers. "I'll show you the flat and then we'll have a sherry and rest our feet. I got some of that walnut-brown. You see I haven't forgotten your tastes even after forty years."

Daphne didn't say it was dry sherry she had then and still preferred. She trotted meekly after Merle. She was just beginning to be aware of the intense heat. Clouds of

warmth seemed to breathe out of the embossed wallpaper
and up through the lush furry carpets.

"I really am thrilled about you coming to live in this
block, dear," said Merle. "This is my little spare room. I
like to think I can put up a friend if I want. Not that many
of them come. Between you and me, dear, people rather
resent my having done so well for myself and all on my
own initiative. People are so mean-spirited—I've noticed
that as I've got older. That's why I was so thrilled when
you agreed to come here. I mean, when *someone* took my
advice."

"You've made it all very nice," said Daphne.

"Well, I always say the flat had the potential and I had
the taste. Of course, yours is much smaller and frankly I
wouldn't say it lends itself to a very ambitious décor. In
your place, the first thing I'd do is have central heating
put in."

"I expect I will if I can afford it."

"You know, Daphne, there are some things we owe it to
ourselves to afford. But you know your own business best
and I wouldn't dream of interfering. If the cold gets you
down you're welcome to come up here at any time. *Any*
time, I mean that. Now this is my drawing room, my
piece de resistance."

Merle opened the door with the air of a girl lifting the
lid of a jewel case that holds a lover's gift.

"What a lot of plants," said Daphne faintly.

"I was always mad about plants. My first business venture was a florist's shop. I could have made a little gold
mine out of it if my partner hadn't been so wickedly vin-
dictive. She was determined to oust me from the first.
D'you like my suite? I had it completely redone in oyster
satin last year and I do think it's a success."

The atmosphere was that of a hothouse. The chairs, the
sofa, the lamps, the little piecrust tables with their loads
of bibelots, were islanded in the center of the large room.
No, not an island perhaps, Daphne thought, but a clearing

in a tropical jungle. Shelves, window sills, white troughs
on white wrought-iron legs, were burgeoned with lush
trailing growth—green, glossy, frondy, all immobile and
all giving forth a strange scent.

"They take up all my time. It's not just the watering
and watching the temperature and so on. Plants know
when you love them. They only flourish in an atmosphere
of love. I honestly don't believe you'd find a better specimen of an *opuntia* in London than mine. I'm particularly
proud of the *peperomias* and the *xygocacti* too. Of course,
I suppose you've seen them growing in their natural hab-
itat with all your mad rushing around those foreign
places."

"We were mostly in Stockholm and New York, Merle."

"Oh, were you? So many years went by when you
never bothered to write to me that I really couldn't keep
pace. I thought about you a lot, of course. I want you to
know you really had my sympathy, moving all the time
and that awful divorce from what's-his-name, and babies
to cope with, and then getting married again and everything. I used to feel how sad it was that I'd made so much
out of my life while you—what's the matter?"

"That plant, Merle. It moved!"

"That's because you touched it. When you touch one of
its mouths it closes up. It's called *Dionaea Muscipula*."

The plant stood alone in a majolica pot within an elab-
orate white stand. It looked very healthy. It had delicate
shiny leaves and from its heart grew five red-gold blossoms. As Daphne peered more closely she saw that these
resembled mouths, just as Merle had put it, far more than
flowers—whiskery mouths, soft and ripe and luscious.
One of these was now closed.

"Doesn't it have a common name?"

"Of course it does. Venus's-flytrap. *Muscipula* means
fly eater, dear."

"Whatever *do* you mean?"

"It eats flies. I've been trying to grow one for years. I was absolutely thrilled when I succeeded."

"Yes, but what d'you mean, it eats flies? It's not an animal."

"It is in a way, dear. The trouble is there aren't many flies here. I feed it on little bits of meat. You've gone rather pale, Daphne. Have you got a headache? We'll have our sherry now and then I'll see if I can catch a fly and you can see it eat it up."

"I'd really much rather not, Merle," said Daphne, backing away from the plant. "I don't want to hurt your feelings but I don't—well, I don't like the idea of catching, free, live things and feeding them to—that."

"Free, live things? We're talking about flies," Merle, large and perfumed, grabbed Daphne's arm and pulled her away. Merle's dress was of red chiffon with trailing sleeves and her fingernails matched it. "The trouble with you," said Merle, "is that you're a mass of nerves and you're much worse now than you were when we were girls. I thank God every day of my life I don't know what it is to be neurotic. Here you are, your sherry. I've put it in a big glass to buck you up. I'm going to make it my business to look after you, Daphne. You don't know anybody else in London, do you?"

"Hardly anybody," said Daphne, sitting down where she couldn't see the Flytrap. "My boys are in the States and my daughter's in Scotland."

"Well, you must come up here every day. No, you won't be intruding. When I first knew you were definitely coming, I said to myself, I'm going to see to it that Daphne isn't lonely. But don't imagine you'll get on with the other tenants in this block. Those of them who aren't standoffish snobs are—well, not the sort of people you'd want to know. But we won't talk about them. We'll talk about us. Unless, of course, you feel your past has been too painful to talk about?"

"I wouldn't quite say—"

"No, you won't care to rake up unpleasant memories. I'll just put a drop more sherry in your glass and then I'll tell you all about my last venture, my agency."

Daphne rested her head against a cushion, brushed away an ivy frond, and prepared to listen.

Merle was scraping slivers of meat from a piece of fillet steak. She was all in diaphanous gold today, an amber chain around her neck, the finery half covered by a frilly apron.

"I used to do that for my babies when they first went on solids," said Daphne.

"Babies, babies. You're always talking about your babies. You've been up here every day for three weeks now and I don't think you've once missed the opportunity to mention your babies and your men. Oh, I'm sorry, dear, I don't mean to upset you, but one really does get so weary of women like you talking about that side of life as if one had actually *missed* something."

"Why are you scraping that meat, Merle?"

"To feed my little Venus. That's her breakfast. Come along. I've got a fly I caught under a sherry glass but I couldn't catch more than one."

The fly was crawling up the inside of the glass, but when Merle approached it, it began to buzz frenziedly against the transparent dome of its prison. Daphne turned her back. She went to the window, the huge plant-filled bay window, and looked out, pretending to be interested in the view. She heard the scrape of glass and a triumphant gasp from Merle. Then Merle began talking to the plant in a gentle, maternal voice.

"This really is a wonderful outlook," said Daphne brightly. "You can see for miles."

Merle said, *"C'est Venus toute entiere a sa proie attachee."*

"I beg your pardon?"

"You never were any good at languages, dear. Oh,

don't pretend you're so mad about that view. You're just being absurdly sensitive about what really amounts to *gardening*. I can't bear that sort of dishonestly. I've finished now, anyway. She's had her breakfast and all her mouths are shut. Who are you waving to?"

"A rather nice young couple who live in the next flat to me."

"Well, please don't." Merle looked down and then drew herself up, all golden pleats and stiff golden curls. "You couldn't know, dear, but those two people are the very end. For one thing, they're not married, I'm sure of that. Of course, that's no business of mine. What is my business is that they've been keeping a dog here—look, that spaniel thing—and it's strictly against the rules to keep animals in these flats."

"What about your Flytrap?"

"Oh, don't be silly! As I was saying, they keep that dog and let it foul the garden. I wrote to the managing agents, but those agents are so lax—they've no respect for me because I'm a single woman, I suppose. But I wrote again the day before yesterday and now I understand they're definitely going to be turned out."

Forty feet below the window, in the parking space between the block and the garden, the boy who wore blue jeans and a leather jacket picked up his dog and placed it on the rear seat of a rather battered car. His companion, a girl with waist-length hair, got into the passenger seat, but the boy hesitated. As Merle brought her face close to the glass, he looked up and raised two wide-splayed fingers.

"Oaf!" said Merle. "The only thing to do with people like that is to ignore them. Can you imagine it, he lets that dog of his foul a really beautiful specimen of *cryptomeria japonica*. Let's forget him and have a nice cup of coffee."

"Merle, how long will those flowers last on that Venus

thing of yours? I mean, they'll soon die away, won't they?"

"No, they won't. They'll last for ages. You know, Daphne, fond as I am of you, I wouldn't leave you alone in this flat for anything. You've a personal hatred of my *muscipula*. You'd like to destroy it."

"I'll put the coffee on," said Daphne.

Merle phoned for a taxi. Then she put her little red address book with all the phone numbers in it into her scarlet patent-leather handbag along with her lipstick, her gold compact, her keys, her check book, and four five-pound notes.

"We could have walked," said Daphne.

"No, we couldn't, dear. When I have a day at the shops I like to feel fresh. I don't want to half kill myself walking there. It's not the cost that's worrying you, is it? Because you know I'll pay. I appreciate the difference between our incomes, Daphne, and if I don't harp on it it's only because I try to be tactful. I want to buy you something, something really nice to wear. It seems such a wicked shame to me those men of yours didn't see to it you were well provided for."

"I've got quite enough clothes, Merle."

"Yes, but all gray and black. The only bright thing you've got is that red hat and you've stopped wearing that."

"I'm old, Merle dear I don't want to get myself up in bright colors. I've had my life."

"Well, I haven't had mine! I mean, I—" Merle bit her lip, getting scarlet lipstick on her teeth.

She walked across the room, picked her ocelot coat off the back of the sofa, and paused in front of the Flytrap. Its soft, flame-colored mouths were open. She tickled them with her fingertips and they snapped shut. Merle giggled. "You know what you remind me of, Daphne? A fly.

That's just what you look like in your gray coat and that funny bit of veil on your hat. A *fly*."

"There's the taxi," said Daphne.

It deposited them outside a large overheated store. Merle dragged Daphne through the jewelry department, the perfumery, past revolving stands with belts on them, past plastic mannequins in lingerie. They went up in the elevators. Merle bought a dress, orange chiffon with sequins all over the skirt.

They went down in the elevator and into the next store. Merle bought face bracer and eau de toilette and a gilt choker. They went up on the escalator. Merle bought a belt of brass links and tried to buy Daphne a green and blue silk scarf. Daphne consented at last to be presented with a pair of stockings, elastic support ones for her veins.

"Now we'll have lunch on the roof garden," said Merle.

"I should like a cup of tea."

"And I'll have a large sherry. But first I must freshen up. I'm dying to spend a penny and do my face."

They queued with their pennies. The Ladies Room had green-marble dressing tables with mirrors all down one side and washbasins down the other. Daphne sat down. Her feet had begun to swell. There were 20 or 30 other women in the room, doing their faces, combing their hair, replacing false eyelashes.

Merle put her scarlet handbag down on a free bit of green marble. She washed her hands, went over and helped herself to a gush of Calèche from the scent-squirting machine, came back, opening and shutting her coat to fan herself. It was even hotter than in her flat.

She sat down and drew her chair to the mirror.

"Where's my handbag?" Merle screamed. "I left my handbag right here! Someone's stolen my handbag. Daphne, Daphne, someone's stolen my handbag!"

* * *

The oyster satin sofa sagged under Merle's weight. Daphne smoothed back the golden curls and put another pad of cotton soaked in cologne on Merle's red corrugated forehead.

"Bit better now?" asked Daphne.

"I'm quite all right. I'm not one of your neurotic women to get into a state over a thing like that. Thank God, I left a spare key with the porter."

"You'll have to have both locks changed, Merle."

"Of course I will eventually. I'll see to it next week. Nobody can get in here, can they? And they don't know who I am. I mean, they don't know whose keys they've got."

"They've got your handbag."

"Daphne dear, I do wish you wouldn't keep stating the obvious. I *know* they've got my handbag. The point is, there was nothing in my handbag to show who I am."

"There was your check book with your name on it."

"My name, dear, in case it's escaped your notice, is M. Smith. Just the initial, and no address. I haven't gone about changing it all my life like you." Merle sat up and took a gulp of walnut-brown sherry.

"The store manager was charming, wasn't he, and the police? I daresay they'll find it, you know. It's a most distinctive handbag, not like that great black thing you cart about with you. My little red one could have gone inside yours. I wish I'd thought to put it there."

"I wish you had," said Daphne.

Daphne's phone rang. It was half-past nine and she was finishing her breakfast, sitting in front of her little electric fire.

Merle sounded very excited. "What do you think? Isn't it marvelous? The store manager's just phoned to say they've found my bag. Well, it wasn't him, it was his secretary, a stupid-sounding woman with one of those put-on accents. However, that's no concern of mine. They found my bag fallen behind a radiator in that Ladies Room. Isn't it an absolute miracle? Of course, the money was gone, but my check book was there and the keys. I'm very glad I didn't take your advice and change those locks yester-day. It never does to act on impulse, Daphne."

"No, I suppose not."

"I've arranged to go down and get my bag at eleven. As soon as I ring off I'm going to phone for a taxi and I want you to come with me, dear. I'll have a quick bath and see to my plants—I've managed to catch a bluebottle for Venus—and then the taxi will be here."

"I'm afraid I can't come," said Daphne.

"Why on earth not?"

Daphne hesitated. Then she said, "I said I hardly know anybody in London and that's true. But I do know this one man, this—well, he was a friend of my second hus-band and he's a widower now and he's coming to have lunch with me, Merle. He's coming at noon and I must be here to see to things."

"A *man?*" said Merle. "*Another* man?"

"I'll look out for your taxi and when I see you come back I'll just pop up and hear all about it, shall I? I'm sorry I can't—"

"Sorry? Sorry for what? I can get my handbag by my-self. I'm quite used to standing on my own feet, thank you." The receiver went down with a crash.

Merle had a bath and put on the orange dress. It was rather showy for day wear, with its sequins and its fringes, but she could never bear to have a new dress and not wear it at once. The ocelot coat would cover most of it. She watered the *peperomias* and painted a little leaf gloss on the ivy. The bluebottle had died in the night, but *dionaea muscipula* didn't seem to mind. She opened her orange, strandy mouths for Merle and devoured the dead bluebottle along with the shreds of fillet steak.

Merle put on her cream silk turban and a long scarf of flame-colored silk. Her spare second-lock key was where she always kept it, underneath the *sanseveria* pot. She double-locked the door and then the taxi took her to the store.

Merle sailed into the manager's office and when the manager told her he had no secretary, had never had anyone phone her flat, and had certainly not found her handbag, she deflated like a fat orange balloon into which someone has stuck a pin.

"You've been the victim of a hoax, Miss Smith."

Merle pulled herself together. She could always do that—she had superb control. No, she didn't want aspirins or brandy or policemen or any of the other aids to quietude offered by the manager. After she had told him he didn't know his job, that if there was a conspiracy against her—as she was sure there must be—he was in it, she floundered down the stairs and flapped her mouth and her arms for a taxi.

When she got home the first thing that struck her as strange was that the door was only single-locked. She could have sworn she had double-locked it, but no doubt her memory was playing tricks and no wonder, the shock she had had. There was a little bit of earth on the hall carpet. Merle didn't like that—earth on her gold Wilton. Inside her ocelot she was sweating. She took off her coat and opened the drawing-room door.

Daphne saw the taxi arrive and Merle bounce out of it, like an orange orchid springing from a black bandbox. Merle looked wild with excitement, her turban all askew. Daphne smiled to herself and shook her head. She set the table and finished making the salad that she knew her friend would like with his lunch and then went upstairs to see Merle.

There was a mirror on each landing. Daphne was so small and thin that she didn't puff much when she had to climb stairs. As she came to the top of each flight she saw a little gray woman trotting to meet her, a woman with smooth white hair and large, rather diffident eyes, who wore a gray wool dress partly covered by a cloudy stole of lace.

She smiled at her reflection. She was old now, but she had had her moments—her joys, her gratifications, her intense pleasures. And soon there was to be a new pleasure, a confrontation she had looked forward to for weeks. Who could tell what would come of it? With a last smile at her gray and fluttery image, Daphne gently pushed open the unlocked door of Merle's flat.

In the Garden of Eden, the green paradisal bower, someone had dropped a bomb. No, they couldn't have done that, for the ceiling was still there and the carpet and the oyster satin furniture, torn now and plastered all over with earth.

Every plant had been broken and torn apart. Leaves lay scattered in heaps like the leaves of autumn, only these were green, succulent, bruised. In the rape of the room, in the midst of ripped foliage, stems bleeding sap, and shards of china lay the Venus's-flytrap, its roots wrenched from their pot and its mouths closed forever.

Merle tried to scream but the noise came out only as a gurgle, the agonized gasp of a scream in a nightmare. She fell on her knees and crawled about. Choking and muttering, she scrabbled in the earth, and picking up torn leaves tried to piece them together like bits of a jigsaw puzzle. She crouched over the Flytrap and nursed it in her hands, keening and swaying to and fro.

She didn't hear the door click shut. It was a long time before she realized Daphne was standing over her, silent, looking down. Merle lifted her red streaming face. Daphne had her hand over her mouth, the hand with the two wedding rings on it. Merle thought Daphne must be covering her mouth to stop herself from laughing—laughing out loud.

Slowly, heavily, Merle got up. Her long orange scarf

was in her hands, stretched taut, twisting, twisting. She was surprised how steady her voice was, how level and sane.

"You did it," she said. "*You* did it. You stole my handbag and took my keys and got me out of here and came in and did all this."

Daphne quivered and shook her head.

"You were so jealous! You'd had nothing, but I had success and happiness and love." Merle's voice went up and the scarf with it. "How you hated me, hated, hated! Hate, hate, poisonous, jealous hate!"

Huge and red and frondy, she descended on Daphne, engulfing her with musky orange petals, twisting the scarf round the frail insect neck, devouring the fly until the fly quivered into stillness . . .

An elderly man in a black Homburg hat crossed the forecourt and went up the steps, a bunch of flowers in his hand.

The boy in the leather jacket took no notice of him. He brushed earth and bits of leaf off his hands and said to the girl with the long hair, "Revenge is sweet." Then he tossed the scarlet handbag that the girl had stolen in the Ladies Room into the back of the car, and he and the girl and the dog got in and drove away.

The Puzzle Garden
by Edward D. Hoch

It had been many months since Michael Vlado's old friend Segar had driven up the twisty roads of the Transylvanian foothills to visit him at the Gypsy village where he was a somewhat uncertain leader. " 'King' only means that I'd be the first to die if the government moved against us," Michael had remarked to his wife Rosanna only the night before. These were not good days to be a Gypsy in Romania. Some of his people had already moved on to Germany, but they had only found a more immediate hell awaiting them there.

So Michael chose to remain in his village, always watching the road for the unexpected. When he recognized Segar's government car that warm spring morning he felt a jolt of alarm. Once a captain in the government militia responsible for law enforcement, Segar had assumed a vague position with the transition government. He could be delivering bad news for Michael's people.

"My old friend!" Segar greeted him with a smile, and Michael immediately relaxed. There was nothing to fear.

"It's been a long time."

Segar nodded sadly. His gray suit seemed worn and drab compared to the bright militia uniform he'd often worn in those years when they first became friends. "I do not have the freedom I once had. I am chained to a bureaucrat's desk eight hours a day."

"At least you managed to escape on this bright May morning."

Segar's smile returned. "I came to ask your help. Have you ever heard of the Garden of the Apostles?"

It was vague in Michael's mind. "On the estate of the Sibiu family, wasn't it? I was only five when the Communist government began the collectivization of agriculture and large estates back in nineteen forty-nine. I remember my mother's concern for the Gypsy farmland when I was growing up, but in the end farmers were permitted to retain half-acre plots for private use. No one here has ever had more than that."

Segar nodded, but it was obvious his interest was in the present rather than the past. "After the overthrow of the Socialist government in nineteen eight-nine, the estate was quietly returned to the rightful heirs of the Sibiu family. The Garden of the Apostles is gradually returning to its past beauty and may someday reopen to the public."

"I am a horse breeder, not a gardener," Michael reminded his friend. "What help could I give you in this matter?"

"It seems that something of great value was buried in the garden long ago, before the Communists seized power. Even Claus Sibiu and his wife have no idea exactly where it's located. Naturally they want me to find it before the grounds are opened to the public."

"You want me for a treasure hunt!"

"In a sense. I thought the puzzle might intrigue you."

"When?"

"Now. Today, if you can get away."

They walked up to the house while Michael spoke with his wife Rosanna. "I'll try to be back tonight, or tomorrow certainly."

She was a long-suffering woman who sought peace among the little wooden animals she skillfully carved. His absences were nothing new. "I will expect you when I see you," she told him. "Are the horses penned?"

"Everything is fine."

She glanced over at Segar. "It is good to see you again. How is life in Bucharest?"

"Improving gradually. There have been no antigovernment protests this month."

"We are thankful for anything these days."

Michael kissed her lightly on the cheek. "I will be back," he said, and then they were gone.

The estate of the Sibiu family was at the base of the foothills where the land finally flattened out on the road south to Bucharest. They turned off the highway at a weathered sign that said Sibiu in barely legible lettering. "Does anyone still come here?" Michael asked.

"If the government is ever stabilized, Claus Sibiu plans to open the grounds to tourists, as in the prewar days. That is why the Garden of the Apostles is being restored."

"Do you know Sibiu?"

"I met him with his wife at a reception in Bucharest a few months back. Last week he phoned me with their problem. They have new growth starting in the gardens and they hope the public will be able to view them soon. However, Claus Sibiu recently uncovered a letter from his father, who died of a heart attack shortly after being forced from his home by the Communists. The letter gave clues to the whereabouts of a statue that the elder Sibiu had hidden in the garden to keep it safe. Claus wondered if I might be able to help decipher it."

"A code?"

"Not really. I gather it's more a puzzle to be solved. They don't want to dig up the entire garden if they can pinpoint where this thing is buried."

Michael smiled. "A treasure hunt, as I said earlier."

"Does it not appeal to you?"

"It might be relaxing after some of the problems I've had to face lately." They'd paused before the big iron gates of the estate, which seemed to show a family crest entwined with vines of metallic ivy. Segar beeped his horn gently and presently a middle-aged woman in khaki pants and a work shirt came to admit them. She was large-boned and handsome in a rugged way, as if much of her life had been lived out of doors.

Michael assumed she was one of the estate's gardeners, and was startled when Segar called out, "Good day, Madame Sibiu. I am here to see your husband."

"Captain Segar!" she greeted him, swinging open the gate for their car.

"Not Captain any longer, I fear. In the new order of things I am only a government bureaucrat. Your husband phoned last week to suggest that I help him in his search for the statue of Cynthia, believed to be hidden in the Garden of the Apostles."

Her quick eyes went from Segar to Michael. "That would be most kind. And you bring with you an assistant?"

"I am Michael Vlado, a poor Gypsy with some knowledge of puzzles. My friend Segar thought I could help."

She nodded. "Park your car inside the gate, off the road, and we will walk to the garden. It is only a short distance from here."

They followed her along a path that had been cut through the haphazard growth of decades. Their drive down from Michael's village had taken much of the afternoon and the shadows of the spring day were already lengthening. Michael tried to remember what he had heard about the Garden of the Apostles. As he remembered it there were twelve sections, one designated for each of the followers of Christ. The flowers and plantings in each were in keeping with the apostle's life and Christian symbolism.

"You and your husband have done wonders here," Segar told her as they emerged from the path onto the open lawn at the front of an old stone mansion badly in need of repairs.

The house, with its dull gray facade and gabled roof,

was a perfect background for the blaze of spring flowers that burst upon Michael's eyes. The Garden of the Apostles, at least in this current reincarnation, was a formal planting of twelve raised beds, each about ten feet square and enclosed by a wooden frame. From where they stood there were three rows of four beds each, running across the front of the house.

"Viewed from the house the order is alphabetical," Mrs. Sibiu explained. "Andrew's garden is here and Thomas, Doubting Thomas is at the opposite corner."

They strolled among the flowerbeds, pausing occasionally to comment on a small tree or a particularly lovely planting. "Everything seems to be in blossom at once," Segar remarked, trying to take it all in.

"Claus and I tried to rebuild the garden using paintings and drawings from medieval monasteries. Most of these show spring gardens, so we have a preponderance of spring blossoms. But there will be blossoms of some sort throughout the summer and autumn." She led them toward the front steps. "Come to the house now. My husband will tell you more about it and explain our particular problem."

As he was mounting the stone steps Michael caught a glimpse of two men ducking out of sight around the corner of the house. "Are those gardeners?" he asked, thinking it odd that they would hide from view.

"Damned Gypsies!" she exclaimed angrily. "They did some work for us and the one in the red kerchief tried to steal our tools."

Segar and Michael exchanged glances but said no more. Inside the house Ida Sibiu ran up the wide front staircase calling to her husband. "Claus—Mr. Segar is here with a friend!"

While they waited, Michael had an opportunity to inspect the sparse but elegant furnishings of the large house. A marble-topped table with thick gilt legs stood in the foyer and on it was a framed photograph of Claus and

Ida Sibiu, on vacation or perhaps in exile, posed at the railing of a cruise ship of some sort. She was almost as tall as he was, and they might have passed for brother and sister. Their smiles in the photograph were virtually identical, as if they were already contemplating the money awaiting them back in a free Romania.

"That was on a cruise to the Greek Islands two years ago," a voice announced from the stairs. "It was our fifth anniversary."

Michael turned to see the man with the fringe of beard and thinning hairline descending the steps. He was a bit thinner than in the photo but still immediately recognizable. Segar came forward to shake his hand. "It is good to see you again, Mr. Sibiu. This is my friend Michael Vlado, who has come to assist us."

Sibiu stepped forward to shake Michael's hand. "Ida told me she'd given you a brief look at the garden."

"Very impressive," Michael told him. "It must take a great deal of work."

"That is Ida's province. She often neglects the house to work in the garden, but she says that is what will bring the tourists." He spoke slowly and carefully, as if unsure of the language. "You can see that our furnishings are sparse."

"This marble-topped table is lovely," Segar told him. "And this wall plaque of a golden moon—"

"Ida found it in Rome during our travels." The plaque was nearly two feet across, perfectly round but with the graceful curve of a half-moon etched on its surface. "She thought at first it might be by Picasso because of that odd representation of the moon's face."

Michael had moved on to a painting of a Roman galley under full sail. "Is this one old?"

"The last century, but not too valuable. The Communists did not even bother to steal it when they went through the house. I used to love it as a child here."

"When were you forced to leave?" Michael asked.

"In the summer of forty-nine when they began seizing property. I was just a boy but my father wanted me safely out of here. The Communists became Socialists in nineteen sixty-five, but no less repressive."

Segar cleared his throat, anxious to get on with the business at hand. "You told me on the telephone that you had found a message left by your father."

"I have it here." He was wearing a short maroon dressing gown over dark pants and a white shirt. From the gown's pocket he drew a folded envelope. "We found this among his papers when they were returned to us by the transition government. Apparently no one had ever opened it over all these years. My father mentions a buried statue which could be very valuable."

Segar accepted the envelope and withdrew a folded sheet of paper. "We had warehouses full of personal papers and possessions seized from the wealthy. You are lucky they could even find this to return it." He read the message with a deepening frown and then passed it on to Michael, who read it aloud:

My son, you have been gone from me only two weeks and already I yearn for your presence. If you should come back I pray that this message reaches you someday. Among the Apostles I have buried a likeness of Cynthia which is unique and valuable. This is for you, my son, and not for those who would destroy our country. Seek out the garden of the last Apostle and there you will find the treasure.

"This is his signature?" Segar asked.

"I believe so. It seems to match others we found among his papers."

"When was this written?" Michael wondered.

"There's a lightly penciled date on the back of the envelope, right here. It says February twenty-four, nineteen forty-nine."

Segar examined the envelope. "Who is Cynthia? An ancestor?"

"No one I'm aware of. My father's books were returned along with his papers, and I tried to find the name in an edition of Bulfinch's *Age of Fable*. It's not there."

"Has any searching been done?" Michael Vlado asked.

"Come into the garden. I will show you."

They followed him out the front door and down the steps to the twelve sections of the Garden of the Apostles. The rosebushes were not quite in blossom, but there were tulips and lilies and even a small magnolia tree in various stages of bloom. They saw now that one bed of the garden had been dug into recently, and an attempt made to repair the damage.

"Our only clue was mention of the garden of the last Apostle," Claus Sibiu explained. "The Apostles are listed four times in the New Testament, in Matthew, Mark, Luke, and the Acts. Each time Judas is listed last. The indication is that he was the last one chosen, but he may be last only because he later betrayed Christ. In any event, we dug up part of this garden and found nothing. A couple of Gypsies camping on the property helped us, but we were unsuccessful. Ida claimed the Gypsies tried to steal our tools and we stopped using them."

"They are still here," Michael said. "We saw them earlier."

"No doubt. The pests are hard to drive off."

"What do you want from us?" Segar asked him.

"If we have to dig up all twelve gardens to find this statue, it will set back progress to open the estate to the public for at least a year. I was hoping the government could offer some solution to the puzzle."

Segar gave a snort. "You need a priest, not a bureaucrat. I have no idea who the last Apostle was, or even the first."

"Simon Peter," Michael said. He remembered that

much, how Christ had come upon Peter and his brother
Andrew casting their fishing net into the sea.

But already the darkness was descending. Any further
examination of the twelve gardens would have to wait until morning. "We have five bedrooms," Sibiu told them.
"Please stay the night and we can examine the place by
the light of day. It is already too late for your return to
Bucharest." He glanced at the watch on his right wrist.

Segar and Michael exchanged glances. The puzzle itself held little interest for Michael, who was inclined to
think that the mysterious statue might well have been dug
up decades ago by the Communist government. Still, the
presence of the two Gypsies on the land interested him.
They might know something, if he could find them again
and speak with them. "We could stay," he told Segar.

His old friend chewed at his lower lip. "I must be in
my office by afternoon, but perhaps we could stay long
enough to have a quick look in the morning. I have no
fondness for driving these roads after dark."

"Very good!" Claus Sibiu seemed pleased. "I ate early
this evening, shortly before your arrival, but Ida can prepare something light for you before you retire. I will look
forward to continuing our analysis of this puzzle in the
morning."

He left them in the large, well-stocked kitchen, and
presently Ida Sibiu appeared wearing an emerald-green
robe. Michael wondered if it was their custom to retire at
nightfall each evening, like the birds.

"I have prepared the largest guest room at the front of
the house," she told them, "overlooking the garden. It has
only one large bed—"

"That's all right," Michael assured her.

She prepared a light supper of soup and cold meat
which tasted good to Michael. Then she joined them at
the table with a bottle of German beer. "You have to forgive us for the food," she apologized, wiping a drop of
blood from a cut she'd inflicted on her left wrist. "We

have not entertained since Claus regained the estate from the government. I've even lost the knack of carving meat!"

"You have not been married long?" Segar asked.

She shrugged. "Nearly seven years. But of course in middle age that is only a small fraction of our lives. I met him in Greece and he would tell me fabulous stories of his great estate back here in Romania. He never thought he would see it again, nor did I. Then the Communist and Socialist governments began to topple. It was all so fast, all at once! Claus made application to the provisional government for the return of his property and no one was more surprised than he when the request was granted. We came back last year to find the place was like a jungle."

"You've done wonders with it."

"But we must open it to the public to generate some income! Claus is not a wealthy man. What money he had was drained away by his years of living in exile. Once we even tried to sneak back into Romania, in disguise, but I was nervous about it and we turned back before we reached home."

"Home. This estate."

She nodded sadly. "For him it was always home. He has told me he wants to be buried here."

Soon after that she showed them to their room. Michael slept restlessly, awakened occasionally by Segar's snoring. Finally, when the first light of dawn slipped into the guest room, he got out of bed and opened the drapes to gaze down at the Garden of the Apostles.

At one of its intersecting paths the body of the Gypsy with the red kerchief was sprawled face down on the graveled earth. There was a knife in the center of his back, and from above it appeared that he'd been dragged to the spot and pinned there by some giant hand.

Michael and Segar, whom Michael awakened hastily from his morning dreams, were unable to find their hosts in the upstairs bedrooms. They finally located Ida Sibiu in the kitchen, where she was just beginning to prepare breakfast. "A body?" she repeated, unbelieving. "In the garden?"

Michael assured her it was true. "It appears to be one of the Gypsies. Is your husband about?"

"He's bathing now. I'll go look with you."

She followed them through the house and out the front door, hanging back a bit when they reached the garden. "It's Erik," she said, apparently recognizing the red kerchief.

"He's dead," Segar confirmed, kneeling by the body. "I'd better use your telephone to call Bucharest. The local authorities aren't equipped to handle this."

"Who could have done it?" Ida asked.

"The other Gypsy?" Segar suggested.

"His name is Bedrich," she volunteered. "They were camped at the back of our property with at least one woman."

"I'll go," Michael decided suddenly, because there was no one else to do it. "If this Bedrich did it he'll be on the run and I can track him."

Segar didn't argue. He'd known Michael Vlado too long for that. "All right, go. You'd better tell your husband what's happened, Mrs. Sibiu, while I phone the authorities."

She pointed the way for Michael and he set off, unarmed, hardly realizing that he'd been out of bed for only twenty minutes. The morning dew lay thick on the grass as he circled the big house and set off toward the rear of the property. He didn't know what he might be facing—a murderer, perhaps, but more likely an abandoned campsite with embers from a fire still glowing in the daylight. If there was only one woman they had probably fought over her. There were no rules in a knife fight, except it would be rare to stab a fellow Gypsy in the back whatever the provocation.

He saw the tent then, a little thing nestled among the firs. Had they left so quickly that the tent had been sacrificed? Not too likely.

He was almost to it when the woman emerged carrying a bucket of morning wash water which she emptied on the ground. She saw him then and was startled. "Bedrich!" she called out.

The second Gypsy emerged, bare-chested, from the tent. He was tall and well-built, with olive skin and a square jaw. "What do you want here?" he asked, speaking in Romany.

They both seemed surprised when Michael replied in the Gypsy language. "Your friend Erik is dead. I have come to ask you about that."

They exchanged glances but he saw no surprise. "The fool was looking for trouble," the woman said. She was dark and pretty in the way that very young women sometimes are, before age plays its tricks.

"Did you kill him?" Michael asked.

"He was my brother," the woman answered. "Erik. I am Esmeralda. Those people at the house killed him because he came searching for their treasure."

Michael turned to the Gypsy named Bedrich, who asked simply, "How did he die?"

"Stabbed in the back, near the center of the Garden of the Apostles."

"We worked for them, for Sibiu and his wife," Bedrich said. "Then she said we stole tools and they ordered us off the property."

"But you are still here."

The man shrugged. "Erik did not want to leave without the treasure. He heard them talking about it. He knew it was somewhere in the garden."

"This was the statue of Cynthia?"

"Yes."

"A goddess?"

It was Esmeralda who answered, possibly because of

her Greek name. "Cynthia is Artemis, the Greek goddess of the hunt, the counterpart to the Roman goddess Diana." She closed her eyes for a moment and then opened them. "I must see my brother's body. Take me to him."

Michael nodded. He could understand the need. When Bedrich followed along too he said nothing. Back at the big house Claus Sibiu had replaced his wife in the garden with Segar. "This is a shock to Ida," he said. "She must rest before she joins us." He looked uncertainly at the Gypsy couple. "So you found them!"

"They were at their camp. They had not run away. Esmeralda is the dead man's sister."

Sibiu frowned. "Why did I never know that?"

She looked away, avoiding his face. "Because you never asked. We were only workers to be accused by your wife when something was missing." The words came from Bedrich, not her, but either might have spoken them.

She saw the body then, only half covered by a burlap sack, and went to it. The knife was still buried in his back and she touched it gently, as if about to pull it free. Then her fingers dropped away and she began to sob quietly, showing real emotion for the first time since Michael brought her the news of her brother's death.

"What about the authorities?" he asked Segar.

"No good news. There are disturbances in the streets of Bucharest. Nothing too serious but all police are on standby. It will be at least tomorrow before they can send someone up here. In the meantime, they quickly point out, I am a former investigative officer for the militia. I am to take charge and conduct my own investigation."

Michael could see he was unhappy with the prospect. "There must be local authorities in this area."

"No one qualified to investigate a murder, I fear. Help in such cases is usually summoned from the cities." He glanced toward the Gypsy Bedrich, who had not joined Esmeralda at her brother's body. "I might as well start with you."

The young Gypsy seemed frightened by the turn of events. "We never stole the tools!" he insisted. "We never killed anybody!"

Claus Sibiu glanced at the watch on his left wrist. "Will you be needing me for the next half-hour, Mr. Segar? I have some phone calls to make. And I want to see how my wife is doing."

"Go ahead."

Esmeralda had returned to Michael's side. "You are a Gypsy too," she said.

"Yes, from Gravita, up in the foothills."

"We must have the body for a traditional burial ceremony. You understand that."

"Of course. Segar will have a few questions first. Tell me about the knife. Did it belong to your brother?"

"It was his."

"Did he always have such dirty hands?"

"What do you mean?"

Michael walked over and indicated the dead man's hands. "There's dirt on them, and under the fingernails too, as if he'd been digging."

"In one of the gardens?"

"Where else? Your brother was after the so-called treasure, wasn't he? His body lies between the gardens of Judas and Jude, at the very center of the layout."

"No Judas," Esmeralda said simply. "He betrayed Christ. He is never honored with the Apostles."

"But there are twelve gardens. You can see that."

"Judas was replaced. The Apostles drew lots for a replacement after he hanged himself."

"There is no marking on any of these gardens," Michael admitted. "I was told they were alphabetical. What was the name of his replacement?"

"I do not remember. It has been years since I studied the Bible with my mother."

Segar had finished questioning the Gypsy Bedrich. "You both must remain on the property until tomorrow," he ordered. "The other police will be arriving then, and may have more questions for you. I will go back to your tent now and look through it. You say you found no statue of Cynthia, but I must be certain it is not among your possessions."

Michael was in the house with Sibiu when he returned. Nothing had been found in or around the Gypsy camp. "Are you sure?" Sibiu asked.

Segar smiled slightly. "My old friend Michael has taught me all the Gypsy tricks. I even kicked away the remains of the campfire and dug underneath it. There was no treasure. Erik did not find it before he was killed."

"Then it's still out there," Michael said. "The statue of Cynthia."

"I'm more disturbed about the killing right now," Sibiu told them in his measured tones. "The government could use this as an excuse for not letting us open the garden."

"Something must be done with the body until tomorrow," Segar told the man. "Do you have any sort of cold storage room in the house?"

There was nothing except a large freezer, and they decided that was too small. The body was wrapped in a plastic bag and carried to the cool basement. Then they set about the problem at hand.

"The statue is out there," Segar stated firmly. "I say everything gets dug up until we find it."

"How will that help us identify the killer?" Michael asked.

"Erik was killed because he guessed or deduced where the statue was buried. If he did it, we can do it."

"You forget he'd camped on the estate for a year or more," Sibiu told them. "He might have seen something."

"According to your father's note the statue was buried over forty years ago, long before Erik was born. Since you and Ida don't know where it is, what could he have seen? Did either of you ever mention your father's message to him?"

"We might have," Sibiu admitted. "That part about the last Apostle."

"Yes, the last Apostle. It didn't mean Judas but the Apostle who replaced Judas. That's where you'll find the statue."

"We looked there!" Claus Sibiu insisted. "We dug it up and the Gypsies helped. The Apostle chosen to replace Judas was Matthias."

"When you say you looked there you mean you looked in the garden assigned to Judas. Don't you see? There never was a Judas garden. He was one of the original twelve, certainly, but he is never honored with the other Apostles. You were too young to remember it, but the twelfth garden was Matthias's from the beginning. It was never the sixth plot, where you dug, but the eighth plot, in proper alphabetical order between Matthew and Peter."

Segar had drawn twelve squares on a sheet of paper, arranged in three rows of four each and labeled as they appeared from the house. "You mean the right-hand plot in the second row?"

"Exactly," Michael replied.

"But Erik wasn't killed there," Sibiu reminded them.

"The killer dragged the body to the middle, to keep it away from Matthias's plot. From the upstairs window I could detect signs of dragging on the gravel. But there's stronger evidence that Matthias is the garden we want. You told us, Claus, that you left here as a child in the summer of nineteen forty-nine, and your father's message says you've been gone two weeks. So the date on the envelope, February twenty-fourth, is not when the letter was written. What does it refer to? I found it in one of your library books last night—the feast of Saint Matthias! That was before I even realized he was the last Apostle."

"Let's get shovels and start digging," Segar suggested.

They went out the front door with Michael leading the way. He paused at the right end of the second row, as seen from the house. The plot for Matthias, even though

it was unmarked. Segar returned with two shovels and he
and Michael plunged them into the dry earth.

Claus gave a sigh. "Ida won't like what you're doing to
her garden."

Michael avoided the well-established tulip bed and the
carpet of lilies of the valley. Instead he went to work
on a patch of disturbed soil, turned over since the last
rain. He'd dug down only two feet before he hit something. "This may be it," he told them. "It's a large plastic
bag. Hand me your knife, Mr. Sibiu."

The man slipped the blade from his belt and passed it
over. Michael made a clean slit and pulled the edges of
the plastic apart.

Something is wrong, he suddenly realized even as he
was doing it. *They didn't have plastic bags like this back
in the forties.*

Then he saw the body, and the dead face staring up at
him was the face of Claus Sibiu, the man who stood behind him at that moment.

Segar gasped at the sight of the uncovered face. "This
is madness! Sibiu, is that a twin?"

"There are forces at work here you cannot imagine,"
Sibiu told them. "Come into the house with me and I will
explain everything."

"The body is fresh," Michael pointed out. "He hasn't
been dead more than a few days, if that long."

"Come into the house," Sibiu repeated.

"No, I think not," Michael replied. He was beginning
to see it all. He was beginning to see too much.

Sibiu's hand came out of his pocket holding a double-
barreled derringer pistol, but Michael still held the knife
in his hand. He rolled to one side as Sibiu fired, and
hurled the knife with an aim he knew was true. It buried
itself in the fleshy part of Sibiu's arm, bringing a high-
pitched yelp of pain.

Then Michael and Segar were both on him, holding

him as Michael peeled away the fringe beard and the false headpiece. "What is this?" Segar demanded.

"It is Ida Sibiu," Michael explained, holding her tightly as he pulled the knife from her arm. "She has murdered her husband and buried him in the garden of Matthias, in place of the moon."

"Moon? What moon?"

"Let me go!" she screeched in a fury, ignoring her arm wound as she wrestled with Michael.

But he held her firm as he answered Segar's question. "The golden moon that hangs on the wall of their house. No one else ever said the treasure was a statue. The message from Claus's father described it as a likeness of Cynthia. I finally remembered that Cynthia is also a poetic term for the moon. You and your husband discovered the hiding place in the garden of Matthias a few days ago. Once it was dug up, you didn't need the pretense anymore. You killed Claus and buried him where the moon had been, then hid the treasure in plain sight on the wall of your house."

"Why would she kill him," Segar asked, "when she knew I was coming to see him?"

"That's just the point. She didn't know."

Segar had produced a pair of handcuffs from the trunk of his car and they bandaged Ida Sibiu's arm wound as best they could before driving to the hospital in a nearby town. "I don't understand any of it," Segar admitted as they waited at the hospital for her wound to be treated and stitched up. "Why would she kill her husband?"

"You'll have to ask her that. She met him in Greece, away from home, and I imagine when they were married seven years ago he filled her mind with visions of great wealth back here in Romania. Then the government collapsed and she got an unexpected look at all the wealth—a decaying mansion and a garden gone to seed. Perhaps she would have left him then if the message from his father hadn't come to light, with its promise of buried treasure. So she stayed on, but when Claus phoned you for help with the puzzle last week he neglected to tell her, probably wanting your arrival kept secret until he knew if you could help."

"So we walked in on her yesterday unannounced?"

"Exactly." Michael watched a nurse helping an old man negotiate the corridor. "In retrospect we have to say she kept her composure very well. You already knew about the statue and the message so she had to show it to us, hoping it wouldn't lead us to the body. As for the disguise, she may have had it ready in case local officials called. Remember, she told us they'd used disguises to slip across borders. All she really needed were the fringe beard for her chin, the wig to make the hair appear thin in front, and some of his clothes. We saw from that picture that they were about the same height, and her face was like his in a sisterly way. She was big-boned, but still a bit thinner than he appeared in the photo. As for the voice, she spoke slowly, in a measured manner, careful to give it a masculine tone. She felt safe because you'd met them only once, and that time at a reception with others present. The rest was easy. We never saw them together and never suspected at first that the wall plaque in plain sight was the buried treasure."

"What about the Gypsies? They knew the Sibius."

"But Esmeralda avoided looking directly at Claus when she came to view her brother's body. He was dressed right and neither of them had reason to doubt his identity."

"You see it all in retrospect," Segar challenged. "Admit it—you were as surprised as I was when we uncovered Claus Sibiu's body!"

"I was surprised," Michael admitted, "but I shouldn't have been. Yesterday Claus wore his watch on his right wrist. This morning it was on his left. Why the change overnight?"

"I didn't notice that," Segar admitted. "Why?"

"Because Ida cut herself while slicing the meat last night—remember? She couldn't risk our noticing the same cut on Claus's wrist so she covered it with the watchband."

Segar nodded finally, beginning to accept it. "After she killed him and buried the body, why didn't she just take that moon plaque and leave?"

"Because Erik the Gypsy was still around, searching for the treasure. Last night, when he started digging with his hands in the garden of Matthias, she stabbed him in the back with his own knife."

Michael Vlado had an answer for everything, except why a woman would kill her husband for a golden plaque that didn't look very much like the moon at all.

One Last Picture
by Sherita Saffer Campbell

Sadie May Ellison walked around the yard clipping the
dead flowers off Mrs. Cramer's rosebushes. The early
morning sun was just touching the heavy stone birdbath
in the center of the garden. Mrs. Cramer was still asleep.
Sadie May clucked her tongue as she looked up at her
employer's window in the big brick house and saw the
heavy drapes still closed to keep out the morning sun.
Sadie May shook her head before she went back to the
roses.

It was going to be hot again today. At her age she
wasn't sure if it was the heat or the cold which gave her
more miseries. The doctor had told her that her arthritic
legs were not built for heavy gardening even when she
was young, but now she wasn't at all equipped to spend
time bending over plants.

The roses were so pretty—pink, red, white, and dripping with dew. They looked almost like shaped party ice
cream ready to eat. She glanced again at the window, as
if her thoughts could penetrate that darned curtain better
than the sun's rays. Roses needed care—mulching, feeding, watering. Sadie May squinted close at the bush she
was working on. Aphids again. Mrs. Cramer had said
she'd keep them off.... She sighed, wishing now she
could be heard behind those drapes. Never mind. There'd
be the charity ball and Mrs. Cramer was totally absorbed
in the June event.

Sadie May walked over to the shed, opened the door,

and stepped inside the dark little building. If I had my life
to live over, she thought, I'd be a gardener instead of . . .
of whatever. Mumbling to herself, she opened the big
cupboard and reached behind the large flower pots she
used for fall re-potting. She dug out her special mixture
for wiping out aphids. She sniffed. Those young land-
scapers that Mrs. Cramer hired could use what they
wanted, they could spray and do all the damage to the
flowers they could, but she had always had luck with the
mixture old Clyde Bellows stirred up for her at the phar-
macy. She shook the can. Old Clyde was in the home now
over to Coldwater, and she doubted that young busybody
pharmacist knew how to mix up a good cold poultice, let
alone a rose aphid killer. Arsenic, Clyde had said, was the
secret ingredient. Mixed with enough other things so as
not to kill the rosebushes.

Sadie May always made the solution in a Tupperware
pitcher she'd bought at some dumb party Mrs. Cramer
had made them both go to. Plastic pitchers to put tea and
milk in, she thought. The world is going to . . . She tried
to think of something awful, then smiled, remembering
her father's favorite expression: "The world's going to
hell in a red wagon."

Sadie May laughed, then looked around guiltily to see
if anyone had heard her. "Parson's still asleep." She
looked up at the window again. "So's the boss." Still
laughing, she shook her head. "It's true; when you start to
sin one way, I guess you just let everything slide."

She went to the rosebush and began to spray the roses
with an antique push thingamagig she'd brought from her
house when she'd left it to go to work, all those years ago
when her father had found out about . . . Never mind,
what's done is done. Mustn't think about it. Except today
. . . today was the day . . . June. She was to have been a
bride those many years ago. Only . . .

Sadie May pushed the sprayer hard. "Don't get moody
and sentimental, my girl," she said aloud to herself. "He

jilted you at the church. Well, you never really got that
far." There was a sigh. "I reckon in the flesh and in the
spirit you never even made it to church." She eyed a bee-
tle, aimed the sprayer, and watched the mist descend on
the creature. She paused in mid-spray. "You just sat in
that stupid train station all day and all night waiting for
some stage-happy tenor who didn't show. And that's
that."

Wasn't long before she was showing, though. "Dumb,
dumb young woman you was." She walked around the
bush looking for more prey. "Whole town knowing I was
there. Whole town knowing why, most likely." She shook
her head. "Mustn't stir up the past." Let sleeping dogs lie
was her mother's motto. Her mother, long dead before the
train station episode.

Maybe if her mother had been alive she'd have been
told not to wait in the station. Would she have listened?
She sprayed harder for a while, then looked again at the
object in her hands. "What a thing to keep as a souvenir
from my homeplace—a rose sprayer. I could have had the
family china."

But Sadie May knew why she had the sprayer. She'd
been spraying the roses at home that day when her father
found her out and came around the side yard screaming at
her. She had left, or he had thrown her out—god, she
didn't even remember any more. She'd left carrying only
the sprayer and listening to the clickety-clack of the
neighbor's lawn mower and the sound of the horses up
and down the street. She'd never even ridden in the new
motor car her father bought to ride around town in.

They didn't make things that lasted like that sprayer
any more. Everyone used them spray cans now. She did,
too, sometimes but . . . maybe she used this to remember.

The bell rang and Sadie May knew Mrs. Cramer was
up. That was the trouble working for someone else. You
never got to do anything you wanted to for very long.
She'd gone from job to job for a while after that long ago

day. She had no education, no training. She had hoped she could save enough to go to college or to the new vocational school. But she never made enough money. She'd try to save, then the job would be over and it would be so long before she got another that her small savings would be gone. She'd been lucky when she got this job, with room and board. Reckon the old parson had talked Mrs. Cramer into it.

Sadie May knew she was too old to work, but she wasn't ready for the home and old Clyde, even after he'd saved her that long ago day, from all that bleeding. Old Clyde even offered to marry her for a while. But that train station had taken too much from her. She had no money, not much Social Security if she quit work. She hated the thought of welfare so she'd worked and worked as some sort of companion for ladies; it was the custom then. Only now not many people needed them. Folks just went full blast all alone. Those who would have hired companions to prepare afternoon teas in the old family homeplaces gave the homeplaces to the local university for a tax write-off, then hied themselves off to a luxurious retirement center as a home base for zapping around the world. Women like herself who had no money tried to find work somewhere and make do. Somehow.

She set the sprayer on the workbench beside the pitcher and went into the house. "The breakfast tray for Mrs. Cramer is ready," the cook said, nodding her head toward the table. Sadie mumbled acknowledgment.

"It ain't right she stay in that bed every morning and make you take food to her, not up them steps," Sharon grumbled.

"It's my job."

"You too old to do it. You need to quit."

"I don't . . . know . . . What would I do?"

"Retire and live off your savings, or . . ."

"I don't have any. It's . . ." The bell rang, more insistent this time.

"She hungry," Sharon grinned.

Sadie sighed at the uselessness of explaining the unexplained, picked up the tray, and left.

The stairs weren't bad, only seven of them to the small elevator Mrs. Cramer had had installed. Sadie May smiled. The cook wasn't much younger than her. Whole bunch of them living in this house were not only "past their prime" as she had heard them young folks speak, but their prime was so far back no one remembered it. Cook just liked to fuss over people, Sadie May knew. She and Sharon didn't either of them have a family or a home.

"I reckon we'd just go to the home with Clyde Bellows, and I just don't like that one bit," she sighed as she rounded the corner into the bedroom.

"Don't like what one bit?" asked Mrs. Cramer as Sadie May carried the tray to the bed.

"Going to the home, me and Sharon."

"What home are you and Sharon going to?" asked Mrs. Cramer, fluffing her pillows. "Have you seen my atomizers and my asthma medicine?"

"Your glasses are on the stand. If you'd put them on, you could . . ."

"Don't get uppity," scowled Mrs. Cramer. "I thought I had my glasses on. I can't seem to see any better with them on than with them off. That's a sign, I guess; I could talk to the doctor again." There was a shishing sound as Mrs. Cramer sprayed her throat. "There. Now I'll have my tray."

Sadie May placed the tray over the old woman's comforter-enveloped legs.

"Now, whose home, dear?"

"I was thinking if me and Sharon retire we wouldn't have nothing to do or nowhere to go, except the home where Clyde Bellows is."

"Nonsense, dear. There's the Masonic home at Fairmont, the Elks home at Crawfordville . . ."

"No. We'd have to go to the old folks home because we won't have no money."

"How many times must I remind you that your home is here with me?" retorted Mrs. Cramer. "Am I working you too hard? If I am ... this coffee is cold."

"That's the milk."

Mrs. Cramer peered into the cup. "Why, of course."

"I was out in the yard working on the roses. You promised to keep the roses ..."

"And you promised to stay out of the yard so often," Mrs. Cramer interrupted. She took a noisy slurp of her coffee. "Today's the day I have to finish with the committee about the ball. I'll be gone all day, so you and Sharon rest."

"Sharon has the rest of the day off."

"You want to come with me? No, that's right; that young man is coming."

"What young man?"

"Well, my dear." Mrs. Cramer stirred her coffee. "I'm sure I don't know, but you got that letter, and a phone call. Some distant relative."

Sadie May sat down. "I'd forgotten."

"How could you forget a visitor? I mean, well, I do believe in all the years you've been here that's the only visitor you've had except the parson. Maybe the lawyer when your father died."

"I guess ... I guess I'd better lay out your clothes for today," Sadie changed the subject.

"Hmmm. I'll wear the light gray summer suit."

"You wore that last time."

"I like my summer suit. I feel ... prominent. Besides, the late Mr. Cramer liked it."

Mrs. Cramer's voice faded in and out as Sadie laid out the clothes. She'd forgotten about the young man coming today. Today was her day. Her wedding day, if that damned hussy Lilly hadn't grabbed off the tenor. Now that wasn't fair. She'd never heard what happened. She just knew it was Lilly told her father about . . . the other. That meant Lilly took the tenor.

Sadie May finished her task and went to her own room, leaving Mrs. Cramer to dress herself. She dug around in the desk searching for the letter she'd wadded up in anger after she'd read it. Finding it, she spread it out on the desktop and pressed and smoothed it so she could read it once again.

"Dear Mrs. Ellison," the letter said, "my name won't mean anything to you, but I'm doing a series of pictures for a magazine and I'll be in the neighborhood. My grandmother was Lilly Wrench. You and she used to be friends."

Sadie May looked out the window as she heard Mrs. Cramer bubbling around in her room. She re-read the letter, then looked again at the roses. Well, she didn't know what he wanted. Him and that grandmother of his. Apples don't fall far from the tree.

She put the crumpled letter back in the desk drawer.

His grandmother had been her closest friend, the only one she'd told about her pregnancy before Lilly left for the stage. Became a big star on the vaudeville circuit, she had. Then just dropped out of sight. Sadie May never heard if or who she married. Back then, with no TV, fan magazines, or, she sniffed, gossip papers, you never knew what happened to people.

"Wonder how he found me?" No matter. Mustn't think about it.

Sadie May took elevator and stairs down to the garden again. The sun was higher now, and the birds were darting in and out of the birdbath. She smelled the sweet, almost funereal, smell of the roses. "More aphids." She made a face, picked up two of them, and squished them between her fingers, watching the gray goo drip on the velvet petals of the roses, marring their beauty with ugliness, the way her day had been marred. She wanted to work in the garden while Mrs. Cramer was gone and not talk to young scallywags.

She went hastily to the shed and got her sprayer again. She began to walk around the roses, spraying and mentally naming each aphid Lilly. A few she named after Lilly's grandson. Two or three times she peered down close and labeled the pests Mrs. Cramer. She was busily enjoying herself and had succeeded in putting aside the awfulness of the day when she glanced towards the back stoop and saw a young man. Lilly's grandson, no doubt.

"Hey there, Mrs. Ellison?" He walked toward her and extended his hand.

She shook it. Shaking hands, she thought. In my day . . . Aloud she asked, "It's right hot. Would you like some lemonade?" Remembering he was young, she added, "Cookies?"

He nodded.

"Well, go on in the house; I'll just clean up." She watched as he went through the door. "Just go on into the sitting room. I'll be right along. Make yourself to home."

The sprayer was empty so she went to the shed and laid down the antique, also taking off her gloves. The pitcher, however, was still partially full. Best take that into the house with me or else I'll forget when he leaves what I was doing, like as not, she thought.

Sadie May set the pitcher on the kitchen counter and washed her hands before rummaging around in the refrigerator for lemons.

"Mind if I come in here?" asked the young man from the other room.

" 'Course not. What's your name again?"

"William. I was named after my grandfather, William Gaither, the Irish tenor."

She was proud that she stopped halving the lemon in time to avoid slicing her hand. Then she continued, putting each section on the glass juicer and twisting it around and around. Wish this was Lilly's damn neck, she thought. She strained the pungent liquid as she poured the juice into a glass pitcher.

"Tenor singer, was he?"

"Yes, ma'am."

"On the stage?"

"Yes, ma'am. Grandma said you knew him, too. Said both you and her chased him and chased him until she got him."

"Umm." Sadie May measured the sugar carefully into the lemon juice.

"Gram is still alive and would sure like to see you and your children. She's got five children and fifteen grand-children and thirty-eight great-grandkids."

"I never married." Sadie May said it simply, quietly. How to tell him her disgrace. Soiled goods, her father had said. Wouldn't do to take on in front of him.

"Oh. She thought you could come and swap stories. She likes to talk about the stamina of young girls now. She was in labor six hours for my mother. She said Mama was so contrary, had a mind of her own even about being born."

While he talked she watched the sugar disappear into the yellow liquid. She thought of that dark alley she'd walked down all alone. Those long dark stairs that went on forever. She'd bled for a long time after. Old Clyde had worked hard to save her.

"I had a time finding you," she heard the boy say. "Finally I went to the church."

She started to turn on the water. In reaching out, she touched the bright orange Tupperware pitcher.

"Yes, Grandmother thought you'd probably have a dozen children and ought to have grandchildren my age, too."

As he droned on she poured the orange pitcher's contents into the glass one and stirred carefully. Then she turned on the cold water.

"Would you get some ice cubes out of the refrigerator?" Her voice sounded natural. "Put them in those two glasses."

She set out a good silver tray and carefully put the pitcher on it. William set the glasses down.

"I'd like to get a picture of you for Grandmother," he said. "Should I take it now, or after we have the lemonade?"

Sadie May paused, looking at the pitcher. "I think," she said, "you'd better take the picture before we drink the lemonade."

A Curtain of Green
by Eudora Welty

Every day one summer in Larkin's Hill, it rained a little. The rain was a regular thing, and would come about two o'clock in the afternoon.

One day, almost as late as five o'clock, the sun was still shining. It seemed almost to spin in a tiny groove in the polished sky, and down below, in the trees along the street and in the rows of flower gardens in the town, every leaf reflected the sun from a hardness like a mirror surface. Nearly all the women sat in the windows of their houses, fanning and sighing, waiting for the rain.

Mrs. Larkin's garden was a large, densely grown plot running downhill behind the small white house where she lived alone now, since the death of her husband. The sun and the rain that beat down so heavily that summer had not kept her from working there daily. Now the intense light like a tweezers picked out her clumsy, small figure in its old pair of men's overalls rolled up at the sleeves and trousers, separated it from the thick leaves, and made it look strange and yellow as she worked with a hoe— over-vigorous, disreputable, and heedless.

Within its border of hedge, high like a wall, and visible only from the upstairs windows of the neighbors, this slanting, tangled garden, more and more over-abundant and confusing, must have become so familiar to Mrs. Larkin that quite possibly by now she was unable to conceive of any other place. Since the accident in which her husband was killed, she had never once been seen anywhere else. Every morning she might be observed walking slowly, almost timidly, out of the white house, wearing a pair of the untidy overalls, often with her hair streaming and tangled where she had neglected to comb it. She would wander about for a little while at first, uncertainly, deep among the plants and wet with their drew, and yet not quite putting out her hand to touch anything. And then a sort of sturdiness would possess her—stabilize her; she would stand still for a moment, as if a blindfold were being removed; and then she would kneel in the flowers and begin to work.

She worked without stopping, almost invisibly, submerged all day among the thick, irregular, sloping beds of plants. The servant would call her at dinnertime, and she would obey; but it was not until it was completely dark that she would truthfully give up her labor and with a drooping, submissive walk appear at the house, slowly opening the small low door at the back. Even the rain would bring only a pause to her. She would move to the shelter of the pear tree, which in mid-April hung heavily almost to the ground in brilliant full leaf, in the center of the garden.

It might seem that the extreme fertility of her garden formed at once a preoccupation and a challenge to Mrs. Larkin. Only by ceaseless activity could she cope with the rich blackness of this soil. Only by cutting, separating, thinning and tying back the clumps of flowers and bushes and vines could she have kept them from overreaching their boundaries and multiplying out of all reason. The daily summer rains could only increase her vigilance and her already excessive energy. And yet, Mrs. Larkin rarely cut, separated, tied back. . . . To a certain extent, she seemed not to seek for order, but to allow an overflowering, as if she consciously ventured forever a little farther, a little deeper, into her life in the garden.

She planted every kind of flower that she could find or order from a catalogue—planted thickly and hastily, without stopping to think, without any regard for the ideas that her neighbors might elect in their club as to what constituted an appropriate vista, or an effect of restfulness, or even harmony of color. Just to what end Mrs. Larkin worked so strenuously in her garden, her neighbors could not see. She certainly never sent a single one of her fine flowers to any of them. They might get sick and die, and she would never send a flower. And if she thought of *beauty* at all (they regarded her stained overalls, now almost of a color with the leaves), she certainly did not strive for it in her garden. It was impossible to enjoy looking at such a place. To the neighbors gazing down from their upstairs windows it had the appearance of a sort of jungle, in which the slight, heedless form of its owner daily lost itself.

At first, after the death of Mr. Larkin—for whose father, after all, the town had been named—they had called upon the widow with decent frequency. But she had not appreciated it, they said to one another. Now, occasionally, they looked down from their bedroom windows as they brushed studiously at their hair in the morning; they found her place in the garden, as they might have run their fingers toward a city on a map of a foreign country, located her from their distance almost in curiosity, and then forgot her.

Early that morning they had heard whistling in the Larkin garden. They had recognized Jamey's tune, and had seen him kneeling in the flowers at Mrs. Larkin's side. He was only the colored boy who worked in the neighborhood by the day. Even Jamey, it was said, Mrs. Larkin would tolerate only now and then. . . .

Throughout the afternoon she had raised her head at intervals to see how fast he was getting along in his transplanting. She had to make him finish before it began to rain. She was busy with the hoe, clearing one of the last patches of uncultivated ground for some new shrubs. She bent under the sunlight, chopping in blunt, rapid, tireless strokes. Once she raised her head far back to stare at the flashing sky. Her eyes were dull and puckered, as if from long impatience or bewilderment. Her mouth was a sharp line. People said she never spoke.

But memory tightened about her easily, without any prelude of warning or even despair. She would see promptly, as if a curtain had been jerked quite unceremoniously away from a little scene, the front porch of the white house, the shady street in front, and the blue automobile in which her husband approached, driving home from work. It was a summer day, a day from the summer before. In the freedom of gaily turning her head, a motion she was now forced by memory to repeat as she hoed the ground, she could see again the tree that was going to fall. There had been no warning. But there was the enormous tree, the fragrant chinaberry tree, suddenly tilting, dark and slow like a cloud, leaning down to her husband. From her place on the front porch she had spoken in a soft voice to him, never so intimate as at that moment, "You can't be hurt." But the tree had fallen, had struck the car exactly so as to crush him to death. She had waited there on the porch for a time afterward, not moving at all—in a sort of recollection—as if to reach under and bring out from obliteration her protective words and to try them once again . . . so as to change the whole happening. It was an accident that was incredible, when her love for her husband was keeping him safe.

She continued to hoe the breaking ground, to beat down the juicy weeds. Presently she became aware that hers was the only motion to continue in the whole slackened place. There was no wind at all now. The cries of the birds had hushed. The sun seemed clamped to the side of the sky. Everything had stopped once again, the stillness had mesmerized the stems of the plants, and all the leaves went suddenly into thickness. The shadow of the pear tree in the center of the garden lay callous on the ground. Across the yard, Jamey knelt, motionless.

"Jamey!" she called angrily.

But her voice hardly carried in the dense garden. She felt all at once terrified, as though her loneliness had been pointed out by some outside force whose finger parted the hedge. She drew her hand for an instant to her breast. An obscure fluttering there frightened her, as though the force babbled to her, The bird that flies within your heart could not divide this cloudy air . . . She stared without expression at the garden. She was clinging to the hoe, and she stared across the green leaves toward Jamey.

A look of docility in the Negro's back as he knelt in the plants began to infuriate her. She started to walk toward him, dragging the hoe vaguely through the flowers behind her. She forced herself to look at him, and noticed him closely for the first time—the way he looked like a child. As he turned his head a little to one side and negligently stirred the dirt with his yellow finger, she saw, with a sort of helpless suspicion and hunger, a soft, rather deprecating smile on his face; he was lost in some impossible dream of his own while he was transplanting the little shoots. He was not even whistling; even that sound was gone.

She walked nearer to him—he must have been deaf!— almost stealthily bearing down upon his laxity and his absorption, as if that glimpse of the side of his face, that turned-away smile, were a teasing, innocent, flickering and beautiful vision—some mirage to her strained and wandering eyes.

Yet a feeling of stricture, of a responding hopelessness almost approaching ferocity, grew with alarming quickness about her. When she was directly behind him she stood quite still for a moment, in the queer sheathed manner she had before beginning her gardening in the morning. Then she raised the hoe above her head; the clumsy sleeves both fell back, exposing the thin, unsunburned whiteness of her arms, the shocking fact of their youth.

She gripped the handle tightly, tightly, as though convinced that the wood of the handle could feel, and that all her strength could indent its surface with pain. The head of Jamey, bent there below her, seemed witless, terrifying, wonderful, almost inaccessible to her, and yet in its explicit nearness meant surely for destruction, with its clustered hot wooly hair, its intricate, glistening ears, its small brown branching streams of sweat, the bowed head holding so obviously and so deadly its ridiculous dream.

Such a head she could strike off, intentionally, so deeply did she know, from the effect of a man's danger and death, its cause in oblivion; and so helpless was she, too helpless to defy the workings of accident, of life and death, of unaccountability. . . . Life and death, she thought, gripping the heavy hoe, life and death, which now meant nothing to her but which she was compelled continually to wield with both her hands, ceaselessly asking, Was it not possible to compensate? to punish? to protest? Pale darkness turned for a moment through the sunlight, like a narrow leaf blown through the garden in a wind.

In that moment, the rain came. The first drop touched her upraised arm. Small, close sounds and coolness touched her.

Sighing, Mrs. Larkin lowered the hoe to the ground and laid it carefully among the growing plants. She stood still where she was, close to Jamey, and listened to the rain falling. It was so gentle. It was so full—the sound of the end of waiting.

In the light from the rain, different from sunlight, everything appeared to gleam unreflecting from within itself in its quiet arcade of identity. The green of the small zinnia shoots was very pure, almost burning. One by one, as the rain reached them, all the individual little plants shone out, and then the branching vines. The pear tree gave a soft rushing noise, like the wings of a bird alighting. She could sense behind her, as if a lamp were lighted in the night, the signal-like whiteness of the house. Then Jamey, as if in the shock of realizing the rain had come, turned his full face toward her, questions and delight intensifying his smile, gathering up his aroused, stretching body. He stammered some disconnected words, shyly.

She did not answer Jamey or move at all. She would not feel anything now except the rain falling. She listened for its scattered soft drops between Jamey's words, its quiet touching of the spears of the iris leaves, and a clear sound like a bell as it began to fall into a pitcher the cook had set on the doorstep.

Finally, Jamey stood there quietly, as if waiting for his money, with his hand trying to brush his confusion away from before his face. The rain fell steadily. A wind of deep wet fragrance beat against her.

Then as if it had swelled and broken over a daily levee, tenderness tore and spun through her sagging body.

It has come, she thought senselessly, her head lifting and her eyes looking without understanding at the sky which had begun to move, to fold nearer in softening, dissolving clouds. It was almost dark. Soon the loud and gentle night of rain would come. It would pound upon the steep roof of the white house. Within, she would lie in her bed and hear the rain. On and on it would fall, beat and fall. The day's work would be over in the garden. She would lie in bed, her arms tired at her sides and in motionless peace: against that which was inexhaustible. There was no defense.

Then Mrs. Larkin sank in one motion down into the flowers and lay there, fainting and streaked with rain. Her face was fully upturned, down among the plants, with the hair beaten away from her forehead and her open eyes closing at once when the rain touched them. Slowly her lips began to part. She seemed to move slightly, in the sad adjustment of a sleeper.

Jamey ran jumping and crouching about her, drawing in his breath alternately at the flowers breaking under his feet and at the shapeless, passive figure on the ground. Then he became quiet, and stood back at a little distance and looked in awe at the unknowing face, white and rested under its bombardment. He remembered how something had filled him with stillness when he felt her standing there behind him looking down at him, and he would not have turned around at that moment for anything in the world. He remembered all the while the oblivious crash of the windows next door being shut when the rain started. . . . But now, in this unseen place, it was he who stood looking at poor Mrs. Larkin.

He bent down and in a horrified, piteous, beseeching voice he began to call her name until she stirred.

"Miss Lark'! Miss Lark'!"

Then he jumped nimbly to his feet and ran out of the garden.

The Scent of Murder
by Frances & Richard Lockridge

Ronnie Beede had been free for forty-eight hours and he had a gun and he was a killer. Throughout Westchester and Putnam counties people locked their doors against Ronnie Beede.

He had escaped from the psychiatric ward of an upstate hospital and since then he had murdered twice. First he had killed a salesman who had picked him up on the road, and after that a girl of sixteen who had been baby-sitting in a house he had broken into for food and clothes. The police were sure of the first: his fingerprints had been found on the salesman's car, which Beede had abandoned when it ran out of gas. They were not so sure about the girl. But her killing had been needless, wanton, and that looked like Ronnie Beede.

They knew a good deal about Beede—almost everything, except where he was. A big blond man in his middle twenties; a good-looking man with a friendly face and a wide, agreeable smile, and a slow, rather diffident way of speaking. The sort of attractive young man anyone might have picked up, even a person who should have known better. Probably the salesman had been bored and lonely when he stopped for Ronnie on a road above Peekskill. Ronnie had slugged him, then strangled him and thrown his body by the roadside. That was needless, too, but it was Ronnie's way. The gun he had now had been in the glove compartment of the salesman's car.

The girl had been killed in Mt. Kisco, and geography

as well as wantonness made the police think of Ronnie Beede. If he was working his way home—killing his way home—Mt. Kisco would be on his route—on the route to a small, unpainted farmhouse on a back road between Brewster and Pawling. His mother waited there—a frail woman with a drawn face who had trembled uncontrollably when Captain M. L. Heimrich of the New York State Police spoke to her, although Heimrich spoke gently, believing that Ronnie was no fault of hers. She thought the fault the army's. "He was always a good boy until he went into the army. The best son a mother ever—" She had been unable to finish.

There was no telling whose fault Ronnie was, but that was not Heimrich's problem—except that, as well as a policeman, he was a man, and mankind worried him. It was easy enough to put a word to Ronnie. He was a paranoic, knowing the world was against him and killing to defend himself against the world. *Mad Killer Strikes Again*—that was the way a New York City tabloid had headlined it that July morning, after the girl's body had been found. The fault? It was not for the police to decide. Their problem was to catch Beede—before he killed again.

The news came on the car radio at four thirty-one in the afternoon. The car, with Sergeant Charles Forniss driving, was two miles east of Katonah on NY 22, heading west toward the barracks at Hawthorne. Forniss set the siren going and the car leaped—leaped through Katonah, with other cars flinching to the curbs; screamed its way north and west for three miles and a little more, and onto a side road and then, almost at once, up a winding driveway between trees.

Forniss knew the way. The Franklins were well-known thereabouts—Arthur Franklin was on the town planning board and the library committee, and Martha Franklin had been active in the garden club, although less lately than in the recent past. It was hard to believe that a thing like this could happen to people like the Franklins.

Their house was isolated, deep in ancient trees. It was probably the isolation and quiet that had brought murder there.

Heimrich and Forniss were the first of the police to arrive. The front door of the house stood open; the screen which had shielded it had been gashed near the knob. In the square hall beyond the door, Arthur Franklin was sitting on a bench—sitting with his wrists resting on his knees and his hands dangling between them. He sat staring at the floor, which was in deep shadow. When Heimrich and Forniss crossed the porch, he got up slowly, heavily, then came to the door and looked at them with almost blank eyes.

"He killed her," Arthur Franklin said. He spoke, Heimrich thought, as if for sometime he had been saying the same words over and over in his mind. "For no reason at all. Anything he wanted—" Franklin did not finish; he pressed the palm of his right hand against his forehead and moved it slowly up his forehead. The hand ground dirt into the skin. He was a handsome man—heavy and in his late forties, but still handsome. He wore stained walking shorts and a blue shirt; he had been kneeling in earth and his knees were grimed with it. "For no reason at all," he repeated, and stepped back so that they could enter the hall.

Martha Franklin lay on the floor, on her back, in blood. She had been a tall woman and looked older by some years than her husband. The dead face was bony—even in death, austere and dominating. Up to now, Heimrich thought, looking down at her, she probably had always got her way. She must, Heimrich found himself thinking, have died in furious surprise that she—*she*—could thus be flouted. She had been shot through the head, from close in. She had fallen with her head toward a marble fireplace.

"I was down in the garden," Franklin said, without being asked. "If only I had been here—" He shook his head, then looked hard at Heimrich. "How many more are you going to let him kill?"

"Him?" Heimrich said.

"This—maniac," Franklin said. "The one in the newspapers. On the radio. What's his name?"

"Beede?" Heimrich said. "Ronnie Beede."

"We'd have given him whatever he wanted," Franklin said. "Food, money—anything he wanted. To kill somebody for—for *nothing*." He looked down at the body of his wife, stunned, moving his head slowly from side to side.

There was no use staying in the hall where death was so visible. There was nothing immediately to be done there, and the others were on their way. Through the open door they could hear sirens, not far off. Gently, Heimrich guided the heavy man from the hall into a living room. "You were in the garden?" Heimrich said. "You didn't see anyone?"

"I heard somebody running," Franklin said. "And a shot. I didn't pay any attention to the shot. You hear them in the country, and it sounded a long way off. But then— somebody running off through the field. From the house." He stopped and stood shaking his head, as if in disbelief. "I was staking up the tomatoes," he said. He repeated it— "staking up the tomatoes"—as if this incongruity was monstrous.

"The garden," Heimrich said. "It's some distance from the house, I take it?"

"Over the hill," Franklin said. "Only place there's enough sun. If—if I'd only been here with her. I—" He shook his head quickly, this time as if to shake shadows out of his mind. "She was resting, probably," he went on. "Heard him break in—you saw the screen?"

"Yes," Heimrich said.

"Went to see what it was," Franklin said. "She would

have. She was like that. And he shot her. Just like that. For no reason at all. For no—"

"Now Mr. Franklin," Heimrich said. "The man you heard running. He ran past the garden?"

"Through the next field," Franklin said. "I was kneeling down among the vines. Had my back to the field. By the time I looked around he was gone. It was this man Beede, wasn't it?"

Heimrich said he supposed so. It had been done Ronnie Beede's way—wantonly, for no reason. "We're doing all—" he began, and stopped, because Arthur Franklin was swaying on his feet. Heimrich moved quickly and caught Franklin around the shoulders. For an instant the man was dead weight in his grasp. Heimrich helped him to a chair, lowered him into it, holding the heavy man's wrists as he let him down, being pulled forward by Franklin's weight. Heimrich's nostrils were pinched.

"All right," Franklin said, after a moment. "It's nothing. Dizzy. Too much sun, maybe. Too much—everything."

"Naturally," Heimrich soothed. He heard a car door slam outside, heard feet on the porch. And then brakes squealed, and another car door opened and closed. The others were showing up. "Just sit and rest a minute, Mr. Franklin," Heimrich said, and went back to the hall.

They were getting cameras out. That came first. "Beede?" Forniss said, and Heimrich said, "Looks like it, doesn't it, Charlie? Mrs. Franklin surprised him and he killed her. And ran. Down past Mr. Franklin's garden. I'll go and have a look."

He went along a path, in the shade first, over a rise and down again, and then into the sun—the full sun a garden needs. It was a fine neat garden. Some day, Heimrich thought, he would like to have a garden like it—with bush limas ripening in long rows and tomato vines tied carefully to stakes. To his right, as he faced the garden, there was a stone fence, and beyond it a field of tall grass and blueberry bushes.

Heimrich went into Mr. Franklin's vegetable garden and squatted among the tomatoes. Mr. Franklin kept the vines trained to three stems by pinching off unwanted shoots. The stubs of many such were on the ground, withering in the sun. Franklin had missed some and Heimrich snipped two or three between thumb and forefinger. He smelled his fingers, nodded, and walked back to the house. He went through the now crowded hall and into the living room. Franklin sat where Heimrich had left him.

Heimrich went up to the seated man, lifted Franklin's right hand, and looked at it, while Franklin stared at him, then began to pull his hand away. The hand was grimed. Heinrich bent down and smelled it.

"What the hell?" Franklin said, and his voice was no longer full—it was sharp alert.

"Now Mr. Franklin," Heimrich said. "You say you were working with the tomato plants?"

"I told you—" Franklin began, then stopped.

"Smell your hands yourself," Heimrich said. "Go on, Mr. Franklin."

But Franklin did not smell his hands. He began to stand up.

"No," Heimrich said, and Franklin sank back.

"Then," Heimrich said, "smell *my* fingers, Mr. Franklin," and held thumb and forefinger in front of Franklin's nose. "Very pungent odor tomato vines have, haven't they?" Heimrich said. "Quite unmistakable. When you handle them, the odor gets on your hands and stays. Until you wash the sap off, and then the water you wash in turns green. You know that, naturally. But—*it's not on your hands now, is it?* I noticed that when you were dizzy and I was helping you. No tomato smell. But—you hadn't washed your hands, had you? You dirtied them, yes—and your knees too—to show you'd just come from the garden. Took advantage of the fact there was a killer on the loose and—*why did you kill her, Mr. Franklin?* Merely because she was hard to live with? Or did she have the money?"

Franklin did not answer. But something happened to his eyes.

That sort of thing occurs now and then—a flaw in a lie is exposed and the lie falls, and the liar with it. Franklin had been careless, Heimrich pointed out to Sergeant Forniss somewhat later. If he had said he was in the garden hoeing beans he might easily have got away with it.

They trapped Ronnie Beede that evening. The trap was his mother's house and they let him walk into it. He was on his knees, with his face buried in his mother's lap, when they took him. He was shaking so hard that the frail woman shook with him.

Three Men in a Garden
by Lord Dunsany

When I feel like reading a detective story, as I suppose most of us often do, I usually read it in the ordinary way—in a book; but sometimes I get a taste for having the story raw—uncooked by any printer, as it were. Then I take a walk along a road that I know, which brings me past a garden in Surrey; and if I choose the right time of day, preferably on a summer's evening, I am likely to find an old detective of my acquaintance, working among his bean rows, of which he is very fond, or doing a little digging, or hacking away his weeds.

Then I have only to lean over his wooden paling a while, and, if he is not too busy, he will lean on his spade or on his hoe, and begin to talk reminiscently. If he just says, "Good evening," I will know by the nod of his head that he has too much work to do among his weeds, or with his digging, to spare much breath for more than politeness; and then, with a nod of my head, I go on my way. But if I find him among his bean rows, where the work seems lighter, and if it is a nice warm golden evening, he will be pretty sure to talk—and so I get my detective story raw. Very likely it will come out of years long past, so that it will be a tale that has long been forgotten, and so all the fresher to me.

One evening, leaning over his paling, I said after I had admired his beans, "What is the strangest case you ever investigated?"

"The strangest?" he said almost at once. "Well, the

157

strangest was when they found a body in a garden—in an Irish garden, it was—and it puzzled them a good deal over there. They asked if one of us would go over and lend a hand; and that was me. It was a lovely little garden in a suburb of Dublin, all full of crocuses, for it was spring, and they had found this body lying on the grass among the clumps of crocuses, shot through the heart."

Of course he began at the end, when he first saw the garden, and then told me bits of evidence by which he pieced it all together, and so got back to the beginning—which is not a very good way to tell a story. So I will tell it as it finally unfolded to me ...

Television was quite new at the time these things happened, and the TV company that was run by the man Straeger was a very little organization then—nothing like what it has grown to now; in fact, I think he was working then for motion pictures although his ambitions were toward TV.

One day Straeger went over to Ireland from the United States and his eyes were blazing with a new idea. He went to see a certain James Maloney, to whom he had some sort of letter of introduction. Straeger rang his bell, was asked in, and told Maloney about his new project— that Maloney should play in a film to be especially made for television. And Maloney said that he had never acted in his life.

"All the better," said Straeger. "You'll be absolutely fresh."

Apparently little details like whether a man could act or not didn't trouble this man Straeger. All he thought about was his wonderful new and original idea. There has been something like it since—a native being killed by a lion in East Africa, and a few other things, but it was absolutely new then.

"You needn't be able to act, my boy," he said to James Maloney. "It is only the wonderful thing you have to do, which has never been done on films before."

"And what's that?" said Maloney.

"Shoot a man," said Straeger.

"Nothing new in that," said Maloney. "I have seen it hundreds of times in films."

"Pooh," said Straeger. "You mean *pretending* to shoot a man—only a blank cartridge in the gun, no real bullet, and then somebody hitting the floor with a big hammer, and the man who was shot falling back onto a sofa. But my stunt is the real thing."

"You mean, shoot him dead?" said Maloney.

"Yes, dead," said Straeger.

"But I wouldn't like to do that to any man," said Maloney.

"Now, see here," said Straeger. "I've got all this worked out. He'll be a man that doesn't much matter in any way. And we'll compensate all concerned—his whole family. And we'll compensate them well, extremely well. Everything will be on us, so don't you worry about it."

"But that would be murder," said Maloney. "And I should be hanged."

"Now, don't go running away with fancy ideas," said Straeger. "We have everything worked out—every detail. To begin with, they don't hang in the country in whose territory it is going to be filmed."

"But I don't want to leave Ireland," said Maloney. "I've got a bit of farming to do here, and one thing and another . . ."

"Now don't you bother about one thing and another," said Straeger, "nor your farming either. Nobody is going to ask you to leave Ireland."

"But I thought you said—" began Maloney.

"And so I did," replied Straeger. "But have you ever heard of extraterritoriality and diplomatic immunity?"

"And what are they?" asked Maloney.

Well, that kind of thing was all new to Maloney, as they hadn't had legations in Ireland for very long then. Mr. Straeger explained it all and told Maloney that the film was to be shot only half a mile from where they were talking in Maloney's house. It was to be filmed in the gar-

den of the Eldoradoan legation. (I have found out that
there is no such country as Eldorado now, but he insisted
on calling it that all through his story.)

Well, Straeger was a smart businessman and he not
only explained extraterritoriality to Maloney, but got him
to understand it; and Straeger added that since there was
no extradition treaty between Eldorado and Ireland, the
moment Maloney stepped out of that garden he would be
free from any legal proceedings whatever—that is, so
long as he kept away from Eldorado.

I never heard why Straeger chose Maloney to act in a
film. Perhaps he may have been the only Irishman that
Straeger knew. But chiefly he was so excited over his
new idea of killing a man in cold blood, directly on film,
that he didn't bother much about whom he got to do it.
And when he had talked away the natural decent feelings
of Maloney, so that there was no longer too much resistance to his mad scheme, Straeger began to flutter the dollars before Maloney's eyes—not the actual dollars, but
easy talk about thousands and thousands of them; and so
he got Maloney.

On the appointed day the two of them went to this garden and met the man who was to be shot, a little man
named Hennessey whom they found waiting for them just
inside the garden, as Straeger had arranged. Straeger and
Maloney entered through a little gate in the side of the
garden and joined Hennessey, who looked like a man who
had been a bit too fond of his drinks for the last few
years; and of course he would have got all the drinks he
wanted from the film producer.

Straeger had explained to Maloney that Hennessey was
married and had two children, but when Maloney began
to protest, Straeger repeated, "Everything will be on us—
don't you worry about it." Maloney was naturally puzzled
at seeing Hennessey there, apparently waiting to be
shot—just as puzzled as he would have been to see a
sheep walking into a butcher's shop all by itself. But

Straeger took him aside and explained that Hennessey was a very simple fellow who thought it was all to be done with a blank cartridge; and his family knew nothing about it except that they were to be well paid. "And so they will be," added Straeger, "very well paid."

The house seemed all shut up—as a matter of fact, it was. There were just these three men in the garden, and nobody else about.

Well, to begin with, it wasn't really the garden of a legation at all—Eldorado's or any other country's. Straeger had just picked a garden whose owners he knew to be away, and Maloney had taken his word for it. Either Maloney must have been a bit of a fool, or Straeger must have been particularly sharp at salesmanship—or perhaps a bit of each.

Well, there they were, the three of them in a garden among the crocuses. And then Straeger set up his camera and pulled out his script and stood Maloney just where he wanted him, saying to him again, "The expenses are all on us." He was just handing him the revolver when Hennessey said suddenly, "No. I'll take that." And before Straeger realized what he was doing, he handed Hennessey the gun. And whether Hennessey was drunk or sober, his mind seemed suddenly illuminated by a clear view of the whole situation. Probably Straeger had let him have one drink too many—too many for Straeger, I mean; and it had revealed Straeger's little game in a flash.

And during that flash Hennessey was not the fool Straeger had calculated him to be. For without saying another word Hennessey shot Straeger dead. Then he and Maloney, having the same dominant interest, which was to leave the premises at once, got into Straeger's car, waiting outside, and drove off as fast as they could. So it was Straeger's body they found lying among the crocuses . . .

"Yes," said the old detective, "that was by far the strangest case I ever investigated. I never really did understand it."

The Ronnie
by K. D. Wentworth

Drawing in the rich, earthy, greenhouse smell, Sarah Hopsteader bent to examine the sleeping vegetable faces nestled among the glossy leaves. "Well," she said to the green-uniformed VegeTot nurseryman. "I'm sure that these Eleanor Roosevelts are quite sweet-natured, just as you say, but I was hoping for something a little more . . ." she hesitated as she caught George's scowl out of the corner of her eye ". . . a little more attractive."

The man nodded. "Perhaps you'd like to see one of our Elvises or James Deans, or . . ." He thought for a moment. "I think we still have a few nice Ronnies left in the back."

Summer sunlight gleamed down through the translucent overhead panels, turning the floating dust motes to airborne flecks of gold as she followed him down the narrow, leafy aisles. Behind her, even without looking, she could feel George spreading his disapproval over her birthday like a noxious fog.

"Listen . . ." George caught at her sleeve. "When Allison sent you that wad of cash for your birthday, she didn't mean you should just throw it away. If you're so hot for a pet, I'll buy you a goddamned goldfish."

Her mouth trembled as she smoothed a humidity-dampened strand of graying hair back into place, knowing from the experience of ten long years that it wasn't smart to go against her husband. Still, several of her friends had bought VegeTots in the last few years, and the little creatures always seemed so dear when she visited, scampering about the house on their stumpy legs, peering up at her with round green faces that always looked like someone famous, and—she sighed—when would she ever have so much money of her own again?

Kneeling down, the nurseryman pulled the dark-spotted foliage back to expose a small, leaf-shrouded form. "This is our Ronnie line, very popular with the politically minded."

Bending over, Sarah saw the dark green vegetable child stir as the muted light struck its closed eyelids, moving one tiny fist as if in protest. "It really does look like him, doesn't it?" She thought for a moment. "Does it—"

"Give speeches?" The nurseryman smiled. "No, I'm afraid that all resemblance to their famous namesakes is purely superficial. Still . . ." Releasing the leaves, he stood up. "They're affectionate and loyal, and almost no trouble at all." He punched a few numbers into the comlink on his wrist. "I'm afraid this lot is so ripe that they'll have to be composted in a few days if they don't sell."

"Composted?" Her lips pressed together, then she brushed the broad leaves aside again, studying the firm little face with its eyebrow ridges and precious dimples. Something about the cast of the eyes even reminded her a little of Myron, her long-dead first husband and Allison's father.

The small mouth opened in what could almost have been a yawn, revealing tiny green vegetable teeth, then closed again. Her heart gave a great leap, and she stood up and brushed the black soil off her jeans. "I'll take this one."

"An excellent choice." Handing her a soft green blanket, he produced a short, sharp knife and, with a single decisive motion, sliced through the thick stem growing from the little creature's head. "This is a very vigorous strain, bred out of our heartiest zucchini stock. It's sure to give you months of pleasure."

Sarah accepted the squirming bundle and held it still while he dabbed yellow dust on the dripping stump on the back of its head.

"You'll need to apply this compound every day until the stalk dries and drops off." Folding the blanket over the dark green body, he pressed a packet into her hand. "Just be sure that it gets at least two hours of real sunlight every day, not just indoor light, and has a shallow pan of water available all the time."

A great tenderness surged through her with the feel of the tiny body through the blanket, but when she looked up, George was scowling down at the small green face. Her arms tightened protectively. It's my money, she thought, then walked back to the front counter to give the clerk her birthday money, hoping that George wouldn't make her pay in a different way for defying him.

"Three hundred dollars!" George glared at the glossy-green Ronnie, playing amidst his blocks on the floor. "And I don't care if it does slightly resemble some half-wit, long-dead president, it can't even talk." He wedged his arms across his pudgy chest. "For three hundred, you could have bought one hell of a mynah bird."

Leaning back in her easy chair, Sarah let his voice run over her until it was like so much rain, all movement and no meaning. At her feet, the Ronnie fiddled with his plastic building blocks, erecting tower after tower that had no chance of standing because he stacked them so crookedly.

He was such a dear, she thought; unlike dogs and cats, he didn't even need to be housebroken and asked for nothing but a patch of sun and a bowl of water to soak his root-feet in each day. In the three months that he had been with her, he had already reached his guaranteed height of two feet with no sign of his growth slowing, obviously a superior VegeTot in every way. Sometimes she even pretended to herself that he was like the real Ronnie had been as a child, and even if it weren't true, she finally understood how lonely she had been before. The house would feel unbearably empty without him now.

"Clever Ronnie," she said as he balanced a large yellow block on top of a smaller red one. Turning his pupilless green eyes to her, the Ronnie reached out to pat her leg with curly, vinelike fingers.

Then George's voice broke back into her musings. "—smells."

"What?" Startled, she looked at his sour expression.

"I said that stupid plant is beginning to smell." He ran a hand back through his thinning gray hair, then took another long pull on the frost-beaded bottle of beer. "I think it's time you sent it back to be composted."

The plastic blocks clattered to the floor. Reaching down, she gathered the Ronnie's cool green body into her arms. "It's all right," she whispered, pressing her cheek against the soft vine tendrils that covered his little head. "Go outside and play in the yard for a while."

He clung to her wrist with persistent ropy fingers, surprising her with the strength of his grip, but when she urged him, he let go and wavered toward the terrace door, balancing precariously on his short stumpy legs. She waited until he had pushed through the little dog door, then turned to George, her face stiff. "You don't have to say such things in front of him."

"*Him?* Don't be ridiculous. That thing is nothing more than a glorified squash." He tipped his head back and blinked at the ceiling. "It probably understands a little body language, maybe the tone of your voice, nothing else."

In the silence between them, the television droned on and on, some bit of nonsense about singing toilet bowls. She took a deep breath, feeling from the heat of her cheeks how flushed her face must be. "He understands every word. You have only to look at his poor little face to see that." Her hands clenched together in her lap. "Besides, he can't be rotting. He's guaranteed for a whole year."

"Well, I don't care." George turned back to the screen. "Just keep the stinking thing away from me."

"But you said that you would take care of him when Allison has the baby." She bit her lip, trying not to think of leaving her Ronnie alone with him. "You promised."

"Well, if I promised, then I guess I'll do it, won't I?" Draining the bottle of beer, he slammed it down so hard that she jumped and bit her lip. "I want another brew."

The autumn made dull, warped mirrors of the street as the taxi brought Sarah back through town from the airport. Her trip to Allison's had been wonderful, of course, and the baby, little Colleen, had been so dear that it had been difficult for her to leave, but Ronnie had been on her mind the whole time.

When the taxi pulled up in front of her house, she stared out at the white-painted brick for a moment. Had she really been gone only a week? The house that she had shared with George Hopsteader for ten long years looked almost unfamiliar. Then she nodded to the cab driver and got out to dash through the chill, pelting rain to the covered front porch. She should have brought an umbrella, of course, but as George was so fond of pointing out, she never remembered things like that. Shivering, she unlocked the door and stepped aside so that the cab driver could deposit her single suitcase inside the threshold. "Thank you," she said, then handed him a handful of bills and waved the change away, knowing that George would be furious if he saw her tip like that.

Leaving the heavy suitcase in the hall, she looked around as she pulled off her dripping coat. "Ronnie?" It would have been best to take him with her, but Allison and her husband lived in a highrise apartment building where he wouldn't have been able to get the sunlight that he needed. Actually, she'd come home from the airport by herself just so that she could have some time alone with him. "Ronnie, where are you?" she called again, but there was no answering whisper of little root-feet hurrying to meet her. Well, maybe he was out on the terrace, she told herself, although he usually didn't stay outside much when it was raining.

Draping her coat over a kitchen chair, she peeked out through the sliding terrace doors into the small yard where the Ronnie loved to play when it was sunny, but there was no sign of him among the potted crape myrtles and azalea bushes. Strange . . . She walked back into the master bedroom and looked in the corner where his little wicker basket stood, so close to her side of the bed that she could dangle her hand down and stroke his head in the night. No Ronnie.

He heart beat faster as she checked her sewing room, the den, the guest bedrooms, but there was no sign of Ronnie's glossy dark green body anywhere. Where could he be?

Coming back into the kitchen, she saw the puddle that her coat had dropped on the floor, so she took it outside for a quick shake, then went to hang it in the hall closet. When she opened the door, something stirred faintly in the far corner. Frightened, she dropped the coat and stumbled back, but then she heard it again, a weak scrabbly sound—and thought that she recognized it.

Falling to her knees, she reached back behind the snow boots, feeling more than seeing, touched something dry and scratchy, and pulled Ronnie's limp, wasted body into the light. His vine-hair was dried and frazzled, his eyes closed, his skin a sallow, faded yellow-green. "Ronnie?" she whispered.

The vine-like fingers moved against hers slightly, then one of them cracked and fell to the floor.

Tears welled up in her eyes. How could this have happened? How long had the poor thing been shut up without sun and water? This was all her fault; she should never have left him.

A warm tear fell on Ronnie's emaciated body and his eyes opened slightly. Water, she told herself, first he must have some water, then she would call the nursery and see what else could be done. Handling the husk-light little yellow-green body carefully, she carried him into the kitchen in the crook of her arm. Filling the sink with cool water, she immersed him up to his chin.

Her fingers shook as she punched the number for VegeTots, Unlimited, and her voice broke as she told the secretary what she needed. After a moment, the green uniformed consultant came on screen, looking doubtful as she haltingly told him the story.

"I don't know, Mrs. Hopsteader." He shook his head. "When they're that far gone, it's usually kinder to bring them in for composting and just start over. Once those interior veins start cracking from lack of moisture, there's not really much that can be done."

Her fingers tightened on the kitchen counter as she stared back at his sympathetic young face. "Composting?" Horror rose up in her throat like a river in dark angry flood. "My Ronnie? You can't be serious. He's only four months old."

"They only last a full year if you take proper care of them." He looked grim. "And being without sun for that long, it could have permanent neural damage. You don't want it to suffer, do you?"

"N—" The answer stuck somewhere in her chest, fighting to remain unsaid.

"Well, let us know if we can be of any assistance."

She only nodded, afraid she would cry if she tried to say more, then punched the connection off. The Ronnie stirred in the sink, making tiny splashes with one of his little arms. Dabbing fiercely at the hot, ready tears that threatened to overwhelm her, she nodded down at his yellow-green face. "Don't worry," she whispered, "it's going to be all right."

As she stroked his poor withered vine-hair, her mind raced ahead, trying to think of what she would say to George when he came home. How could he believe that he could explain this?

Three hours later, she still didn't know what to say to him as she watched Ronnie through the plate glass window, propped up against a crape myrtle out on the rain-drenched terrace, soaking up what little light penetrated through the dull clouds.

She heard the front door open, then close, but she didn't move, indeed felt that she couldn't move if her life depended upon it.

"I thought you were going to call me when you got in." George's voice rumbled through the house like sullen thunder. "So, how are Allison and the brat anyway?"

She opened her mouth to answer, but the stupid, useless tears started as they always did at times like this when she wanted so desperately to be calm and reasonable, adult and secure. She took in a great wrenching breath. "The baby is fine, but . . ." She broke off then, her voice wavering, asked, "Why?"

"Why what?"

She heard the thump of his coat thrown over the counter, then the whish of the refrigerator door opening as he rummaged for the first of his daily six-pack, and finally the tortured creak of the easy chair as he plopped into it. She made herself turn around. "Why—Ronnie?"

"You mean that damn plant?" Twisting the cap off the bottle of beer, he shook the paper open and settled back to read it, one arm tucked behind his head and his black sock feet pointing toward the ceiling. "Haven't seen it for days."

"You said that you'd take care of him." The words almost choked her. "You promised."

"Can't very well water the little bastard if I can't find it." He turned the page.

"You locked him in the closet." Her throat closed up hard and tight. "You left him there for days without water or sun."

He met her eyes briefly over the top of the paper. "So that's where it got to." The paper came up again with a rustle. "I wondered."

"You did it on purpose!"

Then he was up out of the depths of the easy chair faster than any man as soft and lethargic as George Hopsteader had a right to be, his forearm catching her hard across the throat, crushing her back against the cold, smooth glass. "This is *my* house," he said into her face, his breath heavy with beer. "My house that *I* have gone out and worked like a slave for. The minute I'm ready to get rid of that damn squash, I'll put it down the garbage disposal one inch at a time."

He leaned harder against her windpipe until she could think of nothing but the brittleness of the rain-spattered glass beneath her, which could give way any second under their combined weights and send her flying out onto the terrace in a pile of gleaming shards, any of which could slice her throat almost as an afterthought. "George—please," she wheezed as her vision fuzzed and his voice faded to a distant roaring in her ears. "Let me— please—"

Abruptly, he released her, returning to his seat as though nothing had ever happened. "I'm hungry." His voice was gruff. "When's dinner?"

She caught herself against the window, trying to blink the grayness away, fighting to keep from falling to her knees. Outside, the chill autumn rain drummed against the window, streaming down it in rivulets, cascading over the Ronnie's head and outstretched arms as he pressed up against the glass, watching her with staring yellow-green eyes.

* * *

After she got her nerves under control, she slipped out the front door and quietly brought Ronnie in from the rain, sneaking him into the guest bathroom where she stood him in the tub and dried him off with a soft thick towel. Her hands trembled as she heard George clatter through the refrigerator after yet another beer.

How had it come to this, she wondered, lifting Ronnie out and setting him on the tiled floor. Little by little, she had gotten so used to George's casual cruelties and drinking that she sometimes forgot she'd once had another, more civilized life—before her soft-spoken first husband had died.

Taking Ronnie's withered little arm, she peered into the shadow-filled hall, but there was no sign of George. Picking up the Ronnie, she pressed his wasted body to her as she hurried into the master bedroom, treading as quietly as she could.

As soon as they entered the familiar room, the VegeTot wriggled out of her grasp and wobbled over to his basket, still unsteady from dehydration and lack of sunlight. "Oh, Ronnie." She sighed, then tucked him into the soft green blanket in which she'd first brought him home. His unblinking eyes followed her every move, speaking his misery as clearly as if he could talk. Tenderly, she touched the few remaining broken bits of vine-hair that still clung stubbornly to his head.

"When the hell are we gonna get some dinner around here?" George bellowed suddenly from the den.

Her stomach gave a sickening wrench. Dinner . . . dear God, she hadn't given it a thought since that heart-stopping moment when she'd found Ronnie shut up in the closet. "In—in a minute." Gathering the wicker basket into her arms, she hurried toward the door, intending to hide Ronnie in her sewing room until tomorrow.

Suddenly the doorway filled with George's bulk.

"Here." He thrust something large and metallic at her. "I got tired of waiting, so I started dinner for you."

Numbly, she stared at the huge panful of steaming water dangling from his hand, sloshing over at the edges to soak into the rug into dark splotches at her feet. "I—don't understand."

"Well . . ." He leered crookedly at her, his face garish in the half-light from the hall. "We are having *squash* for dinner, aren't we?" Then a belly laugh rolled out of him, filling the room until she thought she would scream.

She tried to avoid his eyes. "Please, George, if you'll just let me by, I'll get busy on dinner."

" 'Please, George,' " he mimicked her in a high falsetto. " 'Please, George!' " He lurched toward her and splashed her shoe with scalding water.

She bit her tongue to keep from crying out as the pain ate through her foot. *If he spilled that on Ronnie . . .* "George," she said, fighting to control her voice, "I'm sorry about dinner. Let me by."

"Hurry up, I'm hungry." Laughing again, he swung the pan toward her, slopping more boiling hot water over her legs. "Or would you rather fry the little bastard?"

How many times had the two of them done this? Light-headed from the pain, she stared at his smirk; they had played this scene a thousand times in a thousand different ways, her pleading while he laughed in her face, hurting her in any way that amused him, then pretending the next day that none of it mattered.

"Stop it!" Her heart thumping so hard that she thought it would escape her chest, she put Ronnie's basket on the floor and hastily shoved it out of sight underneath the bed. "I'm not going to live like this any more."

"Is that so?" He wiped one handback across his face, then set the kettle on the floor and blinked unsteadily at her. "What are you going to do, move?" For some reason, the notion struck him as funny, and he began to snicker again.

She heard a rustling behind her as something husk-light moved. Her heart lurched. "Ronnie, no!"

"I keep telling you that the stupid thing doesn't understand a word you say." George shoved her out of the way and made a grab as the little green face peered out from under the bed.

Her face went ice cold. "Don't touch him!"

George paused, his face hidden in shadows. "Don't worry, darling, you're next." He giggled. "Here, Ronnie, here, you little bastard." He staggered forward, groping under the bed.

"No." She seized his arm. "Go sleep it off."

With an almost casual flick of his wrist, he threw her back against the heavy wooden dresser, cracking her head so hard that the room flickered around her—black—white—black—like a photographic negative. She tried to crawl after him, but her arms and legs seemed to be somewhere else, and it was all she could do to hold onto consciousness.

There was a sudden flurry over by the bed; then she heard George exclaim, "Gotcha!"

Blinking hard, Sarah thought she saw him raise something up in the air with one hand.

"Here's hoping that you make a better dinner than you did a president." He turned around on his knees, reaching for the pan of boiling water.

No, she tried to whisper, but her mouth was a million miles away and none of this could possibly be real.

George laughed again, then stopped abruptly. Hazily, she saw him stagger upright, then tear at his face, which seemed suddenly bulky.

Ronnie! She realized that her lips had moved, but had produced no sound. Why was it that George couldn't bear someone else to love her, even if it was only a poor VegeTot?

George collapsed to his knees, croaking while his hands clawed and beat at something that had fastened it-

self over his mouth and nose. Her vision kept losing focus
as she summoned every remaining bit of strength to reach
out a trembling hand and brush the stubble of Ronnie's
broken vine-hair. Then the room and Ronnie and George
all faded away into a soundless blackness.

"I don't think you should go back to that place."
Allison's face was porcelain-pale as she folded the last
nightgown and packed it into Sarah's suitcase. "I want
you to move to Topeka and watch your new granddaughter grow up. There's some beautiful retirement condos
only a few miles from our complex. You'd like that,
wouldn't you?"

Opening the blind, Sarah looked down at the little park
across the street from the hospital. Bright light still hurt
her eyes, but it soothed her to watch the tiny figures of
children at play, so happy and carefree ... almost like
Ronnie.

"I ... really don't ..." each word came slowly, as
though imported from some faraway country "... don't
know what I want." Her fingers sought the tender back of
her head where the doctors had taken twenty stitches. "I
still have trouble remembering what happened."

"And you ought to leave it that way." Taking her arm,
Allison guided her back to the hospital bed.

Feeling a little dizzy, she lay back against the crisp
white pillow. "You're sure ..." she mumbled. "You're
sure that he's ... gone?"

"The funeral was two days ago." Strain lines reap-
peared around her daughter's eyes. "You remember that,
don't you?"

"No, not ... him." She turned her cheek to the freshly-
laundered pillowcase and closed her eyes, trying hard to
compose her thoughts. "No, I meant, you're sure that—
Ronnie—*Ronnie* is really gone?"

Silence filtered through the room for a long moment.
"Well, it was pretty broken up. The police took what was

left away with the—body, but . . ." She hesitated. "When I went back to pack your clothes, I did find something."

Opening her eyes, Sarah watched her daughter put one hand in her pocket and then draw it out again. In the middle of her outstretched hand lay two slim golden ovoids. She blinked hard to make sure that her shaky vision wasn't betraying her again. No . . . she reached out and took them from the palm of Allison's hand, feeling the smoothness of . . . seeds . . . *squash* seeds.

Watching her closely, Allison sat down beside her and touched her face. "Mom, are you all right?"

Closing her fingers around the firm cool shapes, Sarah met her daughter's eyes. "Do you suppose that those condos have—gardens?"

The Ghost in the Garden
by Dan Crawford

The little village of Merodale sat high in the mountains. It was cool there, and dry, but the ground was so thin, over the rocks of the mountain, that not much food could be grown. The people of Merodale could grow only just barely enough for themselves.

Between Merodale and the three largest mountains that cast their shadows over the village, however, there was a garden. Once, long ago, everyone in Merodale knew, there had been a mighty palace there. The great person who had lived in the palace had had dirt and plants and gardeners brought in to make a beautiful place for his family. There were fruit trees and nut trees and berry bushes and little streams and ponds with fish in them.

The palace had fallen down years ago. No one in Merodale could remember ever seeing it when it wasn't just a pile of stones. But the garden was still there, full of weeds now, and foxes. Every autumn, when the people of Merodale looked over their own tiny plants and trees, they would think about the garden, and how big it was, and how much food they could grow there.

"I wish we could go up to the garden," they'd say. "It would be enough if we could just pick a few apples, or catch a fish in the pond."

Some people did go up to the garden now and then. And they did get apples. They'd hear a rustle in the leaves, and *bang!* an apple would hit them in the forehead, or on the arm. And something nobody could see would go running off through the trees.

Or sometimes a woman would go to the pond to try to catch one of the fish. And a hand would grab hold in her hair and push her head under the water until she nearly drowned. Something she couldn't see would laugh, and splash through the pond as she gasped for breath.

So no one went up to the garden unless they were truly hungry. "There's something in there," they said. "A spirit from the forest, or a demon from the mountains; don't go in."

It had been that way for years and years. Now and then some brave villager would sneak into the garden just to see if the spirit was still there, only to be pushed into the pond or knocked down by apples. So the people of Merodale grew what food they could on the little thin land that they had.

One day a wandering magician chanced to come upon Merodale. The people of Merodale had heard of such men but had never seen one, for few came so far north. For his own part, the magician was glad to see Merodale, for cities and even villages were rare and set far apart, so close to the mountains.

He rested in Merodale for several days, helping the people with such magic as he knew, curing a few sick pigs, bandaging broken arms, and telling them what the weather was going to do. The people gave him a share of their food for this. If he noticed that there wasn't much food, and that it wasn't very good, he never complained.

But he did ask, one afternoon, "Why does no one farm the land over by the trees up there? You might find it good land for growing."

"We can't go up there," whispered Young Josh, the potato farmer. "There's a ghost."

The magician sat up and stared at the trees. "A ghost, is it?" he asked. "What sort of ghost?"

"Are there sorts of ghosts, then?" said Old Linda, the baker. "This is the only ghost we've ever seen."

"I suppose he's seen plenty of ghosts, to know what sorts they are," laughed Vivon, the pigherd. "Aye, and gone to have dinner with them."

The magician stood up. "I've talked with ghosts," he said. "It may be I shall talk with this one."

"Maybe," said Vivon. "Maybe not."

Medina, the mayor, stood up to walk over to the magician's side. "Stranger," she said, "if you could tell the ghost we need to use the garden, you would have our thanks forever."

"I will not live forever," said the magician. "But you may thank me if I come back." He picked up his walking stick and started for the tall trees. The people followed him to the edge of town and then stood to watch until he had disappeared into the shadows.

It wasn't an easy walk. Where there used to be paths, weeds were grown up and tangled. The magician pushed some aside with his walking stick. He came to the heaps of stones that had been a palace once and looked around. There was nothing to see but stones.

He passed under a stone arch and stood in the garden. He could see where the garden paths used to be, but they were dusty with crumbled leaves from years of autumn. Stooping under a vine, he marched toward the pond, scaring a rabbit that had been hiding under a broken bench.

"Are you all that lives here, Bunny?" asked the magician.

Something whistled, and he turned around. His stick was in his hand, and when he saw the apple coming at him, he swung at it and knocked it away.

"Ha!" said someone or something. "Ha ha! Ha ha ha!"

The apple was a hard one and flew across the garden. As the magician watched, it stopped and hung just a few feet from the ground.

"Hee hee!" squealed a voice from over by the apple.

The apple bounced in the air and then came flying back at the magician.

He waited for it, brought his stick around, and knocked it away again.

It sailed over to the pond and landed with a splash. "Oh ho ho!" said the voice. Eight little splashes rippled the pond, going out toward the apple. There was a moment of silence, and then, with another splash, the dripping apple rose into the air again.

"I'm glad you came!" said a voice in the pond. The apple flew up in the air and dropped for whatever it was to catch it. "You're the only person who ever stayed to play!"

"Ah," said the magician. He sat down on the edge of the broken bench. "And who are you?"

The apple came toward the edge of the pool with little splashes moving along underneath it. "Oh, I'm Than," said the voice.

The magician nodded. "Are you a ghost?"

"Of course not!" said the voice. "I'm a boy!" The apple floated over dry land. Beneath it now was a double line of little footprints.

The magician nodded again. "You have been here many years."

"I have not!" said Than. "I will be only six on my next birthday."

"When is that?" said the magician.

"I don't remember," said Than.

The magician crossed his legs. A big wet splotch appeared on the ground before him, as though someone wet had sat down. "Where's your father?" the magician asked.

"My father was a soldier," said Than. "He died in the wars." The apple came to rest in a little pile of leaves.

"How old was he?" asked the magician.

"Oh, he was really old," Than said. The apple rolled

down the pile of leaves and then back up. "Almost thirty, I think."

"Who was your mother?" the magician asked.

The apple bounced up into the air, where Than caught it with invisible hands. "My mother was the daughter of the king. She died when the soldiers came through the palace."

"How old was she?" asked the magician.

"She was very pretty," said Than.

The magician nodded. "But how old was she?"

"I don't know," said Than.

"Was she thirty, too?"

The apple bounced into the air and was caught higher, as though Than was standing up again. "Maybe," said Than. "Let's play."

"In a minute," said the magician. "Do you remember the king's name?"

"Our king?" said Than. "Of course I remember. Our king was Simon of the Mighty Heart."

"Simon of the Mighty Heart?" said the magician. "King Simon died three hundred years ago."

"I knew that he died," said Than.

The magician leaned forward and pointed his stick at the apple. "If Simon was your king, then you are not five years old," he said. "You are three hundred and five."

"I'm not," Than told the magician. "I am five. You want to come see the fish?"

"You died three hundred years ago when the soldiers came through the palace," said the magician.

Than threw the apple at him, but missed. "I did not! I'm not dead!"

The magician stood up and said, "You are older now than your parents ever were. You are dead and you must go to heaven."

"I am not!" said Than, running back toward the pond. "I'm five! And I wouldn't know the way to heaven!"

"You are three hundred and five," said the magician,

"and you have been dead for three hundred years. Go! Heaven lies above the mountains."

"I don't know the way," said Than. His footprints stopped at the very edge of the pond. "I shall get lost. They never let me go into the mountains. They said I could when I was older, and I'm not older. I'm five!"

"You are three hundred and five and you must go," said the magician. He pointed his walking stick at the high peaks of the mountains. "Now go! I order you to go!"

There was a whistle and a wail as something stirred the dust and leaves by Than's footprints. The magician put his hands over his head and closed his eyes. Sticks and dirt flew past his head, and a cold wind screamed.

Then the garden was quiet. The magician opened his eyes. "Than?" he called. "Are you there?"

Nobody laughed or threw an apple. The magician picked up his stick and walked down to Merodale.

"You may go up to the garden," he told the people. "No one will bother you."

And they did. They took away the old stones of the palace and built new paths with them. They tore out all the weeds and brambles and raked up the dead leaves. The fruit trees were given good care so that instead of small, hard apples, they had big ripe ones. The people of Merodale had enough food at last.

And they were never again troubled by the ghost. Except, now and then, when the wind blows cold off the mountains, some people say they hear a tiny, lonely voice calling, "I'm five! I am five!"

Rappaccini's Daughter
by *Nathaniel Hawthorne*

From the Writings of Aubépine

A young man, named Giovanni Guasconti, came, very
long ago, from the more southern region of Italy, to pur-
sue his studies at the University of Padua. Giovanni, who
had but a scanty supply of gold ducats in his pocket, took
lodgings in a high and gloomy chamber of an old edifice,
which looked not unworthy to have been the palace of a
Paduan noble, and which, in fact, exhibited over its entrance the armorial bearings of a family long since ex-
tinct. The young stranger, who was not unstudied in the
great poem of his country, recollected that one of the an-
cestors of this family, and perhaps an occupant of this
very mansion, had been pictured by Dante as a partaker
of the immortal agonies of his Inferno. These reminis-
cences and associations, together with the tendency to
heart-break natural to a young man for the first time out
of his native sphere, caused Giovanni to sigh heavily, as
he looked around the desolate and ill-furnished apartment.

"Holy Virgin, Signor," cried old dame Lisabetta, who,
won by the youth's remarkable beauty of person, was
kindly endeavoring to give the chamber a habitable air,
"what a sigh was that to come out of a young man's
heart! Do you find this old mansion gloomy? For the love
of heaven, then, put your head out of the window, and
you will see as bright sunshine as you have left in Naples."

Guasconti mechanically did as the old woman advised,

but could not quite agree with her that the Paduan sunshine was as cheerful as that of southern Italy. Such as it was, however, it fell upon a garden beneath the window, and expended its fostering influences on a variety of plants, which seemed to have been cultivated with exceeding care.

"Does this garden belong to the house?" asked Giovanni.

"Heaven forbid, Signor!—unless it were fruitful of better pot-herbs than any that grow there now," answered old Lisabetta. "No; that garden is cultivated by the own hands of Signor Giacomo Rappaccini, the famous Doctor, who, I warrant him, has been heard of as far as Naples. It is said that he distils these plants into medicines that are as potent as a charm. Oftentimes you may see the Signor Doctor at work, and perchance the Signora his daughter, too, gathering the strange flowers that grow in the garden."

The old woman had now done what she could for the aspect of the chamber, and, commending the young man to the protection of the saints, took her departure.

Giovanni still found no better occupation than to look down into the garden beneath his window. From its appearance, he judged it to be one of those botanic gardens, which were of earlier date in Padua than elsewhere in Italy, or in the world. Or, not improbably, it might once have been the pleasure-place of an opulent family; for there was the ruin of a marble fountain in the centre, sculptured with rare art, but so wofully shattered that it was impossible to trace the original design from the chaos of remaining fragments. The water, however, continued to gush and sparkle into the sunbeams as cheerfully as ever. A little gurgling sound ascended to the young man's window, and made him feel as if the fountain were an immortal spirit, that sung its song unceasingly, and without heeding the vicissitudes around it; while one century embodied it in marble, and another scattered the perishable garniture on the soil. All about the pool into which the water subsided, grew various plants, that seemed to require a plentiful supply of moisture for the nourishment of gigantic leaves, and, in some instances, flowers gorgeously magnificent. There was one shrub in particular, set in a marble vase in the midst of the pool, that bore a profusion of purple blossoms, each of which had the lustre and richness of a gem; and the whole together made a show so resplendent that it seemed enough to illuminate the garden, even had there been no sunshine. Every portion of the soil was peopled with plants and herbs, which, if less beautiful, still bore tokens of assiduous care; as if all had their individual virtues, known to the scientific mind that fostered them. Some were placed in urns, rich with old carving, and others in common garden-pots; some crept serpent-like along the ground, or climbed on high, using whatever means of ascent was offered them. One plant had wreathed itself round a statue of Vertumnus, which was thus quite veiled and shrouded in a drapery of hanging foliage, so happily arranged that it might have served a sculptor for a study.

While Giovanni stood at the window, he heard a rustling behind a screen of leaves, and became aware that a person was at work in the garden. His figure soon emerged into view, and showed itself to be that of no common laborer, but a tall, emaciated, sallow, and sickly-looking man, dressed in a scholar's garb of black. He was beyond the middle term of life, with grey hair, a thin grey beard, and a face singularly marked with intellect and cultivation, but which could never, even in his more youthful days, have expressed much warmth of heart.

Nothing could exceed the intentness with which this scientific gardener examined every shrub which grew in his path; it seemed as if he was looking into their inmost nature, making observations in regard to their creative essence, and discovering why one leaf grew in this shape, and another in that, and wherefore such and such flowers

differed among themselves in hue and perfume. Nevertheless, in spite of this deep intelligence on his part, there
was no approach to intimacy between himself and these
vegetable existences. On the contrary, he avoided their
actual touch, or the direct inhaling of their odors, with a
caution that impressed Giovanni most disagreeably; for
the man's demeanor was that of one walking among ma-
lignant influences, such as savage beasts, or deadly
snakes, or evil spirits, which, should he allow them one
moment of license, would wreak upon him some terrible
fatality. It was strangely frightful to the young man's
imagination, to see this air of insecurity in a person cul-
tivating a garden, that most simple and innocent of human
toils, and which had been alike the joy and labor of the
unfallen parents of the race. Was this garden, then, the
Eden of the present world?—and this man, with such a
perception of harm in what his own hands caused to
grow, was he the Adam?

The distrustful gardener, while plucking away the dead
leaves or pruning the too luxuriant growth of the shrubs,
defended his hands with a pair of thick gloves. Nor were
these his only armor. When, in his walk through the garden, he came to the magnificent plant that hung its purple
gems beside the marble fountain, he placed a kind of
mask over his mouth and nostrils, as if all this beauty did
but conceal a deadlier malice. But finding his task still
too dangerous, he drew back, removed the mask, and
called loudly, but in the infirm voice of a person affected
with inward disease:

"Beatrice!—Beatrice!"

"Here am I, my father! What would you?" cried a rich
and youthful voice from the window of the opposite
house; a voice as rich as a tropical sunset, and which
made Giovanni, though he knew not why, think of deep
hues of purple or crimson, and of perfumes heavily
delectable.—"Are you in the garden?"

"Yes, Beatrice," answered the gardener, "and I need your help."

Soon there emerged from under a sculptured portal the figure of a young girl, arrayed with as much richness of taste as the most splendid of the flowers, beautiful as the day, and with a bloom so deep and vivid that one shade more would have been too much. She looked redundant with life, health, and energy; all of which attributes were bound down and compressed, as it were, and girdled tensely, in their luxuriance, by her virgin zone. Yet Giovanni's fancy must have grown morbid, while he looked down into the garden; for the impression which the fair stranger made upon him was as if here were another flower, the human sister of those vegetable ones, as beautiful as they—more beautiful than the richest of them—but still to be touched only with a glove, nor to be approached without a mask. As Beatrice came down the garden path, it was observable that she handled and inhaled the odor of several of the plants, which her father had most sedulously avoided.

"Here, Beatrice," said the latter,—"see how many needful offices require to be done to our chief treasure. Yet, shattered as I am, my life might pay the penalty of approaching it so closely as circumstances demand. Henceforth, I fear, this plant must be consigned to your sole charge."

"And gladly will I undertake it," cried again the rich tones of the young lady, as she bent towards the magnificent plant, and opened her arms as if to embrace it. "Yes, my sister, my splendor, it shall be Beatrice's task to nurse and serve thee; and thou shalt reward her with thy kisses and perfumed breath, which to her is as the breath of life!"

Then, with all the tenderness in her manner that was so strikingly expressed in her words, she busied herself with such attentions as the plant seemed to require; and Giovanni, at his lofty window, rubbed his eyes, and almost doubted whether it were a girl tending her favorite flower, or one sister performing the duties of affection to another. The scene soon terminated. Whether Doctor Rappaccini had finished his labors in the garden, or that his watchful eye had caught the stranger's face, he now took his daughter's arm and retired. Night was already closing in; oppressive exhalations seemed to proceed from the plants, and steal upward past the open window; and Giovanni, closing the lattice, went to his couch, and dreamed of a rich flower and beautiful girl. Flower and maiden were different and yet the same, and fraught with some strange peril in either shape.

But there is an influence in the light of morning that tends to rectify whatever errors of fancy, or even of judgment, we may have incurred during the sun's decline, or among the shadows of the night, or in the less wholesome glow of moonshine. Giovanni's first movement on starting from sleep, was to throw open the window, and gaze down into the garden which his dreams had made so fertile of mysteries. He was surprised, and a little ashamed, to find how real and matter-of-fact an affair it proved to be, in the first rays of the sun, which gilded the dewdrops that hung upon leaf and blossom, and, while giving a brighter beauty to each rare flower, brought everything within the limits of ordinary experience. The young man rejoiced, that, in the heart of the barren city, he had the privilege of overlooking this spot of lovely and luxuriant vegetation. It would serve, he said to himself, as a symbolic language, to keep him in communion with Nature. Neither the sickly and thought-worn Doctor Giacomo Rappaccini, it is true, nor his brilliant daughter, were now visible; so that Giovanni could not determine how much of the singularity which he attributed to both, was due to their own qualities, and how much to his wonder-working fancy. But he was inclined to take a most rational view of the whole matter.

In the course of the day, he paid his respects to Signor

Pietro Baglioni, professor of medicine in the University, a physician of eminent repute, to whom Giovanni had brought a letter of introduction. The Professor was an elderly personage, apparently of genial nature, and habits that might almost be called jovial; he kept the young man to dinner, and made himself very agreeable by the freedom and liveliness of his conversation, especially when warmed by a flask or two of Tuscan wine. Giovanni, conceiving that men of science, inhabitants of the same city, must needs be on familiar terms with one another, took an opportunity to mention the name of Doctor Rappaccini. But the Professor did not respond with so much cordiality as he had anticipated.

"Ill would it become a teacher of the divine art of medicine," said Professor Pietro Baglioni, in answer to a question of Giovanni, "to withhold due and well-considered praise of a physician so eminently skilled as Rappaccini. But, on the other hand, I should answer it but scantily to my conscience, were I to permit a worthy youth like yourself, Signor Giovanni, the son of an ancient friend, to imbibe erroneous ideas respecting a man who might hereafter chance to hold your life and death in his hands. The truth is, our worshipful Doctor Rappaccini has as much science as any member of the faculty—with perhaps one single exception—in Padua, or all Italy. But there are certain grave objections to his professional character."

"And what are they?" asked the young man.

"Has my friend Giovanni any disease of body or heart, that he is so inquisitive about physicians?" said the Professor, with a smile. "But as for Rappaccini, it is said of him—and I, who know the man well, can answer for its truth—that he cares infinitely more for science than for mankind. His patients are interesting to him only as subjects for some new experiment. He would sacrifice human life, his own among the rest, or whatever else was dearest to him, for the sake of adding so much as a grain of mustard-seed to the great heap of his accumulated knowledge."

"Methinks he is an awful man, indeed," remarked Guasconti, mentally recalling the cold and purely intellectual aspect of Rappaccini. "And yet, worshipful Professor, is it not a noble spirit? Are there many men capable of so spiritual a love of science?"

"God forbid," answered the Professor, somewhat testily—"at least, unless they take sounder views of the healing art than those adopted by Rappaccini. It is his theory, that all medicinal virtues are comprised within those substances which we term vegetable poisons. These he cultivates with his own hands, and is said even to have produced new varieties of poison, more horribly deleterious than Nature, without the assistance of this learned person, would ever have plagued the world withal. That the Signor Doctor does less mischief than might be expected, with such dangerous substances, is undeniable. Now and then, it must be owned, he has effected—or seemed to effect—a marvellous cure. But, to tell you my private mind, Signor Giovanni, he should receive little credit for such instances of success—they being probably the work of chance—but should be held strictly accountable for his failures, which may justly be considered his own work."

The youth might have taken Baglioni's opinions with many grains of allowance, had he known that there was a professional warfare of long continuance between him and Doctor Rappaccini, in which the latter was generally thought to have gained the advantage. If the reader be inclined to judge for himself, we refer him to certain black-letter tracts on both sides, preserved in the medical department of the University of Padua.

"I know not, most learned Professor," returned Giovanni, after musing on what had been said of Rappaccini's exclusive zeal for science—"I know not how dearly this physician may love his art; but surely there is one object more dear to him. He has a daughter."

"Aha!" cried the Professor with a laugh. "So now our friend Giovanni's secret is out. You have heard of this daughter, whom all the young men in Padua are wild about, though not half a dozen have ever had the good hap to see her face. I know little of the Signora Beatrice, save that Rappaccini is said to have instructed her deeply in his science, and that, young and beautiful as fame reports her, she is already qualified to fill a professor's chair. Perchance her father destines her for mine! Other absurd rumors there be, not worth talking about, or listening to. So now, Signor Giovanni, drink off your glass of Lacryma."

Guasconti returned to his lodgings somewhat heated with the wine he had quaffed, and which caused his brain to swim with strange fantasies in reference to Doctor Rappaccini and the beautiful Beatrice. On his way, happening to pass by a florist's, he bought a fresh bouquet of flowers.

Ascending to his chamber, he seated himself near the window, but within the shadow thrown by the depth of the wall, so that he could look down into the garden with little risk of being discovered. All beneath his eye was a solitude. The strange plants were basking in the sunshine, and now and then nodding gently to one another, as if in acknowledgment of sympathy and kindred. In the midst, by the shattered fountain, grew the magnificent shrub, with its purple gems clustering all over it; they glowed in the air, and gleamed back again out of the depths of the pool, which thus seemed to overflow with colored radiance from the rich reflection that was steeped in it. At first, as we have said, the garden was a solitude. Soon, however,—as Giovanni had half-hoped, half-feared, would be the case,—a figure appeared beneath the antique sculptured portal, and came down between the rows of plants, inhaling their various perfumes, as if she were one of those·beings of old classic fable, that lived upon sweet odors. On again beholding Beatrice, the young man was even startled to perceive how much her beauty exceeded his recollection of it; so brilliant, so vivid was its character, that she glowed amid the sunlight, and, as Giovanni whispered to himself, positively illuminated the more shadowy intervals of the garden path. Her face being now more revealed than on the former occasion, he was struck by its expression of simplicity and sweetness; qualities that had not entered into his idea of her character, and which made him ask anew, what manner of mortal she might be. Nor did he fail again to observe, or imagine, an analogy between the beautiful girl and the gorgeous shrub that hung its gem-like flowers over the fountain; a resemblance which Beatrice seemed to have indulged a fantastic humor in heightening, both by the arrangement of her dress and the selection of its hues.

Approaching the shrub, she threw open her arms, as with a passionate ardor, and drew its branches into an intimate embrace; so intimate, that her features were hidden in its leafy bosom, and her glistening ringlets all intermingled with the flowers.

"Give me thy breath, my sister," exclaimed Beatrice; "for I am faint with common air! And give me this flower of thine, which I separate with gentlest fingers from the stem, and place it close beside my heart."

With these words, the beautiful daughter of Rappaccini plucked one of the richest blossoms of the shrub, and was about to fasten it in her bosom. But now, unless Giovanni's draughts of wine had bewildered his senses, a singular incident occurred. A small orange-colored reptile, of the lizard or chameleon species, chanced to be creeping along the path, just at the feet of Beatrice. It appeared to Giovanni—but, at the distance from which he gazed, he could scarcely have seen anything so minute—it appeared to him, however, that a drop or two of moisture from the broken stem of the flower descended

upon the lizard's head. For an instant, the reptile con-
torted itself violently, and then lay motionless in the sunshine. Beatrice observed this remarkable phenomenon,
and crossed herself, sadly, but without surprise; nor did
she therefore hesitate to arrange the fatal flower in her
bosom. There it blushed, and almost glimmered with the
dazzling effect of a precious stone, adding to her dress
and aspect the one appropriate charm, which nothing else
in the world could have supplied. But Giovanni, out of
the shadow of his window, bent forward and shrank back,
and murmured and trembled.

"Am I awake? Have I my senses?" said he to himself.
"What is this being?—beautiful, shall I call her?—or in-
expressibly terrible?"

Beatrice now strayed carelessly through the garden, approaching closer beneath Giovanni's window, so that he
was compelled to thrust his head quite out of its conceal-
ment in order to gratify the intense and painful curiosity
which she excited. At this moment, there came a beautiful
insect over the garden wall; it had perhaps wandered
through the city and found no flowers nor verdure among
those antique haunts of men, until the heavy perfumes of
Doctor Rappaccini's shrubs had lured it from afar. Without alighting on the flowers, this winged brightness
seemed to be attracted by Beatrice, and lingered in the air
and fluttered about her head. Now, here it could not be
but that Giovanni Guasconti's eyes deceived him. Be that
as it might, he fancied that while Beatrice was gazing at
the insect with childish delight, it grew faint and fell at
her feet;—its bright wings shivered; it was dead—from
no cause that he could discern, unless it were the atmosphere of her breath. Again Beatrice crossed herself and
sighed heavily, as she bent over the dead insect.

An impulsive movement of Giovanni drew her eyes to
the window. There she beheld the beautiful head of the
young man—rather a Grecian than an Italian head, with
fair, regular features, and a glistening of gold among his

ringlets—gazing down upon her like a being that hovered in midair. Scarcely knowing what he did, Giovanni threw down the bouquet which he had hitherto held in his hand.

"Signora," said he, "there are pure and healthful flowers. Wear them for the sake of Giovanni Guasconti!"

"Thanks, Signor," replied Beatrice, with her rich voice, that came forth as it were like a gush of music; and with a mirthful expression half childish and half woman-like. "I accept your gift, and would fain recompense it with this precious purple flower; but if I toss it into the air, it will not reach you. So Signor Guasconti must content himself with my thanks."

She lifted the bouquet from the ground, and then as if inwardly ashamed at having stepped aside from her maidenly reserve to respond to a stranger's greeting, passed swiftly homeward through the garden. But, few as the moments were, it seemed to Giovanni when she was on the point of vanishing beneath the sculptured portal, that his beautiful bouquet was already beginning to wither in her grasp. It was an idle thought; there could be no possibility of distinguishing a faded flower from a fresh one at so great a distance.

For many days after this incident, the young man avoided the window that looked into Doctor Rappaccini's garden, as if something ugly and monstrous would have blasted his eyesight, had he been betrayed into a glance. He felt conscious of having put himself, to a certain extent, within the influence of an unintelligible power, by the communication which he had opened with Beatrice. The wisest course would have been, if his heart were in any real danger, to quit his lodgings and Padua itself, at once; the next wiser, to have accustomed himself, as far as possible, to the familiar and day-light view of Beatrice; thus bringing her rigidly and systematically within the limits of ordinary experience. Least of all, while avoiding her sight, ought Giovanni to have remained so near this extraordinary being, that the proximity and possibility

even of intercourse, should give a kind of substance and
reality to the wild vagaries which his imagination ran riot
continually in producing. Guasconti had not a deep
heart—or at all events, its depths were not sounded
now—but he had a quick fancy, and an ardent southern
temperament, which rose every instant to a higher fever-
pitch. Whether or not Beatrice possessed those terrible
attributes—that fatal breath—the affinity with those so
beautiful and deadly flowers—which were indicated by
what Giovanni had witnessed, she had at least instilled a
fierce and subtle poison into his system. It was not love,
although her rich beauty was a madness to him; nor horror, even while he fancied her spirit to be imbued with the
same baneful essence that seemed to pervade her physical
frame; but a wild offspring of both love and horror that
had each parent in it, and burned like one and shivered
like the other. Giovanni knew not what to dread; still less
did he know what to hope; yet hope and dread kept a con-
tinual warfare in his breast, alternately vanquishing one
another and starting up afresh to renew the contest.
Blessed are all simple emotions, be they dark or bright! It
is the lurid intermixture of the two that produces the illu-
minating blaze of the infernal regions.

Sometimes he endeavored to assuage the fever of his
spirit by a rapid walk through the streets of Padua, or beyond its gates; his footsteps kept time with the throbbings
of his brain, so that the walk was apt to accelerate itself
to a race. One day, he found himself arrested; his arm was
seized by a portly personage who had turned back on recognizing the young man, and expended much breath in
overtaking him.

"Signor Giovanni!—stay, my young friend!" cried he.
"Have you forgotten me? That might well be the case, if
I were as much altered as yourself."

It was Baglioni, whom Giovanni had avoided, ever
since their first meeting, from a doubt that the Professor's
sagacity would look too deeply into his secrets. Endeav-

oring to recover himself, he stared forth wildly from his inner world into the outer one, and spoke like a man in a dream:

"Yes; I am Giovanni Guasconti. You are Professor Pietro Baglioni. Now let me pass!"

"Not yet—not yet, Signor Giovanni Guasconti," said the Professor, smiling, but at the same time scrutinizing the youth with an earnest glance.—"What; did I grow up side by side with your father, and shall his son pass me like a stranger, in these old streets of Padua? Stand still, Signor Giovanni; for we must have a word or two, before we part."

"Speedily, then, most worshipful Professor, speedily!" said Giovanni, with feverish impatience. "Does not your worship see that I am in haste?"

Now, while he was speaking, there came a man in black along the street, stooping and moving feebly, like a person in inferior health. His face was all overspread with a most sickly and sallow hue, but yet so pervaded with an expression of piercing and active intellect, that an observer might easily have overlooked the merely physical attributes, and have seen only this wonderful energy. As he passed, this person exchanged a cold and distant salutation with Baglioni, but fixed his eyes upon Giovanni with an intentness that seemed to bring out whatever was within him worthy of notice. Nevertheless, there was a peculiar quietness in the look, as if taking merely a speculative, not a human, interest in the young man.

"It is Doctor Rappaccini!" whispered the Professor, when the stranger had passed.—"Has he ever seen your face before?"

"Not that I know," answered Giovanni, starting at the name.

"He *has* seen you!—he must have seen you!" said Baglioni, hastily. "For some purpose or other, this man of science is making a study of you. I know that look of his! It is the same that coldly illuminates his face, as he bends

over a bird, a mouse, or a butterfly, which, in pursuance
of some experiment, he has killed by the perfume of a
flower;—a look as deep as Nature itself, but without Nature's warmth of love. Signor Giovanni, I will stake my
life upon it, you are the subject of one of Rappaccini's
experiments!"

"Will you make a fool of me?" cried Giovanni, pas-
sionately. "*That*, Signor Professor, were an untoward experiment."

"Patience, patience!" replied the imperturbable
Professor.—"I tell thee, my poor Giovanni, that
Rappaccini has a scientific interest in thee. Thou hast
fallen into fearful hands! And the Signora Beatrice? What
part does she act in this mystery?"

But Guasconti, finding Baglioni's pertinacity intolera-
ble, here broke away, and was gone before the Professor
could again seize his arm. He looked after the young man
intently, and shook his head.

"This must not be," said Baglioni to himself. "The
youth is the son of my old friend, and shall not come to
any harm from which the arcana of medical science can
preserve him. Besides, it is too insufferable an imperti-
nence in Rappaccini, thus to snatch the lad out of my own
hands, as I may say, and make use of him for his infernal
experiments. This daughter of his! It shall be looked to.
Perchance, most learned Rappaccini, I may foil you
where you little dream of it!"

Meanwhile, Giovanni had pursued a circuitous route,
and at length found himself at the door of his lodgings.
As he crossed the threshold, he was met by old Lisabetta, who smirked and smiled, and was evidently desirous
to attract his attention; vainly, however, as the ebullition
of his feelings had momentarily subsided into a cold and
dull vacuity. He turned his eyes full upon the withered
face that was puckering itself into a smile, but seemed to
behold it not. The old dame, therefore, laid her grasp
upon his cloak.

"Signor!—Signor!" whispered she, still with a smile over the whole breadth of her visage, so that it looked not unlike a grotesque carving in wood, darkened by centuries—"Listen, Signor! There is a private entrance into the garden!"

"What do you say?" exclaimed Giovanni, turning quickly about, as if an inanimate thing should start into feverish life.—"A private entrance into Doctor Rappaccini's garden!"

"Hush! hush!—not so loud!" whispered Lisabetta, putting her hand over his mouth. "Yes; into the worshipful Doctor's garden, where you may see all his fine shrubbery. Many a young man in Padua would give gold to be admitted among those flowers."

Giovanni put a piece of gold into her hand.

"Show me the way," said he.

A surmise, probably excited by his conversation with Baglioni, crossed his mind, that this interposition of old Lisabetta might perchance be connected with the intrigue, whatever were its nature, in which the Professor seemed to suppose that Doctor Rappaccini was involving him. But such a suspicion, though it disturbed Giovanni, was inadequate to restrain him. The instant that he was aware of the possibility of approaching Beatrice, it seemed an absolute necessity of his existence to do so. It mattered not whether she were angel or demon; he was irrevocably within her sphere, and must obey the law that whirled him onward, in ever lessening circles, towards a result which he did not attempt to foreshadow. And yet, strange to say, there came across him a sudden doubt, whether this intense interest on his part were not delusory— whether it were really of so deep and positive a nature as to justify him in now thrusting himself into an incalculable position—whether it were not merely the fantasy of a young man's brain, only slightly, or not at all, connected with his heart!

He paused—hesitated—turned half about—but again

went on. His withered guide led him along several obscure passages, and finally undid a door, through which,
as it was opened, there came the sight and sound of rustling leaves, with the broken sunshine glimmering among
them. Giovanni stepped forth, and forcing himself
through the entanglement of a shrub that wreathed its tendrils over the hidden entrance, he stood beneath his own
window, in the open area of Doctor Rappaccini's garden.

How often is it the case, that, when impossibilities have
come to pass, and dreams have condensed their misty
substance into tangible realities, we find ourselves calm,
and even coldly self-possessed, amid circumstances
which it would have been a delirium of joy or agony to
anticipate! Fate delights to thwart us thus. Passion will
choose his own time to rush upon the scene, and lingers
sluggishly behind, when an appropriate adjustment of events would seem to summon his appearance. So was it
now with Giovanni. Day after day, his pulses had
throbbed with feverish blood, at the improbable idea of an
interview with Beatrice, and of standing with her, face to
face, in this very garden, basking in the Oriental sunshine
of her beauty, and snatching from her full gaze the mystery which he deemed the riddle of his own existence. But
now there was a singular and untimely equanimity within
his breast. He threw a glance around the garden to discover if Beatrice or her father were present, and perceiving that he was alone, began a critical observation of the
plants.

The aspect of one and all of them dissatisfied him;
their gorgeousness seemed fierce, passionate, and even
unnatural. There was hardly an individual shrub which a
wanderer, straying by himself through a forest, would not
have been startled to find growing wild, as if an unearthly
face had glared at him out of the thicket. Several, also,
would have shocked a delicate instinct by an appearance
of artificialness, indicating that there had been such com-
mixture, and, as it were, adultery of various vegetable

species, that the production was no longer of God's making, but the monstrous offspring of man's depraved fancy, glowing with only an evil mockery of beauty. They were probably the result of experiment, which, in one or two cases, had succeeded in mingling plants individually lovely into a compound possessing the questionable and ominous character that distinguished the whole growth of the garden. In fine, Giovanni recognized but two or three plants in the collection, and those of a kind that he well knew to be poisonous. While busy with these contemplations, he heard the rustling of a silken garment, and turning, beheld Beatrice emerging from beneath the sculptured portal.

Giovanni had not considered with himself what should be his deportment; whether he should apologize for his intrusion into the garden, or assume that he was there with the privity, at least, if not by the desire, of Doctor Rappaccini or his daughter. But Beatrice's manner placed him at his ease, though leaving him still in doubt by what agency he had gained admittance. She came lightly along the path, and met him near the broken fountain. There was surprise in her face, but brightened by a simple and kind expression of pleasure.

"You are a connoisseur in flowers, Signor," said Beatrice with a smile, alluding to the bouquet which he had flung her from the window. "It is no marvel, therefore, if the sight of my father's rare collection has tempted you to take a nearer view. If he were here, he could tell you many strange and interesting facts as to the nature and habits of these shrubs, for he has spent a lifetime in such studies, and this garden is his world."

"And yourself, lady"—observed Giovanni—"if fame says true—you, likewise, are deeply skilled in the virtues indicated by these rich blossoms, and these spicy perfumes. Would you deign to be my instructress, I should prove an apter scholar than if taught by Signor Rappaccini himself."

"Are there such idle rumors?" asked Beatrice, with the music of a pleasant laugh. "Do people say that I am skilled in my father's science of plants? What a jest is there! No; though I have grown up among these flowers, I know no more of them than their hues and perfume; and sometimes, methinks I would fain rid myself of even that small knowledge. There are many flowers here, and those not the least brilliant, that shock and offend me, when they meet my eye. But, pray, Signor, do not believe these stories about my science. Believe nothing of me save what you see with your own eyes."

"And must I believe all that I have seen with my own eyes?" asked Giovanni pointedly, while the recollection of former scenes made him shrink. "No, Signora, you demand too little of me. Bid me believe nothing, save what comes from your own lips."

It would appear that Beatrice understood him. There came a deep flush to her cheek; but she looked full into Giovanni's eyes, and responded to his gaze of uneasy suspicion with a queen-like haughtiness.

"I do so bid you, Signor!" she replied. "Forget whatever you may have fancied in regard to me. If true to the outward senses, still it may be false in its essence. But the words of Beatrice Rappaccini's lips are true from the depths of the heart outward. Those you may believe!"

A fervor glowed in her whole aspect, and beamed upon Giovanni's consciousness like the light of truth itself. But while she spoke, there was a fragrance in the atmosphere around her, rich and delightful, though evanescent, yet which the young man, from an indefinable reluctance, scarcely dared to draw into his lungs. It might be the odor of the flowers. Could it be Beatrice's breath, which thus embalmed her words with a strange richness, as if by steeping them in her heart? A faintness passed like a shadow over Giovanni, and flitted away; he seemed to gaze through the beautiful girl's eyes into her transparent soul, and felt no more doubt or fear.

The tinge of passion that had colored Beatrice's manner vanished; she became gay, and appeared to derive a pure delight from her communion with the youth, not unlike what the maiden of a lonely island might have felt, conversing with a voyager from the civilized world. Evidently her experience of life had been confined within the limits of that garden. She talked now about matters as simple as the day-light or summer-clouds, and now asked questions in reference to the city, or Giovanni's distant home, his friends, his mother, and his sisters; questions indicating such seclusion, and such lack of familiarity with modes and forms, that Giovanni responded as if to an infant. Her spirit gushed out before him like a fresh rill, that was just catching its first glimpse of the sunlight, and wondering at the reflections of earth and sky which were flung into its bosom. There came thoughts, too, from a deep source, and fantasies of a gem-like brilliancy, as if diamonds and rubies sparkled upward among the bubbles of the fountain. Ever and anon, there gleamed across the young man's mind a sense of wonder, that he should be walking side by side with the being who had so wrought upon his imagination—whom he had idealized in such hues of terror—in whom he had positively witnessed such manifestations of dreadful attributes—that he should be conversing with Beatrice like a brother, and should find her so human and so maiden-like. But such reflections were only momentary; the effect of her character was too real, not to make itself familiar at once.

In this free intercourse, they had strayed through the garden, and now, after many turns among its avenues, were come to the shattered fountain, beside which grew the magnificent shrub with its treasury of glowing blossoms. A fragrance was diffused from it, which Giovanni recognized as identical with that which he had attributed to Beatrice's breath, but incomparably more powerful. As her eyes fell upon it, Giovanni beheld her press her hand to her bosom, as if her heart were throbbing suddenly and painfully.

"For the first time in my life," murmured she, addressing the shrub, "I had forgotten thee!"

"I remember, Signora," said Giovanni, "that you once promised to reward me with one of these living gems for the bouquet, which I had the happy boldness to fling to your feet. Permit me now to pluck it as a memorial of this interview."

He made a step towards the shrub, with extended hand. But Beatrice darted forward, uttering a shriek that went through his heart like a dagger. She caught his hand, and drew it back with the whole force of her slender figure. Giovanni felt her touch thrilling through his fibres.

"Touch it not!" exclaimed she, in a voice of agony. "Not for thy life! It is fatal!"

Then, hiding her face, she fled from him, and vanished beneath the sculptured portal. As Giovanni followed her with his eyes, he beheld the emaciated figure and pale intelligence of Doctor Rappaccini, who had been watching the scene, he knew not how long, within the shadow of the entrance.

No sooner was Guasconti alone in his chamber, than the image of Beatrice came back to his passionate musings, invested with all the witchery that had been gathering around it ever since his first glimpse of her, and now likewise imbued with a tender warmth of girlish womanhood. She was human: her nature was endowed with all gentle and feminine qualities; she was worthiest to be worshipped; she was capable, surely, on her part, of the height and heroism of love. Those tokens, which he had hitherto considered as proofs of a frightful peculiarity in her physical and moral system, were now either forgotten, or, by the subtle sophistry of passion, transmuted into a golden crown of enchantment, rendering Beatrice the more admirable, by so much as she was the more unique. Whatever had looked ugly, was now beautiful; or, if incapable of such a change, it stole away and hid itself among those shapeless half-ideas, which throng the dim region beyond the daylight of our perfect consciousness. Thus did he spend the night, nor fell asleep, until the dawn had begun to awake the slumbering flowers in Doctor Rappaccini's garden, whither Giovanni's dreams doubtless led him. Up rose the sun in his due season, and flinging his beams upon the young man's eyelids, awoke him to a sense of pain. When thoroughly aroused, he became sensible of a burning and tingling agony in his hand—in his right hand—the very hand which Beatrice had grasped in her own, when he was on the point of plucking one of the gem-like flowers. On the back of that hand there was now a purple print, like that of four small fingers, and the likeness of a slender thumb upon his wrist.

Oh, how stubbornly does love—or even that cunning semblance of love which flourishes in the imagination, but strikes no depth of root into the heart—how stubbornly does it hold its faith, until the moment come, when it is doomed to vanish into thin mist! Giovanni wrapt a handkerchief about his hand, and wondered what evil thing had stung him, and soon forgot his pain in a reverie of Beatrice.

After the first interview, a second was in the inevitable course of what we call fate. A third; a fourth; and a meeting with Beatrice in the garden was no longer an incident in Giovanni's daily life, but the whole space in which he might be said to live; for the anticipation and memory of that ecstatic hour made up the remainder. Nor was it otherwise with the daughter of Rappaccini. She watched for the youth's appearance, and flew to his side with confidence as unreserved as if they had been playmates from early infancy—as if they were such playmates still. If, by any unwonted chance, he failed to come at the appointed moment, she stood beneath the window, and sent up the rich sweetness of her tones to float around him in his chamber, and echo and reverberate throughout his heart—"Giovanni! Giovanni! Why tarriest thou? Come down!"—And down he hastened into that Eden of poisonous flowers.

But, with all this intimate familiarity, there was still a reserve in Beatrice's demeanor, so rigidly and invariably sustained, that the idea of infringing it scarcely occurred to his imagination. By all appreciable signs, they loved; they had looked love, with eyes that conveyed the holy secret from the depths of one soul into the depths of the other, as if it were too sacred to be whispered by the way; they had even spoken love, in those gushes of passion when their spirits darted forth in articulated breath, like tongues of long-hidden flame; and yet there had been no seal of lips, no clasp of hands, nor any slightest caress, such as love claims and hallows. He had never touched one of the gleaming ringlets of her hair; her garment—so marked was the physical barrier between them—had never been waved against him by a breeze. On the few occasions when Giovanni had seemed tempted to over-step the limit, Beatrice grew so sad, so stern, and withal wore such a look of desolate separation, shuddering at it-self, that not a spoken word was requisite to repel him. At such times, he was startled at the horrible suspicions that rose, monster-like, out of the caverns of his heart, and stared him in the face; his love grew thin and faint as the morning-mist; his doubts alone had substance. But when Beatrice's face brightened again, after the momentary shadow, she was transformed at once from the mysteri-ous, questionable being, whom he had watched with so much awe and horror; she was now the beautiful and un-sophisticated girl, whom he felt that his spirit knew with a certainty beyond all other knowledge.

A considerable time had now passed since Giovanni's last meeting with Baglioni. One morning, however, he was disagreeably surprised by a visit from the Professor, whom he had scarcely thought of for whole weeks, and would willingly have forgotten still longer. Given up, as he had long been, to a pervading excitement, he could tolerate no companions, except upon condition of their perfect sympathy with his present state of feeling. Such sympathy was not to be expected from Professor Baglioni.

The visitor chatted carelessly, for a few moments, about the gossip of the city and the University, and then took up another topic.

"I have been reading an old classic author lately," said he, "and met with a story that strangely interested me. Possibly you may remember it. It is of an Indian prince, who sent a beautiful woman as a present to Alexander the Great. She was as lovely as the dawn, and gorgeous as the sunset; but what especially distinguished her was a certain rich perfume in her breath—richer than a garden of Persian roses. Alexander, as was natural to a youthful conqueror, fell in love at first sight with this magnificent stranger. But a certain sage physician, happening to be present, discovered a terrible secret in regard to her."

"And what was that?" asked Giovanni, turning his eyes downward to avoid those of the Professor.

"That this lovely woman," continued Baglioni, with emphasis, "had been nourished with poisons from her birth upward, until her whole nature was so imbued with them, that she herself had become the deadliest poison in existence. Poison was her element of life. With that rich perfume of her breath, she blasted the very air. Her love would have been poison!—her embrace death! Is not this a marvelous tale?"

"A childish fable," answered Giovanni, nervously starting from his chair. "I marvel how your worship finds time to read such nonsense, among your graver studies."

"By the bye," said the Professor, looking uneasily about him, "what singular fragrance is this in your apartment? Is it the perfume of your gloves? It is faint, but delicious, and yet, after all, by no means agreeable. Were I to breathe it long, methinks it would make me ill. It is like the breath of a flower—but I see no flowers in the chamber."

"Nor are there any," replied Giovanni, who had turned pale as the Professor spoke; "nor, I think, is there any fragrance, except in your worship's imagination. Odors, being a sort of element combined of the sensual and the spiritual, are apt to deceive us in this manner. The recollection of a perfume—the bare idea of it—may easily be mistaken for a present reality."

"Aye; but my sober imagination does not often play such tricks," said Baglioni; "and were I to fancy any kind of odor, it would be that of some vile apothecary drug, wherewith my fingers are likely enough to be imbued. Our worshipful friend Rappaccini, as I have heard, tinctures his medicaments with odors richer than those of Araby. Doubtless, likewise, the fair and learned Signora Beatrice would minister to her patients with draughts as sweet as a maiden's breath. But wo to him that sips them!"

Giovanni's face evinced many contending emotions. The tone in which the Professor alluded to the pure and lovely daughter of Rappaccini was a torture to his soul; and yet, the intimation of a view of her character, opposite to his own, gave instantaneous distinctness to a thousand dim suspicions, which now grinned at him like so many demons. But he strove hard to quell them, and to respond to Baglioni with a true lover's perfect faith.

"Signor Professor," said he, "you were my father's friend—perchance, too, it is your purpose to act a friendly part towards his son. I would fain feel nothing towards you, save respect and deference. But I pray you to observe, Signor, that there is one subject on which we must not speak. You know not the Signora Beatrice. You cannot, therefore, estimate the wrong—the blasphemy, I may even say—that is offered to her character by a light or injurious word."

"Giovanni!—my poor Giovanni!" answered the Professor, with a calm expression of pity, "I know this wretched girl far better than yourself. You shall hear the truth in respect to the poisoner Rappaccini, and his poisonous daughter. Yes; poisonous as she is beautiful! Listen; for even should you do violence to my grey hairs, it shall not silence me. That old fable of the Indian woman has become a truth, by the deep and deadly science of Rappaccini, and in the person of the lovely Beatrice!"

Giovanni groaned and hid his face.

"Her father," continued Baglioni, "was not restrained by natural affection from offering up his child, in this horrible manner, as the victim of his insane zeal for science. For—let us do him justice—he is as true a man of science as ever distilled his own heart in an alembic. What, then, will be your fate? Beyond a doubt, you are selected as the material of some new experiment. Perhaps the result is to be death—perhaps a fate more awful still! Rappaccini, with what he calls the interest of science before his eyes, will hesitate at nothing."

"It is a dream!" muttered Giovanni to himself, "surely it is a dream!"

"But," resumed the Professor, "be of good cheer, son of my friend! It is not yet too late for the rescue. Possibly, we may even succeed in bringing back this miserable child within the limits of ordinary nature, from which her father's madness has estranged her. Behold this little silver vase! It was wrought by the hands of the renowned Benvenuto Cellini, and is well worthy to be a love-gift to the fairest dame in Italy. But its contents are invaluable. One little sip of this antidote would have rendered the most virulent poisons of the Borgias innocuous. Doubt not that it will be as efficacious against those of Rappaccini. Bestow the vase, and the precious liquid within it, on your Beatrice, and hopefully await the result."

Baglioni laid a small, exquisitely wrought silver phial

on the table, and withdrew, leaving what he had said to
produce its effect upon the young man's mind.

"We will thwart Rappaccini yet!" thought he, chuckling to himself, as he descended the stairs. "But, let us
confess the truth of him, he is a wonderful man!—a wonderful man indeed! A vile empiric, however, in his prac-
tice, and therefore not to be tolerated by those who
respect the good old rules of the medical profession!"

Throughout Giovanni's whole acquaintance with
Beatrice, he had occasionally, as we have said, been
haunted by dark surmises as to her character. Yet, so thoroughly had she made herself felt by him as a simple, natural, most affectionate and guileless creature, that the
image now held up by Professor Baglioni, looked as
strange and incredible, as if it were not in accordance
with his own original conception. True, there were ugly
recollections connected with his first glimpses of the
beautiful girl; he could not quite forget the bouquet that
withered in her grasp, and the insect that perished amid
the sunny air, by no ostensible agency, save the fragrance
of her breath. These incidents, however, dissolving in the
pure light of her character, had no longer the efficacy of
facts, but were acknowledged as mistaken fantasies, by
whatever testimony of the senses they might appear to be
substantiated. There is something truer and more real,
than what we can see with the eyes, and touch with the
finger. On such better evidence, had Giovanni founded
his confidence in Beatrice, though rather by the necessary
force of her high attributes, than by any deep and gener-
ous faith, on his part. But, now, his spirit was incapable
of sustaining itself at the height to which the early enthusiasm of passion had exalted it; he fell down, grovelling
among earthly doubts, and defiled therewith the pure
whiteness of Beatrice's image. Not that he gave her up;
he did but distrust. He resolved to institute some decisive
test that should satisfy him, once for all, whether there
were those dreadful peculiarities in her physical nature,

which could not be supposed to exist without some corresponding monstrosity of soul. His eyes, gazing down afar, might have deceived him as to the lizard, the insect, and the flowers. But if he could witness, at the distance of a few paces, the sudden blight of one fresh and healthful flower in Beatrice's hand, there would be room for no further question. With this idea, he hastened to the florist's, and purchased a bouquet that was still gemmed with the morning dew-drops.

It was now the customary hour of his daily interview with Beatrice. Before descending into the garden, Giovanni failed not to look at his figure in the mirror; a vanity to be expected in a beautiful young man, yet, as displaying itself at that troubled and feverish moment, the token of a certain shallowness of feeling and insincerity of character. He did gaze, however, and said to himself, that his features had never before possessed so rich a grace, nor his eyes such vivacity, nor his cheeks so warm a hue of superabundant life.

"At least," thought he, "her poison has not yet insinuated itself into my system. I am no flower to perish in her grasp!"

With that thought, he turned his eyes on the bouquet, which he had never once laid aside from his hand. A thrill of indefinable horror shot through his frame, on perceiving that those dewy flowers were already beginning to droop; they wore the aspect of things that had been fresh and lovely, yesterday. Giovanni grew white as marble, and stood motionless before the mirror, staring at his own reflection there, as at the likeness of something frightful. He remembered Baglioni's remark about the fragrance that seemed to pervade the chamber. It must have been the poison in his breath! Then he shuddered—shuddered at himself! Recovering from his stupor, he began to watch, with curious eye, a spider that was busily at work, hanging its web from the antique cornice of the apartment, crossing and re-crossing the artful system of interwoven lines, as vigorous and active a spider as ever dangled from an old ceiling. Giovanni bent towards the insect, and emitted a deep, long breath. The spider suddenly ceased its toil; the web vibrated with a tremor originating in the body of the small artizan. Again Giovanni sent forth a breath, deeper, longer, and imbued with a venomous feeling out of his heart; he knew not whether he were wicked or only desperate. The spider made a convulsive gripe with his limbs, and hung dead across the window.

"Accursed! Accursed!" muttered Giovanni, addressing himself. "Hast thou grown so poisonous, that this deadly insect perishes by thy breath?"

At that moment, a rich, sweet voice came floating up from the garden:—

"Giovanni! Giovanni! It is past the hour! Why tarriest thou! Come down!"

"Yes," muttered Giovanni again. "She is the only being whom my breath may not slay! Would that it might!"

He rushed down, and in an instant, was standing before the bright and loving eyes of Beatrice. A moment ago, his wrath and despair had been so fierce that he could have desired nothing so much as to wither her by a glance. But, with her actual presence, there came influences which had too real an existence to be at once shaken off; recollections of the delicate and benign power of her feminine nature, which had so often enveloped him in a religious calm; recollections of many a holy and passionate outgush of her heart, when the pure fountain had been unsealed from its depths, and made visible in its transparency to his mental eye; recollections which, had Giovanni known how to estimate them, would have assured him that all this ugly mystery was but an earthly illusion, and that, whatever mist of evil might seem to have gathered over her, the real Beatrice was a heavenly angel. Incapable as he was of such high faith, still her presence had not utterly lost its magic. Giovanni's rage was quelled into an aspect of sullen insensibility. Beatrice, with a quick spiritual sense, immediately felt that there was a gulf of blackness between them, which neither he nor she could pass. They walked on together, sad and silent, and came thus to the marble fountain, and to its pool of water on the ground, in the midst of which grew the shrub that bore gemlike blossoms. Giovanni was affrighted at the eager enjoyment—the appetite, as it were—with which he found himself inhaling the fragrance of the flowers.

"Beatrice," asked he abruptly, "whence came this shrub?"

"My father created it," answered she, with simplicity.

"Created it! created it!" repeated Giovanni. "What mean you, Beatrice?"

"He is a man fearfully acquainted with the secrets of nature," replied Beatrice; "and, at the hour when I first drew breath, this plant sprang from the soil, the offspring of his science, of his intellect, while I was but his earthly child. Approach it not!" continued she, observing with terror that Giovanni was drawing nearer to the shrub. "It has qualities that you little dream of. But I, dearest Giovanni,—I grew up and blossomed with the plant, and was nourished with its breath. It was my sister, and I loved it with a human affection: for—alas! hast thou not suspected it? there was an awful doom."

Here Giovanni frowned so darkly upon her that Beatrice paused and trembled. But her faith in his tenderness reassured her, and made her blush that she had doubted for an instant.

"There was an awful doom," she continued,—"the effect of my father's fatal love of science—which estranged me from all society of my kind. Until Heaven sent thee, dearest Giovanni, Oh! how lonely was thy poor Beatrice!"

"Was it a hard doom?" asked Giovanni, fixing his eyes upon her.

"Only of late have I known how hard it was," answered she tenderly. "Oh, yes; but my heart was torpid, and therefore quiet."

Giovanni's rage broke forth from his sullen gloom like a lightning-flash out of a dark cloud.

"Accursed one!" cried he, with venomous scorn and anger. "And finding thy solitude wearisome, thou hast severed me, likewise, from all the warmth of life, and enticed me into thy region of unspeakable horror!"

"Giovanni!" exclaimed Beatrice, turning her large bright eyes upon his face. The force of his words had not found its way into her mind; she was merely thunder-struck.

"Yes, poisonous thing!" repeated Giovanni, beside himself with passion. "Thou hast done it! Thou hast blasted me! Thou hast filled my veins with poison! Thou hast made me as hateful, as ugly, as loathsome and deadly a creature as thyself,—a world's wonder of hideous monstrosity! Now—if our breath be happily as fatal to ourselves as to all others—let us join our lips in one kiss of unutterable hatred, and so die!"

"What has befallen me?" murmured Beatrice, with a low moan out of her heart. "Holy Virgin pity me, a poor heartbroken child!"

"Thou! Dost thou pray?" cried Giovanni, still with the same fiendish scorn. "Thy very prayers, as they come from thy lips, taint the atmosphere with death. Yes, yes; let us pray! Let us to church, and dip our fingers in the holy water at the portal! They that come after us will perish as by a pestilence. Let us sign crosses in the air! It will be scattering curses abroad in the likeness of holy symbols!"

"Giovanni," said Beatrice calmly, for her grief was beyond passion, "why dost thou join thyself with me thus in those terrible words? I, it is true, am the horrible thing thou namest me. But thou!—what hast thou to do, save with one other shudder at my hideous misery, to go forth out of the garden and mingle with thy race, and forget that there ever crawled on earth such a monster as poor Beatrice?"

"Dost thou pretend ignorance?" asked Giovanni, scowling upon her. "Behold! This power have I gained from the pure daughter of Rappaccini!"

There was a swarm of summer-insects flitting through the air, in search of the food promised by the flower-odors of the fatal garden. They circled round Giovanni's head, and were evidently attracted towards him by the same influence which had drawn them, for an instant, within the sphere of several of the shrubs. He sent forth a breath among them, and smiled bitterly at Beatrice, as at least a score of the insects fell dead upon the ground.

"I see it! I see it!" shrieked Beatrice. "It is my father's fatal science! No, no, Giovanni; it was not I! Never, never! I dreamed only to love thee, and be with thee a little time, and so to let thee pass away, leaving but thine image in mine heart. For, Giovanni—believe it—though my body be nourished with poison, my spirit is God's creature, and craves love as its daily food. But my father!—he has united us in this fearful sympathy. Yes; spurn me!—tread upon me!—kill me! Oh, what is death, after such words as thine? But it was not I! Not for a world of bliss would I have done it!"

Giovanni's passion had exhausted itself in its outburst from his lips. There now came across him a sense, mournful, and not without tenderness, of the intimate and peculiar relationship between Beatrice and himself. They stood, as it were, in an utter solitude, which would be made none the less solitary by the densest throng of human life. Ought not, then, the desert of humanity around them to press this insulated pair closer together? If they should be cruel to one another, who was there to be kind to them? Besides, thought Giovanni, might there not still be a hope of his returning within the limits of ordinary nature, and leading Beatrice—the redeemed Beatrice—by the hand? Oh, weak, and selfish, and unworthy spirit, that could dream of an earthly union and earthly happiness as possible, after such deep love had been so bitterly wronged as was Beatrice's love by Giovanni's blighting words! No, no; there could be no such hope. She must pass heavily, with that broken heart, across the borders of

Time—she must bathe her hurts in some fount of Paradise, and forget her grief in the light of immortality—and *there* be well!

But Giovanni did not know it.

"Dear Beatrice," said he, approaching her, while she shrank away, as always at his approach, but now with a different impulse—"dearest Beatrice, our fate is not yet so desperate. Behold! There is a medicine, potent, as a wise physician has assured me, and almost divine in its efficacy. It is composed of ingredients the most opposite to those by which thy awful father has brought this calamity upon thee and me. It is distilled of blessed herbs. Shall we not quaff it together, and thus be purified from evil?"

"Give it me!" said Beatrice, extending her hand to receive the little silver phial which Giovanni took from his bosom. She added, with a peculiar emphasis: "I will drink—but do thou await the result."

She put Baglioni's antidote to her lips; and, at the same moment, the figure of Rappaccini emerged from the portal, and came slowly towards the marble fountain. As he drew near, the pale man of science seemed to gaze with a triumphant expression at the beautiful youth and maiden, as might an artist who should spend his life in achieving a picture or a group of statuary, and finally be satisfied with his success. He paused—his bent form grew erect with conscious power, he spread out his hands over them, in the attitude of a father imploring a blessing upon his children. But those were the same hands that had thrown poison into the stream of their lives! Giovanni trembled. Beatrice shuddered nervously, and pressed her hand upon her heart.

"My daughter," said Rappaccini, "thou art no longer lonely in the world! Pluck one of those precious gems from thy sister shrub, and bid thy bridegroom wear it in his bosom. It will not harm him now! My science, and the sympathy between thee and him, have so wrought within his system, that he now stands apart from common men, as thou dost, daughter of my pride and triumph, from ordinary women. Pass on, then, through the world, most dear to one another, and dreadful to all besides!"

"My father," said Beatrice, feebly—and still, as she spoke, she kept her hand upon her heart—"wherefore didst thou inflict this miserable doom upon thy child?"

"Miserable!" exclaimed Rappaccini. "What mean you, foolish girl? Dost thou deem it misery to be endowed with marvellous gifts, against which no power nor strength could avail an enemy? Misery, to be able to quell the mightiest with a breath? Misery, to be as terrible as thou art beautiful? Wouldst thou, then, have preferred the condition of a weak woman, exposed to all evil, and capable of none?"

"I would fain have been loved, not feared," murmured Beatrice, sinking down upon the ground.—"But now it matters not; I am going, father, where the evil, which thou hast striven to mingle with my being, will pass away like a dream—like the fragrance of these poisonous flowers, which will no longer taint my breath among the flowers of Eden. Farewell, Giovanni! Thy words of hatred are like lead within my heart—but they, too, will fall away as I ascend. Oh, was there not, from the first, more poison in thy nature than in mine?"

To Beatrice—so radically had her earthly part been wrought upon by Rappaccini's skill—as poison had been life, so the powerful antidote was death. And thus the poor victim of man's ingenuity and of thwarted nature, and of the fatality that attends all such efforts of perverted wisdom, perished there, at the feet of her father and Giovanni. Just at that moment, Professor Pietro Baglioni looked forth from the window, and called loudly, in a tone of triumph mixed with horror, to the thunder-stricken man of science:

"Rappaccini! Rappaccini! And is *this* the upshot of your experiment?"

Parrots in My Garden
by Dorothy B. Davis

In September I lost my job. "Attrition," Mr. Peterson told me regretfully. Over his shoulder, through his wide picture window, facing toward Potter's Woods, I watched two big crows straddling a limb of an old tree, huddling over it, pecking intently at the bare wood, getting every last insect out of it before flying off elsewhere, leaving it behind. Mr. Peterson stood erect, at attention. There was nothing he could do about it. "Sorry, Eileen."

And my husband. The week after I lost my job my husband left me, too. He took me by surprise as well. But I should have seen it coming I see now, for there were two crows, not just one, pecking on that buggy old limb outside Mr. Peterson's office. "Attraction," Wayne told me, reproachfully. I could smell the whiskey strong on his breath, nothing new about that, as he rose stiffly from his recliner chair in the den. There was nothing he could do about it either. Not even "Sorry, Eileen." I'd had my job and my husband for over forty years, each.

And Sue Annie, the plump, dowdy, foolish woman Wayne was leaving me for, was a mere child, not yet forty. She'd been my friend. More than that. She had no family, no friends but us, so taking pity on her, I'd treated her as if I were her mother and she my daughter. I'd had no idea the floozy was sneaking around behind my back.

After he broke the story Wayne lurched quickstep away from me into his bedroom, snapped his closet light on with a jerk, strode forthrightly in, began hastily yanking

clothes off hangers, grabbing clothes off shelves, rolling
them up end over end into untidy balls, throwing all with
a vengeance into suitcases and boxes that stood ready
around him, all the while earnestly avoiding my glance.
"It's all your fault," he yelled, looking straight ahead of
him. "What I've been living with all these years. What
I've put up with. How'd I stand it living with an ugly old
fussy old hag bag like you for so long? Always getting in
my way, always telling me what to do. I'll tell you what
to do."

"Same to you and double, you bastard," I yelled back
at him in a voice so loud it surprised even me. "Up yours!
Up Sue Annie's!" The words were out of my mouth before I knew it.

He looked my way then.

Outside now a nasty storm is raging, as only November
knows how to brew. Its wind and rain are rattling my windows, pounding on my doors. You'd think to hear them
that they were trying to get at me, as I sit here all alone.
You'd think to hear them that they were intent on blowing
me away, on ripping me apart. But I'm not afraid. I've
locked my doors. I've shut my windows tight. Rant and
rage and rattle from now to kingdom come! I'm out of
your reach now and forever. Get off my case, you bully
wind!

After he'd thrown everything he felt like into his boxes
and suitcases, Wayne mopped the sweat from his face and
neck with his handkerchief, blew his nose a good solid
blast, and then leered wickedly at me. "Sue Annie is nowhere near as pretty as you used to be," he said. "Sure is
hard to imagine now, but once you were a real knockout."
He cut me to the bone saying that, and he knew it, too.
But I pretended it didn't matter a fig to me. "So when she
first took a shine to me, all I felt was flattered," he said.
He ran his fingers through the few strands he had left of
what used to be his thick curly mop.

"Well, my looks and your hair must've run off to-

gether," I said then as sarcastically as I could, and by the
look on his face I knew I'd hit my mark. His lips and
voice grew harder.

"Until all of a sudden, I was overwhelmed by passion,"
he yelled. I couldn't believe my ears. Wayne? Passion? At
his age? At our age? But, yes, I can believe it now. And
a kind of passion seized him right then and he grabbed
me snugly by my shoulders, his thumbs drilling straight
into my arm sockets, his eyes boring straight into my
eyes. "Suddenly I couldn't resist," he said, as though he
was bragging about it to me. "I was overpowered by a
force bigger than anything I've ever felt before. Even
from you, in the days when you used to be a knockout."
He spat these whiskey words into my face. So I spat right
back at him, a good blob, got him smack in the left eye.
I've always been a good shot.

"She's a young woman, Eileen" is what he scatter-spat
back in my face. His aim has always been lousy. "And
she wants me a whole darned lot. She's a young woman
and she wants me a whole darned lot." He had to repeat
it, as though, even at such close range, I hadn't heard it
the first time. Or maybe he was still trying to convince
himself of it. Then he swiveled abruptly away from me to
survey the room. "So I've taken our savings," he said,
"bought a van, some property, a house." He spoke softly,
scarcely moving his lips, as though he were a ventrilo-
quist, or maybe a dummy, as though he were an actor, delivering an unimportant aside, throwing the words away.
So that's when I knew the jig was up. Here was the mo-
tivation for Sue Annie's crime of stealing a husband—
mine. What some women won't do to get a house these
days. I don't have to be told. Now I know, personally.

"We're leaving for it this afternoon," he said. "To start
a new life. A new family. To keep himself from going to
seed a man's got to keep on sowing his seed." He flung
his arms wide as he said this, as though this were the
grand finale of some soap opera going on in his head, of

which he was the star, of course, or as though he were quoting some new verse he'd found in his Bible. I guess it must have been in Sue Annie's, too.

The wind is pounding like surf against my windows, shifting them back and forth in their frames, with thudding noises, like the sounds boats make hitting up against their slips, when they're being tossed about by a gale.

There was no reasoning with Wayne, of course, about what he was doing. There never had been. He'd always been all jeers. And age hadn't mellowed him, as it does some people. He'd never been one to graciously accept the inevitable. Always said he'd rather go down fighting! Who? I always asked him. Fighting who? Fighting what? Well, now he's gone, fighting the whirlwind, but that's how he wanted it.

Wayne accidentally knocked his precious silver-backed soft-bristled baby hairbrush behind the dresser as he reached to get it, so he went down on hands and knees to fish it out. He'd outgrown the trousers he was wearing. I'd been telling him this for the longest time, but he never listened to me about it, of course. They were green. His trousers. When last sighted, Wayne was wearing his kelly green corduroy too-tight trousers. He always was such a bright, colorful guy. In marked contrast to my own conservativeness, or drabness, as he liked to style it. I always saw us as two birds: he the male bird with the bright, showy plumage, me the homely female, sitting camouflaged on her nest. The shirt Wayne had on with his kelly green too-tight corduroy trousers was cardinal red, his sweater was buttercup yellow. His fatty rear cleavage popped out of his too-tight kelly green trousers when he bent over to retrieve his precious silver-backed soft-bristled baby hairbrush. And it took all my strength to stifle the urge to give him a good hard swift kick in the you-know-where. But I managed to restrain myself. It wouldn't have changed anything, might actually have made things more difficult.

"Where for art thou roaming?" I asked him.

Instead of answering right away, he continued to scrounge around under his dresser, looking for money, I guess. "Alaska," he said at last, as he closed one eye, sighted under the dresser with the other. He must have imagined I was under there somewhere, since that's where he was looking as he answered my question.

"It's cold in Alaska!" I protested. "And it's so far away. And with your age, and your heart condition, and the kind of strenuous life you'll be leading, you'll be dead in less than a week. Why don't you just be sensible and stay here at home with me?" I said this as calmly as I could. I wanted to give him another chance, to be reasonable.

But it wasn't calm enough to suit Wayne. "Now don't you fret about this, Eileen," he said, turning his head sharply and peering up at me from the carpet with a wince, which I hoped came from getting a vicious carpet burn on his cheek. "I know how you can get," he said. "Don't you get like that now. I told you how things are, how they're going to be. Don't get it into your head that there's anything you can do about it now to stop me. There's no way you can. You don't own me, Eileen, and I'm sick of your controlling ways!"

The next thing I knew he was on his way out the door with his warm winter parka.

I followed after him, desperate now. I still couldn't really believe what he was doing, even while he was, even after he had. I cried and pleaded with him as soon as he opened the door and began to actually carry the boxes and suitcases through it and down the walk. I followed after him, begging him to stop, to reconsider, making a regular old fool of myself. How could he do this to me? What was I going to do? At my age? He was leaving me penniless. He'd taken all our savings. At a time when I was jobless. How was I going to pay the taxes? I'd lose the house. How was I going to live? What would I eat? How would I pay the electricity? The oil? What was I going to do? He did not favor me with a reply. But even then, I still couldn't really believe he was leaving me forever. I tried to fight it. Even after he'd slammed the back door shut for the last time. Even after he'd staggered down the walk under the last box. Even after he'd set foot on the vinyl-coated step for the last time and swung himself into the driver's seat of his shiny new powder-blue van, and pulled the door shut with a big bang behind him. Even after he'd gunned the big vehicle down the street and squealed it around the corner.

I could see him then racing around the next corner and the next, then all the way down the long swamp-lined road in a tearing rush to get to the big old house by the sea that Sue Annie rented, where she would be waiting for him, breathless with anticipation, her bags packed, too.

When I went back inside my house I cried and carried on for hours. My mind was filled with thoughts of old people who should know better being overpowered by these urgent forces, these passions bigger than they are, chasing after blooming youth. The truth, as now I'd so painfully learned it, was that deep awful drives, as inevitable as birth, as death, control our relationships. We don't. Forces beyond our mastery do. And these forces dominate our relationships and cause us to act as we do in them. That's the bottom-line truth, and we women must always be wary, always be ready for anything, not be taken by surprise.

Icy rainwater spray is sluicing down my windowpanes now in sheets that look like jelly when it's boiled enough.

I could hardly sleep all that long night, woke up to a clammy feeling of nightmarish dread and searingly painful emptiness. As though there were nothing whatsoever left inside of me. It was nearly impossible for me to face what had happened. Very very early that morning, even before first light, I went outside, and after I rested my

bones on the weathered old bench Wayne had set out for
me once a long time ago, and briefly inhaled the cool
stillness, I worked harder in my garden than I've ever
worked before in my whole gosh darned life. Digging,
digging, planting, planting, smoothing, smoothing. And
when I'd finished, I felt better, although I was enor-
mously tired. So I sat down on the bench, being careful
not to get a deadly splinter from it. My friend Julia nearly
died from one once. Ignored the slight swelling the day
after she'd gotten one in her hand without knowing it. Till
the red line appeared up her arm. She went right away to
emergency, spent a week in intensive care, hovering between life and death. The line between them is splinter
thin.

As I sat there, tired and numb, I looked out at the state
lands that border our lonely little property, at the hundreds of green trees, each one of them puffed out in its
own special way, as the sun, shining strongly, insistently
down on them, highlighted all their leaves so that they all
stood out, separately, together, a shimmering.

As I look through my rain-soaked window now, I see
wet, bare, tendriled, tentacled trees dancing wildly in the
wind, like seaweed caught in the unruly waves of a turbu-
lent tide, and it is so hard for me to imagine how they
looked to me that morning in September, how they appealed to me, even in the midst of my desolation, as I
gazed at them at the precise moment of my very great
shock, which jolted through my whole body with all the
force of electricity, as I was gripped by an overwhelming
mystical experience, saw a miraculous sign meant for me
alone. For bright flashes of kelly green and buttercup yellow and cardinal red were streaking back and forth
through all the trees. The colors Wayne was wearing
when I'd last seen him. And the first crazy thought that
sprang into my mind was, "It's Wayne. It's Wayne. He's
flying back to get me." Yes, I really imagined, if only for
an instant, that it was Wayne flying around up there in his

green corduroy trousers and his red shirt and his yellow
sweater. That's the weird way it was with me that morning. All my misery and all the work I'd been doing, I
guess. But it wasn't Wayne, of course. It was parrots. Two
of them, escaped from some cage somewhere, flying from
tree to tree in the state park that borders our yard, just as
though they were in the Amazon rain forest. They even
flew through my garden, screeching at the top of their
lungs. Having a real good time, ignorant of their impending fate, of course, as such creatures are.

Real salt tears came to me then. I cried about a lot of
things, I guess, but what was most on my mind was that
winter was nearly here. And green and red and yellow
tropical birds perish in the cold.

The day after that I needed a coat to sit outside in my
garden, where I've taken to sitting every day I can now.
I feel less lonely there, communing with nature, kind of.
And as I pulled my coat close about me, I realized the
real cold was on its way, all right, and those parrots were
doomed. I never did see them again. They're dead now.
I'm certain of it. For I know why I saw those parrots.

It's cold in my kitchen now as I sit here, wishing that
winter would not come for me, either. That it would never
come. But winter is coming. It is. For all of us. It is
a-comin' in.

Will my windows never cease their infernal rattling?
It's nearly nighttime dark outside now and it's afternoon.
Afternoon. But I'm as cozy as I can be in here in my hot-
pink bathrobe and my fuzzy purple sweater, and my tur-
quoise blue quilty slippers, and my striped chartreuse and
orange socks, sipping my hot tea toddy. And I have a big
gold bow in my hair, too, that once belonged to Sue Annie.

As I look through my shaking windowpanes at my
dried-up, battened-down garden, and at those trees that
now look to me like skeletons being tossed crazily about
by this wild November wind, I know that somewhere out

there are those parrots, their small lifeless bodies flight-less now, like little sandbags, lying somewhere out there on that soaking ground, being covered and uncovered by those restless swirlings of wet brown leaves, being blown about in the mud and the muck by the angry wind. And I know this just as sure as I know that Wayne and Sue Annie didn't go to Alaska, like he said they were going to. His deed said Florida. But they didn't go to Florida ei-ther. Wayne and Sue Annie, two colorful creatures having a real good time, were as ignorant as the parrots were of their impending fate. I still ache, just thinking about what happened.

Dear whiskey-breath Wayne, such an easy target, as al-ways, even though you tried to flee from me. "I'm still a knockout," I shouted at you, and laughed, as I pulled the trigger. Dear childish Sue Annie, why did you let me take you by surprise? You should have been more wary. Women should always be wary. Wayne was already slumped lifeless over the steering wheel when you came trustingly to the door to meet him. Dressed in bright col-ors, too, like the whore that you were. Your eyes soft with anticipation, wearing that tawdry gold bow in your hair. And there stood I, instead of him, to welcome you in my own inimitable way. What a blast! Yes, Sue Annie, we women must always be wary. We can never tell what lies in store for us in our relationships.

Your house was in a desolate place. Beneath the rocky cliff the sea runs deep. I could have rolled you both down there, inside that tacky powder-blue van. But I wanted to have you nearer to me. I don't like being by myself, never have. Wayne knew that. He should have listened to me, worked things out with me. The police don't suspect a thing, of course. For they, like those very few people who might have noticed, knew, before he even bothered to tell me, that you and he were going far, far away from here, never to return. And so you did. And so you have. Like the parrots, your big flightless bodies are out there in my garden, ripped apart. Wayne's wrapped in his useless parka that he carried just to show me. The two of you lie far beneath that sodden ground, where I buried you so laboriously, where I sowed you—my big seeds—so deep, that fine morning in September, just before the sign of the parrots appeared unto me, to illuminate what I'd done. I buried you away from each other of course. You're out of his reach. He's out of yours. And both of you are far, far away too from the reach of this pelting rain, from the strength of this relentless wind, from this earthly cold, and far beyond the grasp of those overpowering forces that overtook you, those big passions beyond our mastery that control our relationships and how we act in them. Those urgent forces that overtook the two of you, and then—in a shocking and totally surprising way, that long ago day in September—overtook me, too.

The Azalea War
by Wyc Toole

Everybody says it happened because of the dog and the azalea bushes, but I can tell you there was a lot more to it than that. The dog and the azaleas just brought everything into focus and it's scary to think you could get killed that way.

I keep reading and hearing about how all people got to do to solve their problems is to sit down and talk—you know, so they understand each other. Well, I'm not too sure I agree with that any more. It sounds good, but after living out here in a quiet neighborhood where people talk all the time, have nice homes and plenty to eat and still see 'em kill each other, I don't know. Maybe people ain't all that reasonable when something they value—no matter what it is—gets threatened. Maybe talking then just makes it worse. But I'm getting ahead of myself as usual.

What happened was that Charlie Wilson and his wife Mary moved in about two years after Margie—that's my wife—and me. Charlie had a tool and die business somewhere up around the Detroit area before he retired and bought the lot next to mine. He and Mary built a big brick home, ran a cedar fishing dock out into the lake, and seemed to be as satisfied as anybody else I knew.

Not too many people lived out here then and Margie and me saw a lot of the Wilsons. No big friendship, just dinner and bridge a couple of times a week and Charlie and me fished together sometimes. We had a few things in common because I owned a hardware store over in Gainesville for thirty years.

I originally bought my place out here on the lake for the weekends and summers. Kids loved it. Lots of old shady oaks and pines. A big, clear, white sand bottomed lake so clean you could drink out of it. Can't do that any more. Too many people using it now.

After the kids got married and left home, I had a little run-in with heart trouble. I sold the store and our house in town, expanded the cottage, and Margie and me came out to stay. We were almost the first permanent residents on the lake, so it was good to have the Wilsons for company. You probably notice I said "company," not "friends," because Charlie could be pretty hard to get along with sometimes. It was just his nature, I guess. Even looked hard—a big, long, lanky man with heavy bones, a thick head of white hair, and a quick temper. Walked like a caged lion. Never gained a pound, either—no matter what he ate, which was discouraging for somebody like me. I've always been too heavy. But the strongest thing I remember about Charlie was his eyes. They were a cold, pale blue and always seemed to be looking at something far away. Charlie never talked much, either, and when I was around him I usually got the feeling he'd much rather be by himself.

Now Mary, she more than made up for Charlie's lack of conversation. She's a plump little girl with curly white hair that used to be blonde, blue eyes, a pert nose, and straight white teeth. Said she never had a cavity in her life. Probably because her mouth moved so much no germs could get a toehold. That woman could really talk! I never saw her when she was quiet. She rattled on at speeds of about three hundred words a minute with gusts up to three fifty. Still, I liked Mary. She was a good person. Do anything in the world for you.

Charlie and Mary were sort of a separate couple, if you know what I mean. Seemed happy enough, but not much show of affection, didn't have any common interests, and no children. Margie said Mary talked so much because she had been lonely most of her life.

About a year after the Wilsons came, Dave and Sue Patterson moved in. Dave had a chain of shoestores in Ohio before he sold out and came down. They bought the lot next to the Wilsons' and built a stone and cedar home that was really pretty.

The dog I was talking about earlier belonged to Dave. Said he'd had him since he was a puppy. The dog's name was Bear and he was seven or eight years old then. Dave and Bear were real close. If you could hit one with a rock, you could hit the other one. I considered this a blessing because Bear was a *huge* German shepherd with the biggest teeth I ever saw on a dog.

The first thing Dave did after he moved in was to take Bear around to meet all the neighbors. I told Margie I figured it was Dave's way of telling Bear who he couldn't eat. Dave claimed the dog was real gentle when he knew you, but I was never comfortable around him. With a dog that big you never know.

After Dave and Sue came, Margie and me sort of drifted away from the Wilsons. Six people don't make for good bridge games. Charlie and Dave weren't all that close, but Mary and Sue hit it off like sisters from the first day they met. Looked a lot like sisters, too. Sue was another little blonde with a big bosom and blue eyes and she talked as much as Mary did. It was absolutely amazing to watch them talk at each other. I never did understand how they could keep anything straight with both of them talking at the same time, but they did and seemed to enjoy it.

I thought at first that Margie might feel left out with Sue and Mary always being together, but she said not. Said she enjoyed them both, but that it was a lot better the way it was. They needed that kind of constant companionship and she just didn't have time for it.

I understood because Margie and me always been as much friends as husband and wife. Her mother used to say we were like a pair of Irish peat diggers—just give us a place to sit and plenty to eat and drink and we didn't need anyone or anything else to be perfectly happy. It sure wasn't that way for Sue and Mary, though. Neither Charlie nor Dave were much on talking and going places. Funny how different they were in some ways and how alike in others. Even told me they both used to hunt a lot, years back. Seemed proud they took their wives on hunting trips and taught them to shoot. I found it hard to believe Mary and Sue thought this was a fun thing to do. I just never could picture them skinning deer and drinking blood and the other things Dave and Charlie laughed about teaching them. Now, however, Dave and Charlie just fished and worked in their yards and I never got the feeling their wives were all that important to them.

I don't mean they were ugly to the girls or anything like that. They were just loners—two hardheaded, independent men who were having real trouble adjusting to a life without a business to run. Listening to them when they did talk, you soon understood their work had been their lives and that kind of living must have been damn hard on Mary and Sue.

Like not having children. Margie told me they both said their husbands had wanted to wait on having kids until their businesses were solid enough to afford them without stretching either their time or money. So they waited and waited and when they finally had the money, time had run out and it was too late to do anything about it. Sad, too. Mary and Sue loved children. They would have been good mothers.

Anyway, getting back to the trouble. Dave had his dog and Charlie had his azaleas. Tons of them. All over his yard in a million colors. His real treasure, however, was a thick hedge of big Formosa azaleas running along the property line between his house and Dave's. Charlie had planted those bushes right after he moved in, and he was truly proud of them. Perfectly beautiful in the spring. Margie said the color of the flowers was a pale salmon. I don't know much about colors, but I sure did enjoy seeing them in full bloom.

Naturally, Dave's dog thought the best place in the whole world to sleep was in the shade of that big azalea hedge and, as most dogs will, dug holes beside it to lie in. Sometimes Charlie would get all bent outta shape about this, saying Bear was gonna kill his plants. Dave always told him the dog was in his own yard and could damn well dig holes in it if he wanted to. There wasn't much Charlie could do about it other than complain to me. We both knew Dave wasn't going to pay any attention to him. That's how Dave was.

When the real trouble started, though, Bear had gotten older like the rest of us. I guess he was twelve or thirteen by then—half blind, couldn't hear too well, and cranky like some people I know. He didn't run around much, just lay in the yard or on the dock where he could keep an eye on Dave—which is how it happened.

You can hear a lot of different stories now about that day, but I know exactly what went on. I was right there cutting my front lawn. It was in late April. The weather was warm and dry. Charlie was out trimming his azaleas, Dave was weeding the boxwoods along the walk, and Bear was sleeping in the shade of the azalea hedge. Charlie told me later he stepped through the hedge onto Dave's property to get a better angle on a stray branch. He didn't know Bear was there and the back edge of his heel landed on the dog's tail. Bear must have thought he was being attacked because he jumped up, yelped like he'd been gut shot, and bit Charlie.

Fortunately old Bear wasn't as strong as he once was and his teeth only went through Charlie's jeans and about an inch into his leg. Six years earlier Bear would have probably taken off Charlie's foot. Charlie apparently thought he had because he lets out a scream that's louder than Bear's and I stopped my mower to see who was getting killed. What I saw was Charlie dancing around on one foot with blood all over the other one and Bear looking sleepy and confused and licking his tail.

Dave came running over and if he had said something sympathetic it might have ended right then, but Charlie looked so damn silly jumping around on one foot that Dave started laughing. I admit I chuckled some myself.

This didn't go over too well with Charlie. He didn't think it was a bit funny, and Dave's laughing made him madder than he already was. So, cussing Dave, Bear, and the world in general, he hops over to his house and calls the sheriff.

The rest of the day was equally entertaining with all the neighbors gathering in my yard to talk about the great *attack.*

In the meantime, Charlie goes down to the doctor's where he gets a shot and eight stitches and comes home limping like he stepped on a land mine. The sheriff shows up and there is a lot of loud conversation between him, Dave, and Charlie. The upshot of it all being that Dave has got to keep Bear tied up from then on.

Dave does not take kindly to such orders and goes around the neighborhood telling everybody how Charlie caused the trouble by trespassing on his property. He allowed as how the sheriff and Charlie could both go directly to hell because Bear was the one that got hurt first and he had rights like anybody else.

Three days go by and Dave is still letting Bear run loose, so Charlie calls the sheriff again. The sheriff is not a good man to ignore and he comes over mad as a wet cat in a sack. This time he tells Dave that he has to fence Bear in or he'll take him to the pound and have him put to sleep and Dave better believe him this time because he's as serious as a heart attack. I know all this because I was standing right there and heard the whole conversation. What really bothered me, however, was how quiet Dave got right at the end.

Charlie was as pleased with the sheriff's new orders as a kid with a .22 rifle. Came over and told me this would teach Dave to keep his damn dog away from his azaleas. Since I'd had more than enough of their foolishness by now, I told Charlie I thought he was making too much out of a dumb accident. Bear wasn't really a mean dog and he was a little old to be fenced in now. I strongly suggested he drop the whole mess and get the sheriff calmed down before he and Dave got into an argument they couldn't turn off.

Charlie's miserable temper came roaring out in full force and he used some extremely colorful words to tell me to mind my own business. I didn't appreciate what he said very much and kept things going by telling him he was the closest thing I had ever seen to an ass walking around on two legs. Our discussion went downhill rapidly from there. I think it was then I realized that this was the first real battle Charlie had gotten into since he sold his tool and die business, and like an old war horse he was actually enjoying the fight. He intended to win, too. But knowing Dave I wasn't so sure he could.

Dave was as short and round as Charlie was long and lanky. He was bald and wore thick glasses, but his brown eyes had the same steely glint as Charlie's and he was just as stubborn. I suspected that way down he was even meaner. Sue told Margie that Dave came in the house and started cleaning his guns after the sheriff left that day.

Several of us in the neighborhood talked about it and decided Dave would probably cool things down by building Bear a nice fenced-in area in his back yard and then wait a while before trying to get back at Charlie. Especially since the sheriff seemed to be on Charlie's side at the moment. That's the kind of mistake you make when you believe people are reasonable, and if we had been thinking, it would have been very obvious that neither Dave nor Charlie fit into that category. They both knew they were in a war, and neither of them intended to hoist any white flags. In fact, Dave got busy and stirred up more trouble the very next day.

Looking back, I think Dave spotted something when he bought the lot or maybe he just had a hunch the survey work had been a little sloppy in the past. Whatever the reason, his next move was a beauty.

For as long as I can remember the survey work on property around the lake had been done by Hank Thorton. Hank was now in his early seventies and a young fellow named Skip Keyes was taking over. So Dave called Skip and told him he wanted his property lines resurveyed so Charlie wouldn't get an inch that didn't belong to him when he put up the fence.

Skip came out and ran the lines. When he finished and all the stakes were in place, they showed that the old property lines were off about four feet on both sides of the lot. Charlie's azalea hedge was actually *on* Dave's property!

Dave is ecstatic. He calls Charlie out and shows him what Skip says. When Charlie finally understands what Dave is telling him, he gets like emergency red, starts spitting fire and cussing Dave and Skip at the same time. Skip gets pretty upset at the things Charlie is calling him, but Dave is laughing so hard tears are running down his cheeks and he can't even talk. He just whoops and Skip's mouth gets tighter until finally Charlie stops cussing long enough to run in his house and call Hank Thorton.

Hank comes bouncing up in a dirty black pickup truck about thirty minutes later. Charlie shouts at him for a while before Hank limps over to where Skip and his crew are standing watching the show and starts screaming at them for being a gaggle of incompetent fools and idiots. Skip is already mad and he doesn't take this too long before he begins yelling how Hank doesn't know a transit rod from a fishing pole and that the whole area is marked wrong because Hank has been using the wrong "point of beginning" for his surveys. He says it isn't just Dave and Charlie, but that every lot on the lake is four feet off line.

There was a big crowd of neighbors milling around in my yard by now and Skip got everybody's attention when he says all our property is legally screwed up. Hank is furious, of course, and says Skip talks big but he hasn't proved it to him yet. So Skip takes Hank off to show him where he made the mistake and all the neighbors start arguing about what it means if Skip is right.

Somebody must have called the sheriff again, since he drives up in the middle of all the confusion and sits across the road in his patrol car, watching quietly and chewing on a dead cigar butt.

When Skip and Hank get back, Hank is obviously upset. He tells us that as much as he hates to admit it, Skip is right. All the lots have the correct amount of footage along the lake, but the side lines are four feet off. He threw in a lot more fancy words about how we could fix the problem, but it all boiled down to each of the property owners on the lake having to agree to deed four feet of their property to their neighbor. This would make the present surveys legally correct.

Charlie speaks up first and says that's fine with him and was looking around at the rest of us for support when Dave states flatly that it is certainly not agreeable to him. He wants the property he paid for and the damn fence is going on the correct line and he has no intention of discussing the matter any further.

Charlie's fury is pretty impressive even for him. Among all the cuss words you can make out that he intends to sue Dave, Skip, Hank, and anybody else he can think of. This got another burst of laughter out of Dave. Skip told him where he could put his lawyer and Hank said he wasn't going to worry about any lawsuit that would take more years to settle than he had to live. Charlie turns purple and starts kicking the survey stakes out of the ground.

Skip comes alive at this and declares he has had a bel-
lyful of Charlie's stupidity and that pulling up survey
stakes in Florida is a first degree misdemeanor. He yells
for the sheriff, who comes trotting over and tells Charlie
that Skip is not lying. That Charlie better put the stakes
back right now or he could be looking at a thousand dollar fine and a year in jail.

Charlie doesn't want to believe it, but the sheriff's face
doesn't give him any choice. Also, Skip is yelling how he
damn well is going to press charges if the stakes aren't
back where they belong in five minutes. So Charlie takes
a deep breath, grits his teeth, and starts putting the stakes
back in the ground.

While he's doing this, the sheriff is trying to get Skip
calmed down, Dave is sitting on the grass rocking from
side to side totally helpless with laughter, and Charlie is
trying to kill everybody with his eyes.

I figured it was best for us to leave and took all the
neighbors around back of my place for a beer. We could
hear the yelling and the laughing going on out front for
another thirty minutes at least.

The next morning a fencing crew shows up and starts
putting up a six foot high, chain link fence between
Dave's property and Charlie's. Charlie comes out with a
shotgun and the fencing crew picks up steel poles. I call
the sheriff. He was obviously expecting trouble because
he was already there when I went back outside. The sheriff takes Charlie's gun, tells the fencing crew to put down
the poles and start putting up the fence.

Six of the neighbors come over to my yard to watch all
the excitement. We thought the whole mess was funny,
which goes to show how wrong even a group of people
can be.

When I went back in my house, Mary and Sue were in
the kitchen with Margie. They were crying. Dave and
Charlie had told them not to see each other any more and
Charlie was calling real estate agents about selling his

house. Mary and Sue grab onto me and start in about how
I had to do *something* to get Charlie and Dave back to
normal. I told them this was not even a possibility. I had
already tried and neither one of them was close to being
rational. My honest opinion was that if anything was to
be done it had to be pretty drastic and Mary and Sue had
to do it. I was talking about the threat of divorce, but
couldn't bring myself to come right out and say it. Margie
told me I was a *big* help and why didn't I just go eat
lunch down at the hamburger place.

The next few days rocked along quietly. I tried to talk
to Charlie and Dave again, but they wouldn't even speak
to me. I did begin to have a faint hope that if they would
stay away from each other for a while longer, time might
begin to heal the split. That dream died the next day when
Dave came out and started cutting down the azalea hedge.

Charlie sat on his front steps watching him like he was
slicing up one of his kids.

I was disgusted with both of them by now and went in
the house. Mary and Sue were there again with Margie.
They were using our place as neutral ground—slipping
off to talk and be together. I don't know if they were mad
at me or not because they quit talking when I walked in
and that was really unusual. I asked Margie if I could
have some coffee and she just stared at me, too, so I left
and went down to the hamburger place again.

Later in the day, I saw Dave begin digging up what was
left of the azalea hedge. Charlie walked over to the fence
and stood watching the final destruction a full minute before saying, "You shouldn't have done that, Dave. I
warned you. Don't forget that. I warned you!"

Dave acted like Charlie wasn't even there. He kept digging away and throwing the bare roots hard against the
fence so the dirt fell in Charlie's yard. Charlie didn't say
another word. He pounded once on the fence with his
clenched fists, turned and went back to his steps where he

sat with pure hate on his face. I got so nervous I went in-side and watched the ball game.

It was a little after ten that same night when we heard the shots. They were fast and bunched together. Three or four with a pause and one more. Margie and me were in bed reading. She sat straight up and said, "Oh my God, they've done it."

There wasn't any doubt in my mind, either. I called the sheriff's office, pulled on some pants and shoes, grabbed a flashlight, and ran for the fence. I got there about three minutes before the first patrol car, but there was nothing I could do. They were both dead. One on one side of the fence and one on the other. Charlie was holding a .357 magnum and Dave was clutching an old army issue .45. The dog was dead, too. His body was about two feet from Dave's.

Mary and Sue were on opposite sides of the fence also, but close together. It was too dark to see their faces. They were crying or talking—probably both, knowing them. I didn't pay much attention because a .45 and a .357 are big guns and it was a bloody mess. I got sick over by the side of Charlie's house. The sheriff came about that time and stood looking at all the blood and cussing softlike at the two bodies. I swear I saw him wipe tears off his face, but it might have been sweat.

Margie gathered up Sue and Mary and took them to our house to wait on the doctor. It was really a bad night.

I finally got back to bed a bit after one. Margie slipped in beside me about two thirty. I tried to talk with her, but she said she wasn't in the mood. I just wish she had stayed that way.

There wasn't much to the inquest. Everybody knew what had happened and why. When the courts got through, Mary took Charlie back to Michigan to bury him and Sue took Dave to Ohio.

Neither one of them ever came back to the lake. They sold their homes and went down to Longboat Key where they bought a condominium. Margie hears from them off and on. She says they are fine and real happy.

The neighbors all got together and hired an attorney to straighten out the survey problems. So the fence came down and it's quiet out here again. I guess I'm the only one who's still got troubles over the "azalea war"—which is what everybody ended up calling it.

Margie says my problem is that I can't leave well enough alone. I keep picking at something until it unravels on me and then I get upset with what I find out.

"Why do you ask questions if you don't want to know the answers?" she yelled at me. She was right mad.

That was one day about eight months after the shootings when I was sitting on the end of my dock fishing. Margie came out with some iced tea and we started talking. I'll be honest and say she had asked me at least four times not to bring it up, but being me I got off on Dave and Charlie and how I tried to help.

Margie got white around the mouth and says, "I can see you're not going to be satisfied until you get me to admit it."

I should have left it alone, but like an idiot I asked, "Admit what?"

"That you did the right thing. I *wish* you had not told them to do it, but you did and it has worked out all right. I'll give you that."

Usually I know exactly what Margie means, but this time I was lost and said so.

"Don't try that *innocent* act with me, Jack Harrison. I have lived with you *too* long for that to work. I was right there when you told Mary and Sue to kill Dave and Charlie. I certainly did *not* approve of you giving such advice, even if it was the best thing for them to do."

I was totally confused by now and made the mistake of saying, "What in the blue-eyed world are you talking about? Sue and Mary didn't kill anybody. Charlie and Dave shot each other. Everybody knows that."

"Don't be ridiculous!" she snapped. "Charlie and Dave did no such thing. They were having too good a time to end it by shooting each other. You can be terribly dense sometimes. Men like Charlie and Dave love to fight. Sue told me Dave was enjoying his war with Charlie more than anything else he'd done since he retired. Mary said Charlie was the same way. Those two mean men would have happily gone on fighting with each other for years. The two who were miserable were Mary and Sue. It was their old lives all over again and that was hard to face."

"I had no idea they hated their husbands," I said quietly.

"They didn't *hate* anybody," Margie explained patiently. "They loved them—as much as they were allowed to. Their problem was that Charlie and Dave gave them everything but companionship. That was what they needed most. I don't even think they minded Charlie and Dave fighting. They were used to that. They just couldn't accept being lonely again."

"I still don't think they did it," I said defensively.

Margie cocked her head to one side, smiled and asked, "Did anyone ever check to see which gun killed Bear?"

"That never came into question," I admitted. "They proved Dave's gun killed Charlie and Charlie's gun killed Dave and we all knew why."

"You just thought you did," Margie insisted, "but if anyone had taken the time to look into it, they would have found that the same gun that killed Charlie also killed Bear. You know good and well Dave never shot his own dog."

"It could have been an accident," I protested, "but whatever happened I never told Mary and Sue to kill anybody."

"You most certainly did!" she insisted. "You said that something 'drastic' had to be done and they were the only ones who could do it."

"I was talking about divorce!"

"You can say that now, but that is not the way it sounded," she stated firmly. "I knew what you meant as well as they did. I tried to stop them, but they decided you were right.

"I don't know everything that happened that night, but I do know they made up some lie and got Dave and Charlie out to the fence. Then Sue shot Charlie with Dave's gun and Mary shot Dave with Charlie's. The last shot we heard was when Bear saw Dave hurt and went after the only person he could reach—Sue. Sue said the only thing she could do was shoot him. I don't think she ever liked Bear much anyway. Then they put the guns in Charlie's and Dave's hands and started screaming. Everybody was so all-fired smart they decided Charlie and Dave had shot each other and never looked any further for an explanation. Mary said that's what would happen."

"How can you know all this, Margie? You were in bed with me that night."

"When I got them over to our house after the shootings, I asked them and they told me," she replied.

"Then why didn't you tell the sheriff?"

Margie looked shocked. "When it was all *your* idea! Don't be foolish. Now what do you want for lunch?"

The Mushroom Fanciers
by Lawrence Treat

ELLA . . .

We all know her, here in Enderby Village. She's a warm, plump, earthy creature of broken teeth and broken English. We trust her and love her, most of us, and we wonder, all of us, what she lives on.

A pension of some kind. Cora Prichard and Martha, my wife, agree on that much, but however small the amount, Ella gets along well enough. She lives rent-free in that backwoods cabin of the Prichards', and all summer long she survives on what she finds in the forest. By way of gratitude she makes periodic gifts of wild mushrooms—on which subject she is an acknowledged authority.

I'll never forget the first time she came to our house. She'd brought a bucket of mushrooms to our back door just as Martha happened to step outside. Ella offered the lot.

"You like?" she said.

Martha is not only beautiful and loyal and intelligent, but she's polite, and she was far too polite to offend an old woman. Nevertheless, she had no intention of eating any part of that assorted heap of brown, white, and yellow poison, no matter how luscious it looked or how redolent it smelled. But Ella, who has a peasant's insight, would have nothing of Martha's politeness.

"Okee," Ella said. "I cook, we eat." And she stormed into the kitchen, which was where I found them.

I fell in love with Ella on sight, for there was something so real and warm and peasanty about her that I couldn't resist. She knew how to laugh and she knew how to forgive, and she saw right through both Martha and me, who were scared of those mushrooms. So Ella took one of them out of the pan where she was sautéing them and she cut the mushroom into three parts. One part for Martha, one for me, and one for herself. And she popped hers into her mouth.

It was the time-honored way of assuring a guest that you're not trying to poison him. And Ella, there in our brand-new kitchen, acted the part of the hostess putting us at ease. I reacted by getting a bottle of wine, our best, and the three of us sat down and finished both the bottle and the mushrooms. As I recall, we had some meadow mushrooms and some oyster mushrooms, and some of the smaller puffballs. After that we were good friends.

A few days later Martha took up the study of mushrooms, which I found out is called mycology, and when Martha does something she does it thoroughly. She bought all the standard texts on fungi and she boned up on their characteristics. She could spot a "destroying angel" at 50 feet and, as a matter of precaution, she turned her back on all the amanitas. She took long hikes into forest and field. I went with her whenever I had the time, and we usually returned with full baskets.

At home, Martha studied the specimens we'd found. She felt them, sliced them, photographed them, and put them under a water glass and left them there overnight to deposit their spore patterns. She talked about identifying specimens from their veils and gills and pores and caps; she delighted in morels and polypores and boletes; and she went mushrooming with Ella and combined field work with scientific analysis.

In other words, Martha became something of a mycologist, and if she'd been at that fateful party of the Prichards', she would have known at once and nothing would have happened. But unfortunately she'd gone to visit her mother in California and was there for two weeks.

Martha's interest in mushrooms was contagious, and as can happen in a small community like the Bluebird Road area, the fashion quickly spread. The Prichards and Enderbys and Eilers and all the rest of them dealt with Ella. They wanted to pay her for her wild mushrooms, but Ella always refused.

"Is my benefit," she would say, meaning that she was glad to oblige. And she brought morels, campestras, and ceps and chanterelles and chicken of the woods (*Polyporus sulphureus*, Martha insists on calling them) to every house. There developed a kind of gourmet competition in wild-mushroom cookery. Whenever Ella brought someone a large enough supply there was a party. We had our mushrooms sautéed and broiled and stuffed, as well as in mushroom spreads; we had quenelles; we had mushrooms prepared in sour cream and cooked in chafing dishes and marinated and pickled and even raw. The varieties seemed to be endless, and Cora Prichard, having once written a cookbook, felt constrained to lead all the rest.

Martha and I were new in the community, and were and are very much in love. How we happened to get in with the Bluebird Road crowd was a matter of sheer chance. We really weren't in their class. We didn't have their money, their social background, or their lack of morals. In the course of time we found out more or less who was bedding up with whom, and we heard rumors of involvement in corruption, embezzlement, and fraud. Still, they were only rumors—until Malcolm documented them.

Malcolm was the Prichard butler, and he had apparently been steaming open envelopes and listening in on phone extensions for years, and recording it all for future use. I never liked him, nor did he like me. I'm convinced that he investigated me and decided I wasn't worthwhile. I slept only with my own wife, I'd committed no known crimes, and I didn't insult people—which put me down as a complete nobody in Malcolm's book.

Literally. Because he had a book, or at least the manuscript thereof. The title was *Memoirs of a Corrupt Family,* and he apparently had all the residents of Bluebird Road tagged. But he must have had talent, too, because a well-known publisher was all set to buy the book and had offered him a $5000 advance, subject merely to their legal department clearing the text for libel.

The legal department, however, would have none of it, and word reached the Attorney General. He'd been a guest in several of the big houses on Bluebird Road and he tried to sit tight on the whole affair, but found it impossible. Regretfully he informed his friends that there was no way to prevent what he referred to as an undesirable investigation. He remarked casually that in ten days' time he had an appointment with Malcolm, who would be the key witness and had promised to produce proof.

In one way or another Martha and I picked up most of this gossip, and we realized that Malcolm was in grave danger. He had the same idea and he appealed to the police for protection. The result was Detective John Vesey. He arrived a week before Malcolm's scheduled interview with the Attorney General.

Vesey's assignment was a difficult one. Not that he was ill at ease in our local society. He wasn't. He could wear black tie or Ivy League clothes as naturally as any Enderby, and he did. But Vesey must have been aware that the attack on Malcolm, if it came, would be made with the finesse and ingenuity of a Medici. And to defend against it would require considerable perspicacity on Vesey's part.

He didn't look perspicacious. He was a tall, lanky, easy-going guy, and he flirted like the devil with Cora Prichard. Maybe that was part of his job, but if so, he sure overdid it. For Cora was attractive and she knew how to run a love affair right under her husband's nose. She'd had plenty of experience.

Then one day Cora found a couple of fine specimens of *Polyporus sulphureus,* that gigantic bright-colored fungus that can measure a foot or two across and looks like a pile of freshly ironed, ruffle-edged doilies just come from the laundry. And tastes delicious. Naturally, after checking up on their identity, Cora celebrated her find with a party, and that's what this story is about.

"I found two of them," she said to me over the phone. "Isn't that wonderful? We're going to eat one, and the other we'll just look at and admire. Can you come at seven?"

"Delighted," I said, sorry that Martha was away and would miss the party.

The Prichard estate is a large one, complete with an artificial lake containing an island which is just a few feet from shore and is reached by an arched stone bridge. Cora gives her parties on the island.

Most of the island is occupied by what she calls a "pleasure house," and what other people call a pavilion. She visited Japan in her youth and never got over it, and her pleasure house is Japanese in style. It has an expensive porch where cocktails are served and where at least a dozen people can lounge comfortably. From there you reach the dining area and a galley, to which food from the house is brought and where it can be kept hot. In addition to the galley, Prichard, who fancies himself as an outdoor cook, has installed a grill for charcoal cooking.

A couple of Japanese gardeners landscaped the island. Although the pavilion has left not much more than a rim of earth to be landscaped, they have arranged it tastefully, with bonsais and carefully selected rocks.

On the afternoon of the party the gardeners had been working on a corner of the island. Rather than carry their top soil and peat moss over the bridge, they had a plank from shore to island. The plank, just out of sight of the bridge, was about fifteen feet long and barely a foot wide. Cora was telling how the Japanese had brought over their material on a wheelbarrow.

"Such a sense of balance!" she said. "You should have seen them—they're so sure-footed." And she smiled and moved her blonde head just enough for her huge gold-wire earrings to make a faint tinkling sound.

Cora enjoyed her parties. They stimulated her and made her chatty. Although she wasn't clever, she thought she was and the excitement made her eyes flash with blue fire. And, caught up in the thrill of her own exalted fancy, she dressed daringly.

I was part of the circle attracted equally by her high spirits and her low neckline. Lennie Eiler and Ed Broome were there, too. Lennie plays squash every day and sometimes even finds time to stop in for mail at what he calls his office. Ed Broome, dark and saturnine, is a more serious type, but the pair of them along with Peter Prichard, who was standing at the other side of the room and examining the hors d'oeuvres, were reputed to be the major targets of Malcolm's book. Which is another way of saying that all three of them had excellent reasons for muting Malcolm permanently.

Cora, however, was off and running about her Japanese gardeners. "They're experts on mushrooms, too," she said. "They told me the best mushrooms come from Japan, and they're going to send me some samples. Dried, of course."

"Don't they like ours?" Lennie asked.

"Oh, yes. While I was talking to them Ella came in with a whole bucketful. We're going to have them tonight, too, and the gardeners tasted them right from the bucket. 'Very good,' they both said, and they nodded. Like this." Cora, with mock seriousness, nodded, chiefly to make her earrings tinkle again.

"What kind are they?" Ed Broome asked.

"They're the squishy kind," Cora answered. "I never

can remember names. Peter!" She called out to her husband, who had completed his analysis of the hors d'oeuvres. "Peter, what kind did Ella bring this afternoon?"

"I didn't know she'd brought any," he said, approaching her.

"They're the same kind we had a week ago Saturday, when the Davidsons were here. We're having them tonight, along with my *Polyporus.*"

Peter Prichard, dignified and erudite, answered by giving the scientific name. *"Coprinus atramentarius,"* he said. "How are they being prepared?"

"That new recipe of mine," Cora said. "I was working on it and tasting all afternoon. You make a paste, but you start with onions and—" She broke off in laughter. "But I'm not going to give away my secrets in public."

I turned away, and as I did so, I noticed Prichard's expression. He was licking his lips and frowning, like a man who'd just heard some important news and was trying to decide how to handle it. I remember thinking that people can make an awful lot of fuss over a few mushrooms.

Still, the *Polyporus* was worth it. We were due to eat one of them, but the other stood on a small table, with a spotlight focused on the center. It was a beautiful specimen, a bright orangy-yellow, about a foot across and some five inches high. Behind it was Cora's favorite painting, a picture of three white cats done by a Japanese artist.

Cora loves cats. Her current favorite, a long-haired white Persian named Miss Underfoot, came parading across the room. As I watched, she leaped up on the sideboard and then, without hesitating, jumped onto the narrow ledge above it where Cora kept a pair of rare and beautiful vases. The cat squeezed past without touching them and then settled down on the ledge, as if presenting herself as an object of art and asking us to judge which was the lovelier—she or the vases.

Cora waved to some of her guests who were just arriving, and I saw that Vesey was left with Prichard and Eiler and Broome. I stayed within earshot and wondered how they'd handle the situation—a police detective at a party with the three men he'd been assigned to watch.

I could, however, notice no strain. They spoke casually of Wall Street prices and of yesterday's tennis matches. If I expected them to trade veiled insults and to slip an innuendo into every remark, I was disappointed. All three of them acted matter-of-fact, civilized, and rather dull.

Vesey left them a couple of minutes later, and I saw Prichard whisper something to the other two. They nodded and moved off into a corner. There, after a whispered conference, each of them took out a coin. Their expressions were somber as they tossed, in the ancient game of "odd man out." It crossed my mind that they were tossing to decide who would dispose of Vesey. The idea, however, was ridiculous.

Malcolm, wheeling in a lacquered tea wagon with drinks, spoke to me.

"May I serve you, sir?"

There was Scotch, bourbon, and the makings of a martini on the top platform, and I picked bourbon on the rocks. This was a drinking crowd, and he made mine strong.

I studied him while he made my drink. He was as unlikely an author as you could find. He retained the silky, subservient manner of the born lackey, and he'd aged perceptibly since I'd seen him a few weeks before. His cheeks were sunken and his eyes looked feverish.

"Malcolm," I said, "how are you these days?"

"Badly, sir," he said in a low tired voice. "I shouldn't be here."

"Then why don't you leave? Go to town and stay at a hotel."

"Me?" he said in surprise. "I couldn't. I belong here.

Mrs. Prichard needs me." He handed me my glass. "Your drink, sir."

"Thanks," I said. "You don't look at all well."

"I'm under a great strain, sir. I fear for my very life."

"I don't understand you," I said. "Or anyone else around here."

"Perhaps not," he said, and wheeled the tea wagon toward Prichard.

I watched the pantomime of the butler asking his boss what he wanted, and then preparing it. Then Malcolm turned to Lennie Eiler.

"Mr. Eiler," Malcolm said, "I have your specialty, rum and tomato juice. I mixed it ahead of time, so the ice would melt. I hope it's satisfactory, sir."

Malcolm reached down to the lower shelf of the wagon, found a glass with a red brew, and handed it to Eiler.

"Thanks," Eiler said. He held it up to the light. "What a beautiful red," he remarked, and he stared as if he suspected Malcolm of having poisoned the drink. Malcolm dropped his eyes, and for a moment I wondered if the drink really could have been poisoned.

How easy, I thought, to slip something in the one drink that was different in color from all the others. Then I dismissed the possibility. Malcolm would be the most obvious suspect, and he'd still have Prichard and Ed Broome to reckon with.

I watched Malcolm wheel his cart on to the next group. Behind him two maids circulated, carrying a trayload of both *Polyporus* and the mushroom paste, take your pick or have them both. I tasted Cora's new concoction. Delicious.

Nevertheless, I couldn't quite enjoy it. I kept thinking of the interplay between Malcolm and the three men he was accusing. The situation was sinister, unhealthy, and it bothered me. If Malcolm really had something against them, why didn't he clear out, instead of acting as if everything was normal?

Suddenly I couldn't stand the hypocrisy of the whole group here. I wanted a breath of fresh air, and I walked out to the porch.

The sun was dropping behind a clump of birch across the pond, and the light was magically soft. It seemed to settle on the oddly shaped rocks and to reduce the bonsais to an even smaller size than they actually were. I thought longingly of Martha in California, and I wanted to tell her that I had a premonition of impending tragedy. Wrapped up in my thoughts, I had no idea anyone was near me until I heard a cough. I swung around and saw Vesey standing next to me.

"Sorry," he said. "Did I startle you?"

"No. Or rather, I guess anything would have."

"You think something's going to happen tonight, don't you?" Vesey said. "Maybe so. This gang"—he motioned with his head—"they have their own rules. Break one of them, and they impose their own sentence and carry it out. And the idea of a butler writing a book about them—I think that's what bothers them more than anything he can say in it."

"He's one worried butler," I remarked.

Vesey, leaning forward over the railing, stared at the plank connecting the island with the shore. "These people are heavy drinkers," he remarked somberly. "And the way they're going at it, somebody's going to get real drunk and try to walk that thing, and fall in."

"Then move the plank," I said.

"Not my job," Vesey said, turning. As he did so, I glimpsed the gun in the shoulder holster under his jacket.

I stayed where I was for a few moments, staring at the water and feeling more lonesome than ever. Then I, too, went back to the party.

It was in full swing by now. There were, by my later count, fourteen people present, but as far as this story is concerned, the only ones that mattered were Cora and Vesey, and the trio who had tossed coins.

The dinner was informal, with all the servants dismissed, and instead of a large table a few smaller ones were scattered around the room. The arrangement left Prichard in the central spot, where he could exhibit his artistry at the charcoal grill. This evening he was broiling shish kebab, and doing it expertly. He speared the lamb, onions, and tomatoes with a flourish, dipped them in a sauce that Cora had created, and then put the skewers side by side on the rows of racks.

I sat down with Vesey and Myra Jones, who designs textiles. We talked first about designing, and later on about the food, which was superb. The first course was shrimp and lobster salad, garnished lavishly with Ella's inky caps. A vichyssoise followed, but that was as far as Vesey got. He'd had about half of it when he rose abruptly, muttered something, and left the table.

"I hope it's not business," I said.

Myra gave me a funny look, and she put her spoon down and ate nothing more. I was starting in on the shish kebab when suddenly I felt sick. I glanced at Myra and saw that her face was cherry-red and her eyes glassy.

I stood up shakily, jostling my tray and knocking my skewer to the floor. I was in no condition to pick it up, and I rushed out of the room. I made it as far as the porch, where I retched over the railing. When I was able to look around I saw that most of the guests were having the same trouble. I sat down, feeling dizzy and nauseated and completely disinterested in who staggered past me, only to collapse gasping in one of the deckchairs.

I heard Cora, gasping in misery, phone the main house and tell one of the servants to call a doctor. I noticed, too, that Vesey had planted himself on the stone bridge. His job was to watch three men, and although he was in no condition to carry out his assignment he was doing the next best thing—namely, keeping track of whoever crossed the bridge to the mainland. Which, apparently, no one did.

I was too sick to think clearly, but I was aware that, whatever had made us sick, it was not the mushrooms. The Japanese had eaten them raw, and Cora had been tasting them all afternoon without suffering any ill effects. It followed that somebody—and Malcolm was the most likely candidate—had added some kind of poison.

He had good reason to. He was in danger and at least three people here wanted him out of the way before his appointment with the Attorney General. The easiest way to eliminate three people was to poison the lot of us. But Malcolm a mass murderer?

In due time Dr. Ames arrived. He examined a couple of us, saw that our faces were red and swollen, and made his diagnosis. Food poisoning. He prescribed some sedatives, told us to keep warm and not to aspirate when we threw up, and he added wryly that we'd all live. Then he impounded some samples of our dinner and phoned the local Board of Health. They promised to send somebody over to pick up the specimens for analysis.

By the time the doctor left, we were beginning to feel a little better. Vesey had left his watchdog post. Lounging in comparative comfort, he seemed glad to see the doctor cross the bridge and take the gravel path leading to the main house. I decided to speak privately to Vesey and ask him what he thought of the mass poisoning. I was approaching him when Dr. Ames came rushing back.

"There's a detective here, isn't there?" he said breathlessly. "Who—which?"

Vesey, stretched out on a deckchair, answered. "Me. What's the trouble?"

"There's a dead man in the bushes. With a knife in his back."

Vesey hauled himself up, and his voice sounded a little stronger. "Show me," he said. "The rest of you, stay here."

The body was Malcolm's, and Vesey confirmed it after he'd returned to the island, made some sort of examination of the dining room, and then come out to the porch where we were all waiting.

"I'm calling the local police," he announced. "It's their case. I have no official standing here, but I can tell you this much. Malcolm was stabbed with one of those skewers we were all using. I just checked inside and the skewers are all mixed up, no telling whose is missing, so that line of inquiry is out. That's about all I can tell you now, except that nobody can leave."

Although we were recovering, we were a subdued lot. Cora plugged in the big coffee-maker, and one by one we went up to it and helped ourselves. By the time the local police arrived, we were able to answer questions quite lucidly.

We all told the same story. We'd felt sick, we'd been nauseated and dizzy. Nobody could have managed to stagger across the bridge without Vesey seeing him. As for using the plank, that was equally impossible. It would have been tricky enough for a healthy man to cross on a narrow, fifteen-foot plank in the dark, but someone dizzy with nausea? Out of the question. Nevertheless it followed that somebody had, or else that somebody not at the party had killed Malcolm. But in that case, where had the skewer come from?

The police let us all go home shortly after one. I slept soundly, and in the morning I called Martha long-distance and told her the news. She was horrified. She couldn't believe that Ella's mushrooms were at fault, but she wanted to know what kind they were. I couldn't remember the name, so I said I'd call Cora and find out.

I was having breakfast when Ella arrived. She'd heard what had happened, and she'd come to me first.

"You're sure your mushrooms were good, aren't you?" I said.

Ella nodded. "Inky caps. Very good. I eat every day, and the two Japanese eat without sick."

"Then what happened? How do you explain it?"

"No poison," Ella said. "But inky cap—good to eat, but not with drink. Eat and drink together, and then—" She had no words for it, so she made a retching sound.

I jumped up and put my arms around her. "Ella," I said, "you've just solved a murder and—" I gave the matter a second thought, and reversed myself. "Except that you haven't," I said. "I think I know how, but I don't know who."

"Maybe somebody don't drink," Ella said.

"Exactly." I remembered Cora saying the mushrooms were the squishy kind, and then Prichard had identified them, and their Latin name. Prichard, knowledgeable, thorough, must have known the consequences of combining inky caps and alcohol.

I saw it then. In that whispered conference he'd warned Eiler and Broome that everybody was due to be incapacitated, and the three of them had tossed coins to see who would refrain from drinking, stay sober, and kill Malcolm. But which one of the three actually committed the murder? And how could I prove it?

The method was clear and Vesey was probably aware of it, too. With everybody in distress and none of the servants around, the sober killer had taken a skewer, crossed to the mainland on the narrow plank, found and killed Malcolm, then returned via the plank. He'd needed only nerve and a good sense of equilibrium.

Later in the morning I went to the Prichards'. I was told that Cora was in the pleasure house, and I found her there with Vesey. They were looking glum and talking the way people talk about a tragedy after the event.

They greeted me without enthusiasm. "I think I know what happened," I said.

"Great," Vesey said sarcastically. "We know, too. Malcolm was killed, and the Attorney General won't take action against anyone without Malcolm's personal testimony. Any idea *who* killed him?"

"No, but I know how. Those mushrooms were inky caps. Right?"

"*Coprinus atramentarius,*" Cora said, nodding. She had the State Agricultural Bulletin in her lap, and she read from it.

" 'The Inky Cap,' " she said, " 'common on lawns and in gardens from August until late frosts, grows singly or in dense clusters. The cap is especially meaty, and this, along with its pleasant flavor, makes the Inky Cap one of the choice forms for the table.

" 'The Cap is at first egg-shaped, but elongates—' "

"Cora!" I said. "Stop it."

She put the Bulletin down.

"I just spoke to Ella," I said. "She told me that the inky cap is fine, except that in combination with alcohol it can make you sick. And does. I guess we all know the symptoms."

Vesey slapped his hands together. "If somebody last night merely pretended to drink, then—" And Vesey went ahead and outlined a theory exactly like the one I'd figured out. "And what's more," he said, finishing, "the doctor didn't examine us individually. He prescribed the same treatment for all of us, and today there's no way in the world of telling who faked being sick."

"You don't know what you're talking about," Cora said angrily. "My guests are my friends. I know them and I can vouch for them, and I resent your saying that one of them could commit a murder." And, irritably, she threw the mushroom Bulletin to the floor.

I hadn't noticed Miss Underfoot, the white Persian, although I think I'd heard a lapping sound, as if she was drinking something at the other side of the room. Now she made a dive for the Bulletin, and missed. For a ludicrous moment she seemed unable to understand how she could have missed such an easy target. Then, drawing herself up proudly, she stalked off.

It seemed to me that she was wobbly, but she made a fair enough leap up to the sideboard, which had a narrow ledge on which Cora kept the valuable pair of vases. Miss Underfoot took a sight on the ledge and jumped. But she didn't quite make it. She clawed at the edge, hit one of Cora's precious vases, and knocked it down. The vase smashed to bits.

Vesey and I got up at the same moment and rushed over to Miss Underfoot. I got there first, and I picked her up and sniffed.

"Smell her breath," I said excitedly. "She's drunk!"

Vesey grabbed her, sniffed, then dropped her unceremoniously. He crossed the room and picked up the bowl at which Miss Underfoot had been lapping. There were three artificial peonies in it. After removing the peonies he smelled the contents of the bowl.

"Rum," he said. "Rum and tomato juice. Who drinks that?"

"Nobody," Cora said quickly. "I don't know how it got there."

"But I do," I said. "That's Lennie Eiler's drink, and it's the only drink he ever takes. And he was the only one who had a red-colored drink. I saw Malcolm hand him a special glass of it last night. Obviously he dumped the drink in the bowl and stayed sober. But is that enough to convict him?"

Vesey smiled. "When we know a man is guilty," he said, "we manage to get a confession. Don't worry about that."

After the arrest Martha and I had to move away. Apparently the Bluebird Road crowd thought it just wasn't cricket to pin a murder on one of your neighbors. We were so thoroughly ostracized that we sold our house. At a nice profit, I might add. But we have one regret.

We miss Ella and her mushrooms.